SELECTED PRAISE FOR

WHAT WE BURIED

"Irresistible reading."

THE GLOBE AND MAIL

"While *What We Buried* is a superb whodunit, it's also a tale of family secrets and family beliefs. *What We Buried* is a terrific read, with some fabulous secondary characters. Your book club may want to ask each other: How well do you know your grandparents?"

WINNIPEG FREE PRESS

"With unflinching empathy, [Rotenberg] masterfully uncoils the strands of two mysteries as his detective heroes unearth devastating secrets that span continents and generations."

BARBARA KYLE, author of *The Deadly Trade*

"Takes us on a deep and complicated journey, solving puzzles that have mystified Rotenberg's characters and readers throughout his engaging series . . . Sharp and masterfully written, this is storytelling at its best."

DAVID ISRAELSON, journalist and author

"[A] well-written and cinematic new novel."

HELLA ROTTENBERG, journalist and coauthor of
The Cigar Factory of Isay Rottenberg

"Explores the intergenerational trauma of war that lies beneath the surface of modern life. A layered and propulsive thriller."

KATE HILTON, bestselling coauthor of *Bury the Lead*

"At the heart of this fast-paced thriller, there is a dark mystery that has festered for seventy years—a mystery that links unsolved murders in today's world with a Nazi atrocity in a small town in wartime Italy. It is left to Daniel Kennicott to find the connection before it destroys him."

ANNA PORTER, bestselling author of *Gull Island*

"Rotenberg has earned a name for himself with legal thrillers that deftly ramp up the suspense. In the same vein, *What We Buried* keeps us guessing but this time against a backdrop that is darker and more personal. A guaranteed great read."

D. J. McINTOSH, bestselling author of the Mesopotamian Trilogy

"With historical intrigue, evocative locales, and timely themes, Robert Rotenberg's latest novel is a profound and chilling page-turner."

ROBYN HARDING, bestselling author of *The Drowning Woman*

"*What We Buried* is a polished gem of a story, but because it draws on a real and brutal historical event that holds tight to living memory, it turns this seventh outing in the always-riveting Ari Greene series into something very special."

C. C. BENISON, award-winning author of the Father Christmas mystery series

"A rare treat. A thriller with depth and resonance that reaches back into the shadowy past to excavate a Nazi atrocity and expose a contemporary crime."

DANIEL KALLA, bestselling author of *High Society* and *Fit to Die*

ONE MINUTE MORE

ROBERT ROTENBERG

PUBLISHED BY SIMON & SCHUSTER

New York   Amsterdam/Antwerp   London   Toronto   Sydney   New Delhi

SIMON &
SCHUSTER
CANADA

A Division of Simon & Schuster, LLC
166 King Street East, Suite 300
Toronto, Ontario M5A 1J3

The image on page 317 is from the US National Archives and Records Administration.

This Simon & Schuster Canada edition February 2025

SIMON & SCHUSTER CANADA and colophon are trademarks of Simon & Schuster, LLC

For information about special discounts for bulk purchases, please contact Simon & Schuster Special Sales at 1-800-268-3216 or CustomerService@simonandschuster.ca.

Interior design by Wendy Blum

Manufactured in the United States of America

10 9 8 7 6 5 4 3 2 1

Library and Archives Canada Cataloguing in Publication

Title: One minute more / Robert Rotenberg.
Names: Rotenberg, Robert, 1953- author.
Description: Simon & Schuster Canada edition
Identifiers: Canadiana (print) 20240408624 | Canadiana (ebook) 20240408659 |
ISBN 9781668078778 (softcover) | ISBN 9781668078815 (EPUB)
Subjects: LCGFT: Thrillers (Fiction) | LCGFT: Novels.
Classification: LCC PS8635.O7367 O54 2025 | DDC C813/.6—dc23

ISBN 978-1-6680-7877-8
ISBN 978-1-6680-7881-5 (ebook)

For my brother David Rotenberg

1953–2023

"I like Mr. Gorbachev, we can do business together!"

British prime minister Margaret Thatcher

MONDAY

JULY 4, 1988

GREENE

75 HOURS MORE

IF ONLY HE HADN'T agreed to take this foolish assignment, Ari Greene thought, he could have spent the long weekend sunning himself on the dock at his girlfriend Meredith's family cottage north of Toronto. Or maybe the two of them could have taken a canoe and paddled over to their secret beach, where they could swim in private.

But no.

Instead, here he was heading down Rue Canusa, the main street of Stanstead, Quebec, a small town plunked squarely on the Quebec–Vermont border. His destination: the little US customs booth at the end of the road.

It was ten o'clock and the day was already warm. He opened the booth's glass door, stepped inside, and heard it close behind him with a loud clang. The air in the small room was stifling. A red-haired border guard sat alone behind a steel desk that looked as if it had been there since Pearl Harbor. A metal nameplate on his otherwise empty desk identified him as Officer Trevor Hickey.

Greene looked around. The walls of the booth were painted a deadly dull shade of beige. The only decoration, if you could call it that, was a wood-framed photo of a beaming President Ronald Reagan and his wife,

Nancy. The picture was too small for the wall, and it was hung higher than it should have been. The effect, Greene thought, was both absurd and sad at the same time.

He returned his gaze to Hickey, who gave him a look that seemed to be a toxic mixture of resignation and resentment.

"Good morning," Greene said. He thrust his arm across the desk to shake hands. "Ari Greene, Toronto Police Force. I believe you were expecting me."

Hickey gave a barely perceptible nod, as if to say he wasn't going to agree to anything or even deign to speak to Greene. At least not yet. He made no effort to rise to greet Greene or to shake his hand.

"You'll want to see my ID," Greene said, pulling his hand back and retrieving his badge and police identification card from his wallet.

Hickey put his hand out for both items and, like a bored theatre usher taking a customer's ticket before a show, glanced at them for a nanosecond. Still without saying a word, he rose from his chair. The man was tall and skinny, a long carrot-topped drink of water, Greene thought as he watched Hickey disappear through the door behind him.

Greene looked back through the glass door onto Canusa Street. A huge banner stretched across it announcing: WELCOME TO THE 1988 CAN/US JULY FOURTH PARADE. The sidewalk on the north side was filling up with rows of families dressed in red-and-white T-shirts, waving Canadian flags. On the south side, the scene repeated itself, with everyone wearing all-American red, white, and blue along with an equally healthy dose of American flags.

He heard the door behind Hickey's desk open, and a moment later the border guard walked back in holding a piece of long teletype paper.

"Officer, would you mind rolling up the sleeve of your left arm?" Hickey asked Greene, breaking his silence at last.

He's checking out my scar on the outer side of my arm to confirm my ID, Greene realized as he rolled up his shirt over his elbow. When he was a teenager, Greene fell through a glass door. The cut was so deep it took more than four hundred stitches to sew him back up, leaving a permanent scar. He had the habit of rubbing it when he was anxious.

Hickey glanced at the scar, handed Greene back his badge and his ID, and smiled. "I just got off the phone with Washington to check your clearance. You fit the description to a tee."

He passed over the telex. Greene read: "Ari Greene, Caucasian, five foot eleven inches, 185 pounds, dark hair, blue-green eyes, right-handed, scar on left forearm. Police constable, Metropolitan Toronto Police Force, five years since 1983. Single. No dependents."

Greene passed the telex back to Hickey without saying a word. It was his turn to remain silent.

"My orders are to let you cross the border during the parade, as you wish," Hickey said. He checked his watch.

Greene nodded. He resisted the urge to rub his scar.

"They didn't tell me why," Hickey said.

Greene shrugged. He watched Hickey pick up a metal pen and twirl it between his fingers.

"Officer Greene," he said, "I know you're not at liberty to inform me of the purpose of your mission."

Greene just looked at him.

Hickey pointed to the photo of President Reagan. "I also know that my president and the other G7 world leaders, and the Russian prime minister, are all gathering in your city, Toronto, soon."

"They arrive later today." Greene flashed his best smile.

That broke the ice. Hickey laughed. Clicked his pen open and shut, open and shut, gave a conspiratorial look around the customs booth.

"I for one am glad you're here. For the last three years I've taken nothing but flack for trying to tighten up security during this parade." He pointed through the glass door down the main street. "They've held this parade since the 1930s, and to the locals it's the most important day of the year. As far as I'm concerned, it's a nightmare."

He pulled out a clipboard from his desk and passed it across to Greene.

On it was a chart that Hickey had made of everything and everyone scheduled to be in the parade. It was meticulously detailed, each entry written in a tight, neat script.

Picky, picky, Greene thought, swallowing a smile.

"This lists what you can expect to see out there," Hickey said, pointing to each item with the tip of his pen. "Sixteen floats, four marching bands, three police cars, two fire trucks, a bunch of local politicians, the Shriners clowns—all in colourful yellow upside-down clown costumes festooned with fluffy red balls, some driving in circles in their tiny putt-putt cars, others walking among the crowds. Those were the numbers last year. This year things aren't as well organized. I tried. Believe me I tried."

"Must be frustrating," Greene said.

"No one wanted to listen, so now I'm grounded," Hickey said. "Under strict orders to stay put in this booth until the show's over." He walked around the desk and came uncomfortably close to Greene.

This guy was more intense than a laser beam.

"I'll watch from here and keep an eye on things," Hickey said.

Greene nodded, trying to convey how thankful he was for the offer of assistance. But all he could think was: Calm down, Picky, it's a meaningless small-town parade. And Greene was only here on this wild-goose chase to keep his boss happy.

"We'll work together on this." Hickey was speaking in a hushed voice now, still at close range.

"Sure." Greene bit down hard on his lower lip.

Hickey took Greene's hand and shook it firmly. "I'll stay at my post. You'll be on duty in the field."

Hickey's gaze was so fierce that Greene searched for somewhere else to look. His eyes wandered over the border guard's shoulder to the photo of Nancy and Ronald Reagan. For a second, he thought he saw old Ronnie wink.

WINTERS

75 HOURS MORE

"COME ON, BABY, DON'T give out on me now," Josh Winters called to his "Red, Rusty, and Trusty" Volvo, as he loved to call his old car. It was a phrase coined by another professor in the history department at the University of Vermont, who claimed the car and Winters were one and the same.

There were many valid points of comparison. Winters's politics were "red"—he wasn't some run-of-the-mill leftist, but a full-fledged neo-Trotskyite revisionist. He looked "rusty"—now in his late forties, Josh's wild auburn hair and beard were turning grey. Most of all he was "trusty"—despite his radical politics and outrageous appearance, Winters was one of the hardest-working academics in the department.

He did the lion's share of the housework too. His wife, Arlene, travelled so much—thanks to her job at that rip-off international bank—that he was alone most nights with their three daughters.

Last winter he'd come up with the idea of finding a summer retreat. When he saw the ad for this place in the *Burlington Free Press*, it sounded "too Josh" to resist. Imagine: an abandoned old farmhouse right up on the Quebec–Vermont border, miles from anywhere, no phone, no electricity, no plumbing. Let his colleagues rent their overpriced little cottages on the Cape for a thousand dollars a week. For twenty-five grand he'd bought his own piece of paradise.

Predictably, his fellow professors had all laughed when he told them about his purchase.

"What's the place look like?" one asked.

"Well, I haven't seen it yet," he was forced to admit.

"It's a perfect Josh move," the department head declared. "As far away from America as you can get and still be inside the border."

Thank goodness for his daughters. They loved the idea. All through the spring, Josh spent countless nights with them at the kitchen table, mapping out their organic herb and vegetable garden and designing their own anti-capitalist croquet game. He'd read them *Das Kapital*, *Animal Farm*, and *Lord of the Rings*—all three volumes.

Arlene was not amused. "Joshua, yes, we spent two months living out of a tent when we backpacked through Guatemala," she said. "But that was twenty years, and three kids, ago."

This morning she'd insisted on staying back with the girls at the bed-and-breakfast in St. Albans they'd rented for the weekend, while Josh went out to find "the damn shack." Josh had told her she was being a spoilsport. But now he was driving back and forth on the lumpy gravel road for the third darn time, stones flying up and pinging the floor of his old vehicle in a steady rat-a-tat that seemed to grow louder with every pass. He couldn't find the stupid driveway, never mind the farmhouse, and all he could think was that it was a good thing he was alone and his family wasn't with him.

His car hit a huge rut in the road, and Josh had to squeeze the steering wheel to keep from driving off into the ditch. Behind him, he heard his prized collection of brittle Robert Johnson 78 records flop around in the trunk and he said a silent prayer for their good health. What was he doing on this deserted, off-the-beaten-path road?

By his fourth pass, even Josh's indefatigable spirit was beginning to flag. Then, at last, he spotted an overgrown trail running up the hill. This had to be it. There was no way his trusty Volvo could squeeze through, so he parked on the side of the road, moved some branches out of the way, and started to walk.

And walk.

The trail kept narrowing, a swarm of mosquitoes pouncing on his now-sweaty beard and hair. In his excitement, he'd forgotten to check on his records. He was about to give up and turn back when he caught a glimpse of a building in the distance. A few minutes later his spirits were soaring as he ran around the tumbledown, two-story farmhouse. It had a solid stone foundation, a classic wraparound porch and, inside, wide-plank pine floors. Best of all were the magnificent windows in the living room, which gave a clear view all the way to the Canadian border.

Down in the valley he could see a road running between two towns, Stanstead, Quebec, and Derby Line, Vermont, where a colourful array of marching bands and decorated floats were readying for the Fourth of July parade. He could hear the musicians tuning their instruments. Someone was playing a trumpet, and the sound wafted up from below like a hawk cruising on an upstream wind current.

Winters, a man forever in motion, was transfixed. He stopped, put his hand on an old wood porch railing, and listened. Out of the cacophony of sound, the trumpeter's rendition of "God Bless America" emerged and, despite himself, Winters smiled.

Seconds later, he was skipping back down the hill, humming the patriotic song to himself, the same song he'd refused to sing since his first antiwar march two decades earlier. He snatched a thick branch for a walking stick and, laughing out loud, twirled it in the air above his head.

"Whoopee!" he cried out at the top of his lungs, running now, like a child rushing home for dinner. When he got back to his car, he started dancing, spinning wildly, twirling the branch over his head like a cheerleader at a football game with an oversized baton.

"America, America," he sang to the woods.

Then he saw the young woman.

She was riding an old-fashioned bike with a big backpack strapped to the back. She rounded the corner of the deserted road, pedaling hard, before she saw him and jammed on her brakes.

She looked shocked. He couldn't blame her. The whole situation was absurd.

"Welcome to paradise," Josh said, taking a deep bow.

The woman looked around, as if she expected another crazy man to jump out of the woods at her.

"Don't worry, I'm the only one here," he said, pointing the stick up the hill. "We just took possession of a farmhouse up the road."

The woman nodded. Dismounted. She hadn't responded.

Although Josh had taught attractive students his whole life, he'd made a point of never putting any stock in a woman's looks. He was interested in their brains. He'd never once even thought of straying with a student.

But there was something about this woman that seemed different than the usual coed. Yes, she was remarkably good-looking, as many of them were. But it was her face. Symmetrical. Like a fashion model's. Entrancing. And her eyes, a dark brooding brown colour, so dark they were almost black. The only flaw was her left eye, which he could see drifted slightly off-centre. It was noticeable, probably because otherwise she had a perfect face.

He realized that, although he hadn't intended to, he'd been staring at her. "This is the first time I've seen the place," he said, turning away, "that's why I'm so excited."

Still, she didn't say a word. What was it? Maybe she was a foreign summer student and didn't understand English. But most of them knew a few basic words: "Hello. How are you. My name is Isha."

Maybe it was the branch he was holding. Perhaps she was scared.

"Sorry about this stick, I didn't mean to frighten you," he said, shrugged, and lobbed it into the woods.

Still no answer. She hadn't moved a muscle.

"I've got to unload the car," he said, walking over to the trunk, talking over his shoulder. "Then get my wife and kids in St. Albans. We have three girls. They're going to love this place."

He turned back to her and at last she moved. She'd put her bicycle on its kickstand and stood beside it. As if she'd decided to do something.

Strange.

Why did she have that large backpack on her bike? What was she doing on a bike up here in the middle of nowhere? Why was she still staring at him that way? What was her next move going to be? For some reason he felt a shiver go up his spine. Maybe it hadn't been such a smart idea to come to this remote location by himself.

He felt naked. Alone. And now unarmed.

"I'm going to start with my old record collection," he said, speaking louder and slower. "Extremely rare. I call them my babies. I have to handle them gently."

He turned back to the car, opened the trunk, and pulled out a plastic milk carton filled with his Robert Johnsons. Despite the bumpy ride, the old records all appeared to be intact.

He peered back over his shoulder and saw the woman reach inside her jacket. He was relieved. He'd been right about her not speaking English. She must be carrying one of those pocket dictionaries, he thought, the way he had needed one when he went to the Soviet Union three years earlier.

He relaxed.

What an idiot he'd been. He felt guilty about being suspicious of her because she was "foreign." That was the kind of thinking the right-wing professors in his department had. What the hell, he'd even been singing "God Bless America" out loud. Ha, he laughed to himself: it *was* a good thing he was here alone.

He reached back in the trunk, pulled out an L.L.Bean blanket, and draped it with care over the record-filled milk carton like a father swaddling his first child. He did this every time he moved his records and loved to joke that he was keeping his Johnsons safe.

"It is not a long walk and if you are interested, you can come take a look at the house. It's old, but boy does it have potential," he said as he closed the trunk.

He turned and started back toward the driveway, smiling.

She was still staring at him. Then, with alarming speed, she jumped in front, blocking his way.

What the heck?

He saw what she had in her hand. It wasn't a dictionary.

He gasped.

He backed up, away from her.

"Please, please. Arlene, my girls . . . "

Her eyes kept zeroing in on him as she stepped closer.

"Emma is going to college next year, Samantha is studying Latin, Katherine is a bookworm . . . "

He retreated two more steps. Bumped into the back of the car. He was trapped. She moved in closer and raised her arm.

"Arlene, my wife, I love her so mu—"

He tried to say more, but he could no longer speak. A moment later his grip on the milk carton slipped and he watched helplessly as his Johnsons spilled out onto the rocky rutted road and splintered into a thousand pieces.

KEON

74.5 HOURS MORE

TORONTO POLICE CHIEF CHARLES Keon was good at many things, but waiting wasn't one of them. When the force was doing a dangerous stakeout, or a jury was deliberating on a murder case, or one of his officers had been gunned down and was in the hospital, he felt like a caged bear stuck in his office. He'd stomp around and drive his secretary, Miss Rose, crazy with hundreds of requests, until he'd grab a radio and hit the street.

Nothing made him feel better than marching out of police headquarters. Forget the fancy limos those politicians wanted him to drive around in. He preferred to walk the streets, as he'd done for the first twenty-five years of his career. Or hail a cab if he had to. He needed to be with his officers—assisting with a stakeout, pacing the courthouse halls, or holding the hands of an anxious spouse.

But with the G7 leaders coming to his city for three days, starting tomorrow and doing their final public appearance at one o'clock on their last day, right now there was no crime scene, no courtroom, no hospital for him to go to. Nothing to do but hope he'd hear from Ari Greene, the talented young cop he'd sent down to the Quebec–Vermont border after getting an anonymous tip that an assassin was about to cross into Canada, was on his way to the summit.

He hadn't heard anything yet from Greene's partner, Nora Bering. Keon had stationed her at a hotel down the street to be on twenty-four-hour duty as Greene's backup to follow up on any leads Greene might stumble on. Plus, report on Greene's progress to him.

Three years earlier, Keon had picked Bering for a special assignment, and it had gone horribly wrong. She was still furious with him and had refused his efforts to apologize to her.

So for Keon, this was a win-win. Greene was smart and resourceful, a good pick for this long-shot assignment. And Keon would get a chance to work with Bering and try for some personal redemption.

Meanwhile, every day Keon had to sit through the Security Assessment Meeting with so-called security experts from each of the G7 countries. With three thousand of the world's leading financial and economic journalists converging on Toronto, needing to be taken care of twenty-four hours a day, you would have thought these get-togethers would be serious affairs.

They were supposed to compare notes and strategies. Instead, they spent half of the time bragging about their expensive new equipment: message beepers, fax machines, and even new portable phones. And the other half of the time they gossiped about the leaders: Who would take Italy's foreign minister to the racetrack? Would there be English breakfast tea for Margaret Thatcher? The Japanese prime minister Takeshita wanted to stand beside President Reagan at the final "family photo" to be taken on the last day in the internal quadrangle at Hart House, a classic English university–style building at the centre of the University of Toronto. Who was caring for the two beavers brought to Toronto and living in the man-made pond on the site? The juiciest tidbit of all was their constant speculation about French prime minister François Mitterrand: Would he bring his wife or his mistress? Or both?

They tolerated Keon's presence, as if he were a poor nephew visiting his rich uncle's mansion on the hill. If the hotshots thought Keon would be wowed by their high-tech gadgetry and their "expertise," they were dead wrong.

"I've never been to a meeting where we caught a criminal," he'd told hundreds of politicians, bureaucrats, and overeager lieutenants in his ten-plus years as chief. "You want to stop crime, get out on the street and look for it."

This gang of self-righteous G7 bureaucrats wouldn't know a street if they tripped over a curb, Keon thought. Yesterday, he had told them about his tip that an assassin was coming across the border headed for the summit, gunning for all seven leaders, and Russian president Mikhail Gorbachev, who was invited as a special guest with "observer status."

You'd think that would have gotten them off their duffs. Not on your life.

"And the source of this 'tip' is whom?" asked James (call me Jimmy) Jameson, the pompous chief of G7 security who ran these get-togethers. An all-American preppy, right down to his khaki pants, blue blazer, round glasses, and ever-present bow tie—a different one each day. The day's colourful choice was bright yellow with red polka dots.

"For the last two months, a select group of officers have shaken down every contact they have in Toronto," Keon said, matching Jameson's stare. In fact, he didn't know the source—it was anonymous—but he wasn't going to reveal that to these bean counters. He shrugged. "The source is confidential."

"Very helpful, Chief Keon," Jameson said, rolling his eyes.

Could the guy be more condescending?

"We get two or three so-called assassination tips a day," Jameson said. "I'm sure your force can follow up on this one."

Keon made a show of shaking his head. He wanted them to think he was angry. Just the opposite. He was pleased. Now he'd followed their "protocol," presented his intelligence, and had it duly recorded in the minutes.

If these arrogant prigs weren't interested, all the better. Now he could pursue this lead as he saw fit, without anyone looking over his shoulder.

Keon got up from his desk and walked over to his fourth-story window, grasped the acrylic stick attached to the Venetian blinds, and twirled it between his thumb and forefinger. The slats blinked open and shut. Open and shut. Open and shut.

"Chief Keon, there's a call from Mr. Jameson's office," Miss Rose's voice cackled over the intercom. "They may have to move today's meeting back to four o'clock. I'll let you know when they call back to confirm."

This nonsense had been going on for the last two weeks. Jameson was constantly either late for meetings or "moving them back," as if Keon and the others were mere pawns on his chessboard.

Why not cancel the useless meeting, Keon thought as he strode over to his desk and clicked on the intercom. "Grrrr," he said, growling like a lion. "Same old, same old with these people. Hurry up and wait, wait, wait. Let me guess, he sends his sincere apologies." He heard Miss Rose laugh as he clicked the intercom off.

He opened his top desk drawer and removed a handmade calendar he'd drawn on a dry cleaner's shirt cardboard. With a thin black felt pen, he crossed out the 12:00 p.m. meeting and scrawled in 4:00 p.m. He turned the pen upside down and counted. He looked up at the big clock on the wall across from his desk. He'd placed it there so when he was interviewing someone in his office, he could casually look over their shoulder to check the time without being noticed. It was 10:30.

The leaders were arriving this afternoon and would be here for three days. Their last public appearance was at one o'clock on the last day. Three times twenty-four equals seventy-two hours. Add another two and a half hours. Seventy-four and a half hours more.

He slipped his handmade calendar back in his desk, stood, and looked around his office: thirty-six years of accumulated plaques, citations, trophies, photographs since he'd joined the police force as a recruit. A lifetime of long days and longer nights.

No one knew he was getting ready to retire. Not his wife, not even Miss Rose. But he was ready—if he could just get through these next seventy-four and a half hours.

He hit the switch on his intercom again. "Miss Rose, I'm going to walk. Please have my radio ready for me."

"Sir, do you want to try one of the new portable telephones? We received our first one for you this week. The police board wants to—"

"I know, I know. They want to *modernize* the force. They say I have to stop resisting all this new technology."

"Well, sir, people are starting to use them. In that movie you said you enjoyed, *Wall Street*—"

"I saw it. Michael Douglas talking into one of those big contraptions while he's on the beach. These technocrats at these meetings were showing theirs off the other day. They look more like mallets than phones."

A few nights ago, when Miss Rose had gone home, curiosity got the better of him and he opened the box of the portable phone that she'd put beside her desk. It was a heavy white thing, more than twice the size of his hand, with a black plastic aerial that stuck way out. He'd heard that the phone had been nicknamed the "Motorola Brick" and it sure felt heavy enough. In a pinch, he thought, he could use it to smash someone on the head or poke someone's eye out. Probably its most useful function.

"If you have it with you, Chief Keon," Miss Rose said, "I'll be able to patch through important calls directly to you."

"What's wrong with my radio?"

"These are like real telephones. You can call anyone, even if they're not on the force. We won't have to route calls through the radio room so the newspaper scanners can't listen in."

Keon sighed. "I surrender. Bring one in. I bet there's some trick to make the darn thing work."

"Well, you do have to drain the battery all the way down before you recharge it."

"I knew it," he said.

"Can I get you anything else, sir?"

"How about a time machine to transport me three days and three hours into the future?"

They laughed. He snapped off the intercom and shook his head. The next three days were going to seem like a lifetime.

HICKEY

74.5 HOURS MORE

FOR FIFTY-THREE CONSECUTIVE YEARS the Shriners' "Right on the Border" Fourth of July parade—"A Great Example of Canada–US Cooperation"—had gone off like clockwork. Even during the gas-starved summers during World War II, the locals managed to scrape together enough volunteers and ration tickets to put on their cherished local pageant. And it felt as if he'd lived through all fifty-three of them, Hickey thought as he sat in his customs booth and peered down the street tracking the parade.

Ever since the 1920s when Al Capone ran whiskey through this border, the town had been famous for its casual attitude about the lines on the map. The border bisected a library, a curling club, and even a bar, where it went right through a pool table.

When Hickey had arrived here three years earlier, a twenty-year veteran fresh from five tough years down on the southern Texas border, this place had more leaks than a colander. It drove him around the bend.

He shook his head at the memory as he watched the spectacle play out before him. This is supposed to be an international border, not a country fairground. You'd never know it today, he thought as he watched the costumed, upside-down Shriner clowns, who were "walking on their hands" as they pranced up and down along the parade route. They'd march for a while, then zigzag across the street, entertaining the crowds as if the border didn't exist at all. Total chaos. He was the only one who noticed or cared. Everyone else was too busy basking in the bright sunlight. One big party.

He peered down at his handwritten list and one by one ticked off the floats, marching bands, putt-putt cars, and six clowns as they made their way down Canusa Street.

During his first year here, Hickey had tried to put some order into the parade. "How can you guarantee that someone illegal won't slip across the border in all the hubbub?" he'd asked his pampered, sleepy staff. But his concerns fell on uninterested ears. Predictable.

The second year, he put his foot down. Insisted every parade group prepare a detailed itinerary and fill out a three-page questionnaire on the background of each participant. He set a firm deadline: ninety days before the parade so there would be time to run security checks and issue photo passes. His sullen staff worked double-overtime to handle the paperwork.

The backlash was immediate. The Franco-Vermont International Trade Association, the Border Guards Union, the local Canadian and American press—they all complained: the forms weren't translated into French, the filing deadline was too early, the spirit of international friendship had been stripped from the historic parade.

You name it, they bitched about it.

A month later some geek bureaucrat in Washington filed a report about Hickey's staff's excessive overtime and unauthorized use of funds. Hickey got papered for it and had to go through a "job reevaluation" at the regional headquarters in Burlington. By the time they were done with him it was all he could do to save his job.

As part of the deal, he'd agreed to forgo work on this year's parade and never leave his booth until it was over. Now all he could do was stay imprisoned here and watch. And count. After more than two decades in the service, he couldn't watch anything without counting it.

He'd strung his binoculars around his neck. Now he lifted them again and began to tally things up. Twelve tractors, tick; six marching bands, tick; nineteen promotional vehicles—mostly trucks, everything from Marg's Lovely Lawn and Garden Centre to Ricky's Guns 'n' Ammo Shop. Tick, tick, tick. Both towns rolled out all their best civic hardware: one fire truck and police car each, and the snowplow they shared. More ticks.

The parade hit a bottleneck and slowed to a snail's pace. He kept counting. Twelve Shriners in their cars. Tick. Seven upside-down clowns.

Wait.

He did a double take. The upside-down clowns. Last year there were six. He'd seen two beside the Derby Line volunteer fire truck, two in front of the float for Marcel's Hardware, and two were behind the pink late-model Cadillac from Wanda's Wonderful Hair Salon. But he had counted a seventh clown. A moment later they were all mingling with the crowd, overlapping and switching positions. The parade started to move again.

"No, no, no," Hickey muttered to himself. This was *exactly* the thing he was trying to stop. Seven. He was sure he'd counted seven upside-down clowns. There were only supposed to be six.

The parade was picking up speed, travelling again down the street. Could he have got it wrong? He checked his clipboard. He looked through his binoculars again, right down the borderline. One, two. There were three and four. And five and six. Number seven was nowhere to be seen.

The seventh clown was missing.

Disappeared.

Vanished.

He thought about the visit from the Toronto cop. The upcoming G7 summit being held there starting tomorrow. Hickey's years of experience screamed out at him: something is wrong. He yanked the binoculars off his neck and smashed them down on his metal desk. He took his parade list, coiled it into a cone shape, and started hitting it into his open palm. He paced in a tight circle. Like a prisoner in a cell.

He looked around his booth and stopped at the portrait of Ronald

Reagan and his wife, Nancy, smiling down on him. "I can feel it, Mr. President," he whispered. His breath was coming hard. "One of them crossed over into Canada and disappeared. It's my job to protect you."

He gritted his teeth, turned to the front door, and wrenched it open. A flood of music from the marching bands blasted in. He stepped outside and barely heard the door slam shut behind him.

GREENE

74.5 HOURS MORE

GREENE WANDERED THROUGH THE parade, not at all certain what he was looking for. The wide avenue was packed with what felt like a never-ending line of tacky floats, punctuated by brassy high school marching bands and clowns in their yellow costumes. Both sides of the road were lined with families waving their Canadian and American flags.

Two boys from the Canadian side scurried out into the road to scoop up some candy one of the upside-down clowns had tossed their way. The boys were obviously twins, and the clown stopped and bowed. The boys laughed and high-fived one of his "feet" before rushing back to their parents.

The clown stopped in front of Greene. He found himself staring at the costume. The illusion was so powerful he had to force himself to picture that the man's feet were on the ground and not up in the air. He searched up and down for eyeholes until he found two slight openings hidden in the folds on the top of the pants. Clever.

The clown seemed to understand his curiosity. Seemed to be looking back at him. He nodded. The clown nodded back and lingered for a long moment before heading toward the Canadian side. Greene kept walking along the parade route. The whole pageant was extraordinarily informal. The border had all but disappeared.

No wonder Picky Hickey was so uptight. This was no place for a by-the-book type like him. Not today, at least. His bosses must have chained Hickey to his post for the good of his health. What was a guy like Hickey doing in a town like this? Greene chuckled to himself. What was *he* doing here?

One of the Shriner putt-putt cars, doing a wild figure eight, skidded toward him. Greene jumped out of the way. He found a gap between a float from Howie's Hardware and one from Home Fixins and skipped over to the American side.

It was liberating, being able to stroll across the border. He wandered among the crowd for a minute or two. Looking back toward the Canadian side, he saw a flash of red hair bobbing above the crowd. Greene stretched up onto his toes to get a better look. Yes. It was Hickey, out of his booth. What was he up to?

Greene started to walk back across the road to the Canadian side, squinting in the bright sunshine. Now the Newport High School marching band was in the way. The musicians were so tightly packed there was no room to cut through. Why do they need so many trombone players, Greene cursed as he looked for an opening. Finally, he spotted a gap in the trumpet section. He started to dart through.

Someone seized his arm. He turned. It was a studious-looking man, probably in his early fifties, with horn-rimmed glasses and a surprisingly firm grip.

"Sir, could you please wait until we pass," the man said. "My staff and students have worked all year to perform in this parade. I'm sure you can understand."

"Sorry," Greene said. Just my luck, he thought as he looked at the long line of the band. The school principal is telling me to behave.

HICKEY

74.5 HOURS MORE

HICKEY SPED DOWN THE road on the Canadian side and stopped to look at the neat row of houses behind the three-deep crowd of spectators.

"*Excusez-moi, s'il vous plait,*" someone yelled.

Everyone was speaking French. Damn foreign languages. Three years here and he still couldn't understand a word. Like on the Texas border, everyone speaking Spanish, and he didn't understand a thing. They'd thrown that at him too, in his job reevaluation.

For a few seconds he was back there on the banks of the Rio Grande. His Navajo guide teaching him to track illegals: "Scour the land, look for small things out of place—those are your clues."

"*Bougez!*" another person in the crowd called out at him.

He stared down at his feet in frustration. He couldn't see a thing.

"The earth never lies," his guide had said. "Read the ground."

Hickey bent down and picked out the outline of four oversized fingers on a patch of dirt between the concrete and the roadside grass. They pointed north off the road.

He popped back up and cut through the crowd. Moments later he found himself looking at two small houses with a thick row of cedar bushes running between them. A well-worn footpath led to a small gap in the greenery. He turned back to look at the parade. Everyone was watching it, no one was watching him.

He slipped through the gap and in a few steps was in a well-kept backyard. After the noise of the parade, it was remarkably quiet. The only sound came from an ornate water fountain tinkling gently in the centre of the tidy lawn. There was the mint scent of fresh-cut grass.

To his left was a screened-in porch with a crucifix on the wall. To his right, in the far back corner of the lawn, stood a life-size plastic sculpture of the Nativity—Jesus in the manger, with the three Magi looking over Mary's bare shoulder—waiting to be illuminated on the front lawn every December.

Summer storage, Hickey thought with a sneer.

Hickey felt like a fool. He'd left his booth, despite his orders to stay there during the parade. Now he was an intruder. He'd crossed the border illegally. Even worse, he was trespassing on private property—in a foreign country. He turned to leave.

He took a last look at the porch. An old lady was sitting in a rocking chair, wrapped in a knitted blanket. He hadn't noticed her before. She must be asleep, Hickey thought. But she seemed so still. The rocking chair wasn't rocking. He took a step toward her.

Out of the corner of his eye, he saw a flash of yellow behind the Nativity sculpture. He swung around.

He was surprised to see one of the Shriner clowns move out from behind the plastic Magi. The top part of the costume had been folded down over the bottom part, and he was even more surprised to see that the person inside it was a young woman. He'd thought all the Shriners were old men.

"Excuse me," Hickey said. "I didn't mean to intrude."

The woman didn't move.

Great, Hickey thought. She probably doesn't speak a word of English.

"I believe," he said, speaking slowly, "you may have crossed the border illegally."

She just kept staring at him.

Hickey tried to remember the word in French for "believe." So he said: "*Excusez-moi, mademoiselle, je—*"

She took a step toward him.

He smiled at her.

She didn't smile back.

She lifted her right arm. Hickey saw what was in her hand. He tried to retreat. But it was too late.

Why, he thought, as he toppled to the ground, hadn't he followed orders and stayed in his booth?

GREENE

74.25 HOURS MORE

GREENE HAD NO CHOICE but to step back while the marching band passed slowly in front of him, stopped, swung their instruments for a few seconds, then continued on. Stop. Start. After the trumpeters, there were the clarinets, the baton twirlers, the tuba players, and at long last the drummers. Newport High must bus kids in from half the state, Greene thought.

When the last band member passed him by, he broke into a run, dodging the putt-putt cars driving in turbulent crazy eights, and made it back over to the Canadian side.

Where was Hickey? It had taken Greene too long to cross Canusa Street, and in that time the border guard had vanished. Greene scanned the long row of neat houses, each with clean front lawns.

He stared down at his feet, searching for any clue. In the dirt he saw a faint boot mark. He looked in the direction it was headed. There was a row of dense cedar bushes between two houses. Drawing closer, he saw a small footpath on the lawn where the grass had been worn away, leading through a small gap in the shrubbery.

He glanced behind him. The crowd's attention was still on the parade.

He heard the boom of the drums, the squeak of the clarinets, and the bass of the trombones. He could even pick out some voices. A small boy: "*Où est le fire engine, Maman?*" A tired father: "Just five more minutes, Zachary, then we'll get you a candy." An anxious-sounding female: "Excuse me, pardon, could I get through? *Puis-je passer?*"

He approached the bushes and examined them. A small ball of red cloth was stuck on one of the branches. He picked it off and put it in his front pocket.

Something wasn't right.

He went through the bushes and found himself on a path between the two houses. After the din of the parade, it was astoundingly quiet. A footpath led to the backyard to his right, where a low-lying gate had been left open.

He entered, step-by-step. There was a gaudy water fountain in the centre, but otherwise everything was still.

He crept forward.

Agent Hickey lay prone on the ground a few feet in front of him.

Motionless.

Greene reached into his jacket, drew his gun from his holster, and swept the yard. He couldn't see anyone. Bending low, he rushed to Hickey. The border guard's head was turned to the side, his eyes upturned. Greene shook his shoulder. He didn't move. Checked his pulse. Nothing.

Still in a deep crouch, Greene backed up until he felt the edge of the open gate behind him. Basic training: keep the scene in front, keep an escape route to your rear.

He quickly took in the whole scene. To his right was a screened-in porch. In front of him was a wide, neatly trimmed lawn with the fountain right in the middle. Back in the far-right corner was a plastic Christmas Nativity sculpture. There was no other possible hiding place.

He looked back at the porch. An old lady sat in a rocking chair. Motionless. She could be asleep. Greene watched her chest carefully. Nothing moved. Turning back to keep his eyes on the backyard, he opened the door to the porch, slipped in, and went to the old lady. She wasn't breathing. He felt for her pulse. Nothing. She was dead too.

He had to act fast.

He bolted across the lawn, past the fountain, and threw his back against the Nativity sculpture. He swept the yard with his gun to confirm there were no other hiding spots. There weren't.

He tried to steady his breathing and listen. All he could hear was the pulsing blood in his brain. Nothing from the far side of the sculpture. Silence. If someone was hiding there, he was a professional killer. Had he seen or heard Greene enter the backyard?

There was no time to waste. The parade would be over in a few minutes.

Greene tiptoed to the end of the sculpture and rubbed the scar on his left arm, comforted by the familiar roughness.

He ducked down, pointed his gun upward, took a deep breath, and jumped.

BERING

74.25 HOURS MORE

OFFICER NORA BERING HATED everything about this assignment. Being cooped up in an airless room at the Jarvis Hotel, steps away from police headquarters. Stuck here twenty-four hours a day. Forced to do nothing. Don't leave. Wait.

Chief Keon had stationed Bering here to back up her partner, Ari Greene, while he was down on the Quebec border following this "tip" about an assassin. Talk about looking for a needle in a haystack. Keon had installed a new phone because, he said, they needed a secure line far away from police scanners and radios and the prying eyes and ears of the press. He told them they couldn't tell their families about this assignment, so they'd made up a silly story about being put on emergency traffic duty for the summit.

She shook her head. The chief really was grasping at straws. But could she blame him? The most powerful people on the planet were coming to his city. Their safety was in his hands.

She looked at the clock radio on the desk. It was quarter to eleven. She'd devised a strict exercise regimen to keep herself sane while she was shut up in this room. Every hour she was doing alternately forty sit-ups or forty push-ups. She'd done her sit-ups at ten. Push-ups were next.

The one good thing was, if by chance Keon was right about this tip of his, Bering would be here for Greene. She'd met him five years earlier on the first day of police college, two of the older recruits, seated next to each other. They'd struck up a friendship immediately, even though they were from such different backgrounds.

Bering's father came from a strict Mennonite family, dedicated pacifists who refused to fight in World War II. One afternoon in 1941, he snuck off the family farm, walked eight miles to town, went to the recruiting office, and signed up. He fought in France for three years, and when he came home he was banished. He moved to a farm in the country, where he still lived, and he never saw anyone in his family again.

Like Bering, Greene was an only child. His father was a Holocaust survivor. Her father had abandoned his religion to fight in the war, and his father had fought the Nazis to survive. Perhaps those were the things that connected them.

They'd been partners since graduating and always called each other by their last names—never Nora and Ari. They liked to joke that they were each other's missing siblings.

She stared at the phone. Don't you dare ring, she half whispered to herself. No news was good news. No calls meant that nothing had happened to Greene. Even better, that she didn't have to talk to Keon. She was still mad at him for what had happened three years ago.

She glanced again at her clock radio. Thirteen minutes to go until she could hit the floor and do forty push-ups.

GREENE

74.25 HOURS MORE

NOTHING.

Not a thing was behind the sculpture. Only grass and open space. Greene lowered his gun. The air rushed out of his lungs. His muscles went slack. He must have just missed the killer. Whomever Hickey had followed here worked fast.

A row of low fences separated the backyard from the neighbours on both sides. Greene's options were narrowing. The longer he stayed here the more likely someone would show up.

He could run back out to the street and get assistance. He played out the scenario: rush to the customs booth, but with Hickey dead there would be no one else there. No, he'd have to notify the local cops. But they'd hold him until they confirmed his identity, especially since he was armed. By that time, the family would be back from the parade. They'd find their dead grandmother. The backyard would be sealed off and he'd be stuck here for hours.

Meanwhile, the killer, whom Hickey must have followed here, would be a million miles away.

He could hop a fence, but that would be a mistake. Too slow. Increase the chances he'd be seen. He might even get shot.

No.

The only way out was the way he came in.

Still, two people were dead. Everything in his training fought against leaving. It was drilled into police recruits from day one: first cop at the scene of a crime has primary responsibility; secure the scene, don't touch or disturb anything, contact your partner, call for help.

If only he were back in Toronto, Greene would use his radio to call this in, and cordon off the backyard. But he wasn't in Toronto. He didn't have a radio. His partner, Bering, was four hundred miles away. Even worse, he was dressed in civilian clothes, alone in a backyard in Quebec filled with fresh corpses. The one local person who knew he was a cop was silenced forever.

And Greene had a gun in his hand.

Move, he told himself as he slipped his gun back in its holster. Move.

Every cell in his brain told him to hurry, but he stopped. Checked the yard again. There must be something. A clue. He didn't want to leave empty-handed. His eyes lit upon another red ball stuck to the outer edge of the sculpture. It was the same as the one he'd taken from the bushes.

He hesitated. Never disturb a crime scene, never touch evidence with your bare hands. He lowered the sleeve of his jacket to cover his fingers, then teased the ball free and tucked it into his front pocket with the other one. He raced back across the lawn toward the gate, the way he had come in five minutes earlier.

Five minutes that felt like an eternity.

MARINA

74 HOURS MORE

"NO PLAN CAN COVER every contingency," Alisander had told Marina hundreds, maybe thousands, of times during her years of training. "You must be in peak physical condition, you must know everything possible about the places you will travel through to get to your destination, you must never, ever hesitate to kill, and you must be resourceful. Your ability to think on your feet will be your greatest asset."

As always, Alisander was right, Marina thought as she stepped onto the 11:00 bus destined for Montreal. She sat in an aisle seat in the middle of the bus, plopped her big backpack on the seat beside her—to make it difficult for anyone to sit there—and pulled out a well-thumbed copy of *L'Étranger*. Now she was wearing a flowery dress, her eyes hidden by a pair of sunglasses. She even had a Montreal Expos baseball cap, which she pulled down low over her forehead. All part of the plan to make her look like a typical, self-absorbed university student slouched over her latest book. Blend in with the crowd.

Training had been her life since she was four years old. The dark night when Alisander took her. Saved her. Taught her. Since then, she was never again allowed to speak her own language. By the time she was fourteen she could stay awake for three days at a stretch and hike 150 miles a week through the mountains of Afghanistan. Four years ago, when she turned eighteen, she was given this assignment.

She began her course of intensive study. Read everything about northern Vermont, southern Quebec, Montreal, and the various routes to Toronto. And the details of the plan. She pored over newspapers and magazines, watched videotapes of television programs and movies, and listened to hours of radio broadcasts. Now her English and French were flawless. So was her physique and physical stamina.

"You'll be unknown," Alisander said. "They'll have no photographs or fingerprints of you, no records of any kind. You'll be like the wind rifling through their curtains, then you'll be gone."

She thought of all that had happened this morning. Alisander would be proud of her. She *had* been resourceful.

First, there had been the man with the red beard near his farmhouse. He'd taken her by surprise. She thought he was an undercover police officer until he told her about his new farmhouse and his wife and daughters back in the town. His family wouldn't be expecting him for a few hours. Too late to cause her any problem.

"When in doubt, kill." Alisander's words rang in her ears. "Never hesitate. Always kill."

The man fell instantly, spraying his records out down the hill. No one would suspect she'd poisoned him. They'd think: overweight middle-aged man has heart attack while unloading heavy boxes from his car.

Marina checked her watch. It was 10:58. The bus was scheduled to leave in two minutes. She peered over her book and looked up the aisle. The bus driver's seat was empty. Hurry up, she thought.

After she killed the red-bearded man, it was a simple matter to ride the last mile to the border, duck into the woods to hide the bike, change into her clown costume, and slip unnoticed into the parade. Crossing the border was easy, just as Alisander said it would be. She saw the house he had picked out for her and entered the backyard to change out of her costume behind that odd sculpture in the far corner of the lawn. The old lady on the porch surprised her, but killing her only took a few seconds. When they found her, they'd think she'd died in her sleep.

Marina was behind the sculpture getting out of the costume when the American border guard showed up. Her third surprise of the morning.

She had to kill him too, even though she knew his death would draw immediate attention. Act fast, she told herself, and she did. His body lay in the yard, and she thought about dragging him behind the sculpture, but there was no time. She flung the costume over the fence, got out of the backyard and, forcing herself to walk, slipped through the crowd. "Never run unless you are being chased, always try to blend in" was another one of the lessons Alisander had taught her.

It was a long walk to the Rock Island bus station where, as they'd planned, a bus to Montreal was leaving every fifteen minutes.

She opened her book that Alisander had given her: *L'Étranger—The Stranger.* Seems fitting, she thought, smiling to herself.

The bus was almost filled up, and except for her, they were all old people. But where was the driver? Had someone found the dead border guard? Were the police going to block the road? Should she get off the bus?

She started to read her book: "Mother died today. Or was it yesterday?"

Mother. Marina had a vague memory of her mother, before Alisander took her away. Or was she given away? She'd always secretly wondered.

She checked her watch again. One minute to go. Still no bus driver. What should she do?

She closed her book and was about to stand up.

Wait.

Someone was coming onto the bus. A man in uniform.

She reopened the book and peeked over it.

The man bounded up the stairs and walked down the aisle, looking at all the passengers. She felt panic rise in her stomach. Was he a police officer? She slunk back down and slid her tongue over her back-right tooth to the spot where, two years earlier, a dental surgeon had carved out a hiding place. It would be easy to flip the cap off with her tongue and swallow the cyanide pill lodged there. She had practiced it so many times with a placebo.

Wait.

The man, overweight with a weird moustache, wasn't a police officer. He was the bus driver.

She let out a breath. Slid her tongue back away from her tooth. The driver lingered near her, and she kept her face down, pretending to read her book. Soon she saw him turn around and lumber back to the front of the bus. He sat down in the driver's seat, pulled a lever, closed the door, and fired up the engine.

She was safe. She felt the tension leave her body. In a few seconds they'd be on their way. Getting across the border had been a huge challenge, and she'd done it.

KEON

74 HOURS MORE

"EXCUSE ME, CHIEF KEON," Miss Rose's voice chirped over the intercom.

"Yes," he replied, perhaps too quickly.

"Confirmed. The meeting's pushed back now to four this afternoon."

"Happy days!" he said, popping out of his chair. He was close to sixty-five and still nimble. A minute later he was positively jaunty, the big, newfangled portable phone in his hand, as he passed through the front lobby, gave the surprised sergeant at the reception desk a firm salute, and shoved the front door open, a wide smile on his face like a convict getting out of the penitentiary.

The Toronto police headquarters was a shabby, redbrick three-story building that fronted onto the top of Jarvis, one of the oldest streets in the city. Chillingly cold in winter, horribly hot and humid in summer, one of the building's two elevators always seemed to be closed for repairs, the washrooms were ridiculously small, and the cafeteria consisted of three vending machines: a pop machine, a coffee machine, and a snack machine. There was never a day when all three worked at the same time.

He crossed Jarvis and looked back at his redbrick home away from home with parentlike affection. He loved every inefficient thing about it. But the building's days were numbered. As with everything else in the booming Toronto of the late 1980s, the police force was going upscale and heading downtown. Soon it would be ensconced in the new, ultramodern headquarters on College Street—all marble, polished granite, and poured concrete with a ten-story atrium, an upscale cafeteria that served cappuccinos and lattes, stainless-steel sinks in the washrooms, and offices with windows that didn't open. The Old Lady of Jarvis Street—as the locals and regulars called it—was slated to be torn down within a year.

Keon wore a short-sleeved white shirt over a white undershirt, worn grey pants, and stolid black shoes. He still parted his steely grey hair with a hard line down the left side. A few years ago he had, reluctantly, stopped wearing a hat. Old-fashioned. A throwback. That's how he looked. But he reveled in all the changes, both good and bad, he'd seen in Toronto since he moved here as an underweight Irish immigrant child of eight.

Back then, Toronto was a dull, closed city. No buses or streetcars ran on Sundays. As a compromise the city fathers in their wisdom allowed the Toronto Maple Leafs, the city's minor-league baseball team, to play on the "Lord's Day," but the games had to end by four o'clock in the afternoon. He remembered going to a doubleheader with his father and the second game being shut down in the seventh inning.

"British puritans," his Irish grandfather, Liam, used to complain. "This city's so flat it makes you think maybe the world isn't round. The Scottish bankers built it with straight streets and their Presbyterian rules to make it so boring people would have nothing to do but work."

A streetcar slowed to a stop, and Keon joined the long line to enter. He could have flashed his badge for a free ride, but he didn't want to. Without thinking, he dug into his pocket and pulled out a five-dollar bill.

The driver frowned. "Exact change, buddy, we only take exact change. Where you been for the last two years?"

Flustered, Keon reached back into his pocket and pulled out a handful of coins. The traffic light turned green. The car behind the streetcar honked its horn. The streetcar driver was getting impatient. Keon piled the coins into the metal fare box.

"Need a transfer?" the driver asked with studied indifference.

"Transfer? Sure, thanks."

The driver tore off a long, thin piece of printed paper and passed it to Keon. "Make sure you don't lose it," he said.

Keon found a seat by a window near the back and watched the city roll by, then took the subway east to his old stomping grounds. The darkness in the tunnel was complete. But he knew what was coming up.

At the turn of the century, the city built a massive expansion bridge across the Don River Valley to join the east end to downtown. Back then the politicians had the foresight to add a rail line under the road above that sat dormant for more than fifty years until the subway was added in 1962.

Back in 1912, when the Prince of Wales opened the bridge, no one realized this would become Toronto's favourite suicide spot. Early on in his career as a cop, the chief had learned of the shocking regularity of the always-unreported death jumps.

Kathump, kathump, kathump. The train made a clicking sound as it burst out of the tunnel into the light and rushed across the bridge.

"Mummy, look, a train, a train," a boy called out to his mother, pointing to tracks below in the valley.

Keon looked down at the tracks, then the river, the place he'd almost drowned when he was a kid before his best friend had rescued him. Then, on the other side of the river, the spot where the judge had landed when he jumped.

"Nora," he whispered to himself, "if I'd known it would happen, I would have never . . . "

All roads seem to lead back to here, he thought, as the train threw him into the darkness of the tunnel on the far side of the valley.

MARINA

74 HOURS MORE

MARINA SAW THE BUS driver hesitate. Something had caught his eye. Why weren't they moving?

Stay calm. Don't move.

She watched as the driver swung the door back open and someone else came on the bus.

What was going on?

It was the man she had stopped to stare at for a moment during the parade while she was in the costume. She'd recognized his face from among the jumble of the thousands of newspapers she'd read and photographs she'd seen in her preparation. He had a fit build, warm, almost boyish features, distinctive blue-green eyes, thick black hair. Try as she might, she couldn't remember who he was.

She watched him lean over and talk to the driver. As Alisander had taught her, she'd taken a seat halfway down the bus, not too close for the driver to notice her but close enough for her to hear any conversations he had with passengers and also near enough to the door for her to get off the bus fast.

She closed her eyes behind her sunglasses, stilled her breathing, didn't move.

As part of her years of training, Alisander made her go blindfolded for days, sometimes a whole week, to develop her sense of hearing. "Blind people can hear better," he had lectured her, "not because their hearing is stronger, but because they have fewer distractions. You must learn to shut down all of your other senses to hear better, Marina. It could save your life."

Years of practice improved her hearing remarkably. She learned to close, or narrow, her eyes so she could hardly see, still her body, and concentrate on every sound. Even those at the outer limits of her range.

Now she squeezed her eyes shut and listened hard.

"If you can wait a minute more," the man from the parade was saying to the driver in stilted French. So he was English, probably not from Quebec. She opened her eyes in time to see him take something out of his coat pocket and flash it at the driver. It glinted in the sunlight for a moment. Marina realized what it was. A badge. The man must be a police officer.

She saw the driver shrug. He left the door open while the policeman made his way down the aisle. Marina picked up her book again. She could hear his footsteps. He was getting closer. Play the part, she told herself: you're a student, pull down your baseball cap, read your book. He'd stopped right beside her. She felt him look down at her. She didn't move, didn't acknowledge his presence.

Keep reading. Be calm. Stay still.

She let her eyes drift off the page.

Ignore him. Be oblivious.

Silently, she slid her right hand, which was hidden from his view, into her pocket for her weapon. Her head started to pound, and her mouth went dry. He was so close she could feel the heat of his body. Smell his fresh sweat. He'd been running.

He hadn't moved. She had to do something. It would be suspicious if she ignored him. She turned in his direction and her sunglasses slipped off and fell to the floor.

"*Merde*," she whispered.

He bent down, retrieved them, and handed them back to her. Their eyes met. She gave him a wan smile, took the sunglasses from his hand, slid them back on, and returned to her book. She'd seen a bulge under the left breast pocket of his jacket and caught a glimpse of a gun strapped inside. For sure he was a policeman.

She thought he was going to say something to her. Would it be in English or French? He wasn't moving.

Keep your eyes on the book.

She read the first line again.

"Mother died today. Or was it yesterday?"

At last she heard footsteps and he started to walk toward the end of the bus. She filled her lungs with fresh oxygen. Moments later he walked past her, without stopping, and went straight to the front of the bus and started talking to the driver. She squeezed her eyes shut again.

"I'll wait for the next bus," she heard him say, and heard footsteps descend, then the bus door closed again.

The driver disengaged the brake and they started to move.

At last.

Marina closed her book and put her head back against the seat. Scanning her memory. A police officer. Not from Quebec. That was it. She remembered now. She'd seen his photo in a newspaper article about two young Toronto police officers, a man and a woman. They tracked down a missing high school student. People thought the girl was a runaway, but the two officers, on their own initiative, had found her locked in a basement and arrested her kidnapper.

Marina couldn't remember his name, but that didn't matter. She remembered his face. She remembered thinking he was handsome, and she'd been right. She slunk down lower in her seat as she pieced together what had just happened. A few minutes ago, this police officer must have found the dead bodies in the backyard. He'd run over to the bus station—that's why he was sweaty—to try to catch the killer. He's from Toronto, that means he's here looking for an assassin.

She broke into a smile at her next thought.

Looking for an assassin, but he doesn't know he's looking for me.

BERING

74 HOURS MORE

BERING HAD JUST FINISHED her fortieth push-up when the phone rang. She was startled, rushed over to pick up the receiver. Who would it be, Greene or Keon?

"Bering," she said.

"It's me," Greene said. "I have a lot to tell you, and I'm not quite sure what it all means."

"I'm listening." She grabbed her notebook and flipped to a blank page. She heard the stress in his voice.

He told her about meeting Hickey, the uptight American border guard in his little customs booth. About the parade, how he followed Hickey into the backyard on the Quebec side and found him dead on the ground. The old lady in her rocking chair on the porch. Dead too. His split-second decision to run back to the bus station.

The words came tumbling out of him in a torrent.

"Slow down," she said. "One step at a time. Are you sure the old lady was dead?"

"Not breathing. Not moving. No pulse."

She flipped her notebook to a fresh page and kept writing.

"Hickey must have caught this guy by surprise and that's what got him killed," Greene said. "The killer had to get away fast, so that's why he left Hickey's body out in the open. There's no train service down here. The only other way out is the bus. I know it's a long shot, but—"

"Okay, okay," Bering said. "Now you're at the bus station—"

"I got here just as a bus was about to leave for Montreal. I boarded it and checked out the passengers. Mostly old people, a few families, a young woman who looked like a student. The youngest man on board, besides the bus driver, was at least sixty years old. I got out, crossed the street, and called you."

Bering was onto the third page of her notes. Her mind racing. Maybe Keon wasn't so crazy after all. What if there really was an assassin heading to Toronto determined to kill the G7?

"How about the local cops?" she asked.

"We have to inform them," Greene said, echoing her thoughts.

Bering realized she was breathing hard. She took a deep breath.

"What if Keon is right?" Greene asked her. "Two people are dead."

"Two that we know of," she said. She had to think through the next move with Greene. "When does the next bus leave for Montreal?"

"There's one every fifteen minutes. I've been watching the people boarding the next bus. Not one of them looks to be under sixty-five," he said. "What do you think? Should I get on it?"

She stopped writing. "What are the other options?" she asked him.

"I stay here. Call the cops—"

"And you'll be stuck there for hours."

Neither of them spoke. The importance of the decision they had to make in the next few seconds felt like a weight they were both struggling to lift.

"I need to decide," Greene said. "The bus driver's closing the luggage rack under the bus. He's about to get on it."

"Take it," Bering said. "Call me the second you get off in Montreal. I'll call Keon and we'll inform the local cops."

She looked out the window down at the street traffic. People in short sleeves and sun hats, laughing, talking, passing by without a care in the world.

"One more thing," she said.

"Quick. I've got to go."

"Greene," she said. "Be careful."

LEVELLIER

74 HOURS MORE

FOR RENE LEVELLIER IT had to be the most boring bus route on the whole lower-Quebec circuit. He was halfway through his four-month stint and, *mon Dieu*, he could hardly wait for it to be over. Montreal to Stanstead, Stanstead to Montreal—the same darn circuit twice a day. Dull, dull, dull.

It wasn't just the scenery that was uninteresting, but the women: retirees, mothers with whining children, even nuns going to and from the convent on the shores of Lake Memphremagog. What an ugly collection. Day after day, not a decent female to look at, never mind try to sidle up to at the end of the trip.

No kidding. Levellier knew he had a reputation among his friends at the bus line for success with his female passengers. He even had a special signal he gave the dispatchers in the booth at the Montreal station, when he had a good-looking prospect aboard about to unload.

This morning, as he was getting ready to leave, he was thrilled when, watching from the nearby café, he saw the pretty university student walk briskly up to the bus, running shoes, flowery hippie dress, sunglasses, Montreal Expos baseball cap tucked low over her head, effortlessly carrying a big knapsack over one shoulder—all that aerobic exercise, Levellier thought. He gave her his most winning smile as she passed him. But she ignored him as she went by and climbed onto the bus. He knew the type. Snob. Probably sleeping with some married professor.

He ambled over to the bus, closed the luggage compartment, went on board, and looked through his wide rearview mirror for her among the old-age home—as he liked to call the people on his bus for this run. He could see she'd taken an aisle seat halfway into the bus and had buried her pretty face in a book. Still wearing her sunglasses.

He was about to put the bus in gear when a cop from Toronto came on board looking for someone. He noticed the young woman too. He stopped and gave her the eye. But she didn't bite. What a cold fish. Still, Levellier was glad to have her on board for the fantasy value if nothing else. Wouldn't the boys back at the station be jealous if he snagged this one?

The trip north was predicably uneventful. Total bore. At the bus station in Montreal, when the passengers began to disembark, he flicked the headlights on and off five times.

"*Merde*, five flashes," Yves Simard said to his fellow colleagues perched behind the one-way glass in the second-floor traffic control office. "That's Rene's highest rating. Francis, come have a look."

From their covert watching post, the two men watched as a depressing collection of old people, mostly women, made their way off the bus. Then she came out. Sunglasses, wearing an Expos baseball cap, flowery hippie dress. A real looker, you could tell.

And there was Rene, trying to make small talk, good luck! She ignored him, put her oversized backpack on one shoulder, and was gone. Poor Rene. He looked up at them. Shrugging, he signaled with his right forefinger: "I'll be back in a minute." And off he went, following her at a safe distance.

Oh, Rene, they all laughed, he can never take no for an answer!

BERING

74 HOURS MORE

BERING HUNG UP THE phone after talking with Greene and took a deep breath. She knew what she had to do. But that didn't make it any easier.

She glanced longingly at the place on the floor where she did her workouts, changed quickly into her street clothes, and within a minute was out the door. At the end of the hallway a new recruit officer was manning a security desk. Bering had dealt with him yesterday when she'd needed to get some supplies.

"Hello, Officer Mudhar." Bering didn't break stride as she approached him.

Mudhar looked up, surprised.

"Officer Bering, can I get you something?"

"Don't worry about it." Bering strode past him.

Mudhar began to rise. "Do you need a lift? The chief gave me a cruiser, it's parked right outside. The chief told me that under no circumstances—"

"No lift. And don't worry, I'll take care of the chief." She pulled open the heavy fire door, stepped out onto the stairway, and seconds later she was out on Jarvis Street.

Bering found it odd to be on the street out of uniform. Especially this street, where she'd started her career. When she first joined the force, she was a natural for the so-called morality squad. Young, attractive, and smart, for a year she spent her nights working the notorious "Jarvis Street Track"—a collection of downtown streets frequented by men who would drive around looking for prostitutes. Bering, dressed in a skimpy skirt and high heels, her long hair flowing in the wind, waited for a ceaseless stream of johns to pull over and proposition her.

The price list shifted according to the season. Twenty-five dollars for a hand job, fifty for a blow job, and a hundred for an hour were the base rates. On cold nights, or when traffic was bad because the Maple Leafs were playing a hockey game around the corner at the Gardens, the numbers could double. She'd direct them to a parking lot, where her partner, Ari Greene, was waiting in an unmarked car to arrest them.

She walked at full speed up Jarvis to police headquarters. We're going to miss this old dump, she thought as she pulled open the front door, waved to the sergeant at the reception desk, and cut up the back stairs.

When she got to Keon's outer door, she stopped to catch her breath. Looking at Keon's name stenciled on the glass door, the old emotions washed over her. The rage still inhabited part of her being.

She let the moment pass and turned the bent metal knob.

Keon's ever-loyal secretary, Miss Rose, looked up from her desk. She looked older, Bering thought, but still had that solid Scottish stoicism about her. Forever the trooper.

"Sorry to barge in on you like this, Carol," Bering said. "I need to see him, right now."

"Nora. I thought you were at the Jarvis Hotel and were going to call." Instinctively, Rose seized her notepad.

"This is too important for a call. It can't wait."

"I understand, but Chief Keon isn't here."

"What?" Bering came right up and stood over her. "Where the hell is he?" She was almost shouting.

"He's out walking. You know how he does this when he's worried."

Bering took a step back and nodded.

"I can't stop him. It's better than having him pace around the office. He hates being cooped up." Rose looked down. "No one realizes how much he misses being on the street. Nora, I know he's sorry about what happened at the bridge three years ago and involving you in it . . . "

"Let's not get into that now," Bering said, tightening her jaw. "Get him on his radio."

Rose frowned. "He doesn't have his radio with him."

"Why not?"

"He has one of the new portable phones. It's his first time using it."

"I've heard about them. Can you call him on it?"

"I can try." Rose dialed a number on her desk phone and passed the receiver to Bering. She heard an odd ringing sound, then Keon's voice, but it was faint. The line was full of static.

"It's Nora. Can you hear me? This is urgent."

"Nora?"

"Yes, where are you?"

The phone went dead. Bering turned back to Rose.

"The connection just died. What's going on?"

"He's not good with it. I warned him to turn it off when he wasn't using it or the battery would die."

"Great." Bering frowned.

"He called in twice, the last time was about ten minutes ago."

"Did he say where he was?"

Rose looked down at her notebook. "About to get on the Bloor subway heading east."

Bering looked directly at Rose. The thought struck them both at the same time.

"He's going back to the bridge, isn't he?" Bering said. The implications of her words hung in the air between the two women, the unspoken meaning clear to both of them.

"Damn it." Bering turned to leave.

Just then, Rose's phone rang.

She grabbed it. "Chief Keon's office," she said in her normal singsong voice. "Yes, yes, sir . . . Officer Bering wants to talk to you . . . No, she's right here."

Rose handed the phone to Bering.

Before she took it, Bering flicked her head toward the door, telling Rose to leave the room.

As soon as Rose closed the door behind her, Bering spoke into the phone. "Charlie," she said, not bothering to introduce herself, "listen."

GREENE

72.5 HOURS MORE

FOR THE LAST HOUR and a half, Greene had been staring out the bus window as the flat countryside of southern Quebec flashed by. The driver was making slow progress north on the way to Montreal. Frustrating. If Greene were back in Toronto, he could be in touch with Bering and the dispatcher on his police radio. But there was no way he could communicate with anyone until he got off this darn bus. Such a helpless feeling.

At long last he saw the high-rise buildings of the city and Mount Royal behind them come into view. It seemed to take forever to cross the high bridge over the wide St. Lawrence River, and even longer for the driver to navigate through the narrow streets of Old Montreal. At last they pulled into the bus terminal.

Greene was the first one off. There was a bank of pay phones on the far wall and he sprinted over to them. They were all being used. He realized he didn't have any quarters. There was a small food stand, and there was a line up there too. When he finally got to the front, he used his fractured French to buy a chocolate bar so he could get some change.

He was hungry. Starving. After all he'd been through in the last few hours, the adrenaline was seeping out of his body. He ripped the wrapping off the chocolate bar and took a bite, then another as he rushed back to the phones. One was free. He put in a quarter and asked the operator, again using his French as best he could, to put in a collect call.

"Where are you?" Bering said once he got through to her.

"Bus terminal," he said, mumbling as he swallowed his third bite, nervously jiggling the remaining change lodged deep in his pocket.

"It's hard to hear you."

"I'm at the bus terminal in Montreal," he said, his voice cleared. He looked around to confirm that no one could overhear him. "Just got in. What can you tell me? What did the chief say?"

Bering updated him on everything she'd done since they'd last spoken. She and Keon had worked out an action plan: the RCMP had a pathologist doing autopsies on the border guard and the old lady on the porch. Greene had been right about her, she was dead too. The local police and the Sûreté du Québec—the provincial police—were on scene. They'd thrown up a roadblock north of Stanstead. So far they hadn't found anyone suspicious.

"I doubt they will at this point," he said.

"Agreed. But there's more. They searched the perimeter around the backyard and found a Shriner's clown suit had been thrown over the fence into the neighbour's yard."

"What?" Greene said, shaking his head.

"The cop who found it told me she had the impression that it had been tossed there in a hurry. I'm assuming there were Shriner clowns at the parade."

"Lots of them. I didn't count them, but Hickey, that's the name of the American border guard, had a list. He was obsessive about numbers."

"Good point. We'll check that."

Greene nodded. His mind was whirling. He reached into his pocket, where he'd put the two fluffy red balls he'd taken from the cedar branches, and took them out.

"Ask that cop if the costume had red cotton balls sewn on to it and if two are missing," he said. "I found a couple stuck to a bush on my way into the backyard."

"Okay, find a bag and bag them, and we'll send them to forensics."

Greene looked around to make sure there was still no one in earshot. The coast was still clear.

"It fits, doesn't it?" he said. "Hickey must have done a count of the number of clowns that were supposed to be in the parade. I couldn't figure out why he left his booth because he'd been ordered to stay there. He must have counted an extra clown. Poor guy."

"Our working assumption right now is that Hickey surprised the killer. He killed Hickey, threw the suit away, then killed the old lady and took off."

A thought occurred to Greene. If he'd arrived in the backyard a minute or two earlier, he might have caught the killer. Or he could have been a third dead body on the ground.

"I bet I just missed him," he told Bering. "I was delayed getting across the street by a high school marching band. If I hadn't—"

"Don't go there," Bering said. "We've told the FBI and they're crawling over northern Vermont. I want to know if there were any other suspicious deaths there."

There was a pause on the phone.

"I had a lot of time on that bus to go over everything in my head," he told her. "Try to put myself in this guy's shoes. The summit starts tomorrow. He knows that with an American border guard dead on Canadian soil, and the old lady in the same backyard dead too, the heat will be on to find him. He'll want to get to Toronto ASAP."

"Makes sense to me," she said. "What's your next move?"

"I've been thinking about that too," he said. "I'm going to talk to the people here at the bus terminal to find out if they saw anyone suspicious. Then I thought I'd get a hotel room, shower, catch some sleep, and write out my report, including a list of everyone I can remember who was on the two buses in Stanstead."

"That's what I thought you should do," Bering said. "I reserved you a room at the Queen Elizabeth hotel—it's right above the train station. And I checked. They have a fax machine, so you can send your report in to me."

"Thanks," he said. "I'll call you when I wake up. Assuming nothing else happens, I'll hop on the evening train back home and we'll have to pick up his trail, somehow, tomorrow morning when I'm back in Toronto."

"Yes," Bering said. "Somehow."

They both paused again. As if neither was quite ready to hang up.

"I know what you're thinking," he said, breaking the silence. "Don't worry. I'll be careful."

She laughed and he put the phone back on its receiver. There was a line of people waiting their turn behind him. He walked to the station's controller's office. At the door, he showed his badge and asked the pair of dispatchers working there, again in his fractured French, if they'd seen anyone unusual come off the buses from Stanstead.

"*Non*," the man who said his name was Yves said. "*Toujours le même vieux dans cette route.*"

"*Oui*," the other man, named Francis, said, agreeing with his coworker that it was always old people on that route.

"*Mais*," Yves said, smiling at his colleague. "*Il y avait la fille que Rene suivait.*"

They looked at each other and chuckled. Greene didn't understand what they meant. It took him a few minutes speaking in English and French to get the story. A bus driver named Rene Levellier had followed a woman off the bus that came in before Greene's bus. Apparently this fellow named Rene did this often and it was somewhat of a joke among his peers.

She was probably the same woman he'd seen on the bus, Greene thought. The one who dropped her sunglasses.

Dead end.

He thanked the two men and walked out of the station. On the street, the sidewalks were packed with people strolling in the sunshine, talking and laughing, eating and drinking on outdoor patios. Families, packs of teenagers, hand-holding couples. Everyone going about their normal lives. Not one of them concerned that there could be an assassin on the loose and that, at some time in the next few days, he could turn the whole world upside down.

LEVELLIER

72.5 HOURS MORE

LEVELLIER KNEW HIS CHANCES with this beauty were a hundred to one, but why not, he thought as he trailed her, making a point of keeping his distance. What did he have to lose? A slap in the face—he'd had that before. Many times. Maybe she's new to Montreal, he thought. Maybe she needs someone to show her around.

He followed her, not too closely, as she walked briskly out of the bus station, across Boulevard René-Lévesque and disappeared into the Place Ville Marie. Man, oh man, what a body, Levellier thought as he was forced to stop at the streetlight. She was headed toward the Metro. He imagined the professor waiting for her at his home, while his family was parked at their cottage in the Laurentians. Lucky bastard.

Levellier was starting to feel foolish. He was about to turn back, but the streetlight changed. Might as well go underground and buy the boys some coffee. You never know, I might catch one last glimpse of her. Besides, he couldn't return to the bus station too soon—everyone would really make fun of him.

He went down to the underground mall and looked around. There was no sign of her. As he passed a row of phone booths, he spotted her backpack. And there she was. No baseball cap or sunglasses anymore, but he was sure it was her. Must be calling the professor, he thought, to make sure the coast is clear.

There was a newspaper kiosk a few steps away. He bought a copy of the *Star*, his favourite tabloid. The front-page story was about Celine Dion, the songbird of Quebec. Levellier couldn't believe what he was reading. Dion was taking English lessons and her next album would feature three songs in English. He shook his head. Before you know it, she'll end up living in Hollywood, he thought. She'll pretend she never spoke a word of French, like Mr. Jeopardy, Alex Trebek.

Levellier peered over his paper at the phone booth and casually watched the woman. He saw her pick up the receiver and put in lots of coins. A local call wouldn't be that expensive. Must be long-distance. Maybe the professor's family was off in Paris, and he was up in the Laurentians waiting for her call. She finished dialing. Her face was beautiful. And her eyes were so dark. Warm and inviting, even if the left one was a little off-centre.

He focused on her mouth. That was when the strangest thing of all happened. After years of communicating with dispatchers across bustling bus terminals and passengers at the end of noisy buses, Levellier had become an adept lip-reader. He could pick out the name of any city or town in Quebec.

He watched her closely. She didn't say hello or goodbye or anything else. She said one word before she hung up.

He had no doubt what that word was: "Montreal."

WHITECASTLE

72.5 HOURS MORE

ANGUS WHITECASTLE'S USUALLY NERVOUS hands were not acting up too badly today, he thought as he put the phone down, scooped up some rich soil, and filled an old clay pot to an inch below the brim. It was the third pot in succession that he was planting with red geraniums, the ones for which he was famous, or perhaps infamous.

Yes, his geraniums, the former prime minister of Great Britain chuckled to himself, wiping his impatient hands on his muddied blue-and-white-striped gardening apron. He put the pots into an old wicker garden basket and carried them down the fieldstone path that meandered through his lush perennial garden until he came to the stone wall that surrounded his estate.

Every day this week he'd formed a triangle of geranium pots on the waist-level ledge, arranging them so the point of the triangle was directed toward the house, the base toward the road. Today he reversed the direction, and slipped a folded piece of paper under the pot closest to the road.

Contrary to his pokey image in the media, Whitecastle was a tall man, well over six feet five inches, with tough ruddy skin and a full head of light brown hair. When people first met him, they were struck by how much more powerful he seemed in person than they had expected after seeing all those awful pictures of him in the press.

He twisted his hands together. How the journalists had loved to make fun of him and his gardening. He remembered some horrifying headlines: "Our Potting Prime Minister" accompanied a grainy photo of him, white hat scrunched down on his head, working away in his greenhouse; "Agile Angus" and an equally grainy shot of him bending down to pick up a fallen robin.

Poor Linda Chen, his hapless press secretary, tried valiantly to help. It was no use. Whitecastle remembered talking to her after a particularly ghastly set of photographs came out. "Mr. Prime Minister," Chen had said, "perhaps you would consider learning to play tennis, or maybe take up jogging."

"Don't be ridiculous," Whitecastle said.

"Then, sir, might you purchase another hat?"

"A new gardening hat? That's what I need to rise in the polls? My white hat belonged to my grandfather Harry, for goodness' sake."

"Yes, well, precisely . . . "

On and on it went to no avail. Whitecastle never changed his gardening hat and he never came back in the polls. He knew he wouldn't. If the British people threw out Winston Churchill after he won World War II, sooner or later they were going to toss him out too. So, like any good gardener, he planned for the next season.

Whitecastle picked up his basket, checked his watch, and walked leisurely away from the wall. He thought back to when he'd met Alisander and how this had all begun. Well before he entered politics, he was a lecturer in international law at the London School of Economics.

"Good morning, I'm Professor Angus Whitecastle," he had said the first day of class. "I thought it might be interesting to start by examining the following question: What effect will the current oil crisis have on international trade and treaties in the next decade?"

A strikingly handsome man in the back row raised his hand.

"Yes," Whitecastle said.

"There is no oil crisis," the man said. His voice was deep and resonant. "In my country, Afghanistan, oil reserves are at their highest levels ever. What has changed is our willingness to sell at scandalously low prices. Oil revenues represent sixty-two percent of our gross national product. That is why we've nationalized all the British and American oil companies. Now that we've gained control over the means of production, the 'crisis' is in the West until the first world nations are prepared to pay fair market price."

Every head in the class turned to look at the speaker. The women liked what they saw. Alisander's dense black hair cascaded across his wide forehead and down onto his broad shoulders. Set off against his deep brown skin, his intense blue eyes seemed to capture the light in the room and beam it back out with extraordinary intensity.

He must be from the south, Whitecastle thought. Alexander the Great came through the Khyber Pass. That would account for the blue eyes and the name.

From that moment on, battle was joined between the right-wing professor and his left-wing student. Throughout the fall term, they dueled. It was the kind of intellectual intensity Whitecastle loved. Alisander, he learned, was the rebellious son of a wealthy Afghani tea estate owner. He was brilliant. He had charisma. Despite their differences, Whitecastle grew enamored with Alisander's analytical mind. And amazed at the parade of striking women who seemed to hang on to his every word.

One night at the start of the winter session, Whitecastle was working late in his office when he heard a tap on his door.

"Come in," he said.

The door opened slowly. To Whitecastle's amazement, Alisander stood there, a child, a young girl, asleep on his shoulder. At his side was yet another beautiful woman.

"Professor, I'm sorry to intrude. We've just learned that our government has been overthrown. This is my wife, Sherani. My daughter, Cloe. Sherani's father is the minister of defence and he's been executed. We are in great danger."

Whitecastle kicked back his chair and rushed to comfort them. "Alisander, this is horrific. What can I do?"

"We need refuge."

"Of course. Anything." Whitecastle immediately called his wife, Deborah, and told her to prepare the guest room.

A few minutes later they sat together in a cab. Whitecastle wasn't sure what shocked him the most. Was it the horrific news? Was it that Alisander had a wife and child? Or was it that Alisander had chosen to trust him, Professor Whitecastle, his great intellectual rival, for sanctuary?

Alisander stared out the window at the darkened city streets, his eyes ablaze in fury. He turned to Whitecastle. "You were right, Professor. I was wrong."

"About what, Alisander?"

"About Marxism. It's a fraud. The Russians. You tried to warn me. We were fools. We supported them against the West, and now look. This is what they did to my country and to my family."

For the rest of the term, Alisander, his wife, and daughter stayed at Whitecastle's house. Then, despite Whitecastle's vociferous pleas that they not leave, they chose to go home. It was a decision with dire consequences.

Whitecastle shook his head at the sad memory. He stooped down at an apparently empty patch in his garden. He ran his hands over the ground and felt the tips of some emerging asparagus buds. Asparagus is rewarding for a gardener, he thought. They require such patience. For three years you must let the shoots grow and chop them off, returning all the energy to the bulb. In the fourth year you can harvest.

Yes, it had been worth the wait, he thought as he straightened up and considered the one-word message he'd left under his geranium pot. "Montreal."

Alisander had set up this system that he called a "double blind" so there would be no direct link back to him. He didn't want any long-distance calls from Canada to Afghanistan. And in the unlikely event something was traced back to Whitecastle, well, as the former PM he was always getting crank calls.

Whitecastle heard a motorcycle make its way down the deserted country lane on the far side of the wall, as it had at the end of every day this week. Instead of driving past, as it had before, this time the motorcycle slowed to a stop for a few seconds beside the geranium pots before it raced off.

He walked back toward the wall. Despite himself, he let his mind drift forward in time a few days. Picture it: The seven world leaders and the Russian president are dead. The world is stunned. In America the vice president takes office, but here in England it's more complicated. The cabinet meets in an emergency session.

Whitecastle smiled at the thought. He's the last living prime minister, the clambering press wants to know his reaction to the assassinations. He looks straight at the cameras and says: "I am shocked and appalled." He believes that at a time of such crisis "calm heads and experienced bipartisan leadership is needed." What will his role be? a journalist asks. He says with supreme modesty: "I'm here to serve the nation in any way."

In this crucial moment, the public will see his steady, old-fashioned ways as a tremendous virtue. The press will remember the dignity he brought to the office. Pundits will point out his many years of experience. Winston Churchill came back after his great postwar defeat, so why not Angus Whitecastle?

Don't get too far ahead of yourself, he thought. Something on a geranium in the far pot caught his eye. To most people it would have looked fine. But near the bottom of the stem he saw the beginning of rot.

He flicked his arm forward and, like a curled-up snake lunging at its unsuspecting prey, snapped the offending twig off with one hard tug.

A smile played across his face. The thing about geraniums that most people don't understand, Whitecastle thought as he dropped the twig to the ground and crushed it under his boot on the stone terrace, is that you have to be ruthless.

Bloody ruthless.

KEON

69 HOURS MORE

KEON SWUNG HIS BATTERED brown leather briefcase onto the polished mahogany table and slowly unpacked a pad of lined paper, a Bic ballpoint pen, and a drugstore-bought pair of reading glasses.

He looked around the wood-paneled room at the glum faces of the eight other members of the Daily Security Assessment Committee.

At most of their previous meetings, Keon had made a point of keeping his comments to a minimum and leaving as soon as possible. This time he intended to do the same thing.

He scanned the faces of the other men and women at the table before he focused on Jameson, wearing yet another bow tie—blue-and-yellow-striped—who always started the meetings.

"The last of the remaining leaders will be arriving in Toronto today," Jameson said, pronouncing "Toronto" with an annoying emphasis on the first syllable. "Chief Keon, we haven't heard much from you all week. Do you wish to address the committee with an update?"

Keon grimaced, slipped on his reading glasses, and picked up the pad of paper. He kept his head down and spoke in a steady monotone. It was a technique he'd perfected over years of giving press conferences. Whenever he didn't really want people to pay attention, he found that droning on in detail, and making no eye contact with his audience, was the best way to ensure no one listened too carefully.

"I have three matters," he said. "First, as was reported in the press this morning, there was a fire last night in a back alley two blocks from where President Reagan is staying at the Royal York Hotel. We had five units on scene within two minutes of the blaze, plus a helicopter overhead. The fire was contained in a steel drum. At first, we suspected it was set by protesters from the so-called tent city, but officers from 52 Division established it was started by two street people. They've been charged, and we'll delay their bail hearing until after the summit."

That last line provoked approving nods around the table.

"Second, yesterday afternoon we arrested a known member of the IRA, who is in Canada illegally. He's now on an immigration hold. The British press is having a field day with this, but he's not going anywhere for at least a week."

More nods.

"Last, we've uncovered three illegal backroom poker games, and a dozen worm pickers who are illegals. And the Right of Prostitutes organization has objected to the street cleanup actions the force has undertaken in the last few weeks."

Keon looked up. He took off his cheap reading glasses and stuffed them back into his briefcase. "That's my report," he said with a "No news is good news" shrug. "If you don't mind I'd like to get back—"

"There's one point I don't think you covered." It was Jameson.

Keon took his time. He capped the Bic pen and put it in his coat pocket. He shut the briefcase with a loud click.

"What was that?" Keon asked.

"What about that 'lead' you mentioned at the last meeting that you told the committee you were going to follow up on?"

Keon stared directly at Jameson. The guy had a smirk on his face. Keon knew what was going on. By now Jameson must know something was up.

He would have heard that Bering had the FBI scouring northern Vermont for dead bodies. He was testing Keon, and Keon wished he could reach across the table and pull off the arrogant jerk's bow tie.

Instead Keon started to laugh.

"Mr. Jameson, as you said the other day, there are a plethora of leads and fake leads coming in all the time. I'm sure none of you wishes to be burdened with a report on every one of them." Keon again scanned the faces seated at the table and elicited nods of agreement. "As soon as I've got something to report, you'll be the first to know."

Keon stood up to leave. He took one last look around. Everyone was looking down at their agenda to see what the next item of business was.

Everyone except Jameson.

LARKIN

65 HOURS MORE

ALAN LARKIN WASN'T THE type to come to a bar like this: valet parking, men in designer suits, stylish women dressed to the nines. He was more at home drinking imported beer in the cozy confines of the McGill graduate student union bar.

He'd come downtown to get a dose of reality, away from his life-in-a-garret university existence. He had a decision to make. He was about to admit to himself that his academic career was over.

What a misfit he was, he thought as he saw the third man in the last hour go up to the bar and take a seat next to the comely woman on the end stool. Even in this good-looking crowd she was radiant. Larkin noticed the bartender, a tough old goat, couldn't keep his eyes off her. Larkin knew he'd never be able to go up and talk to someone like that. He didn't fit in academia, and he sure as hell didn't fit in an upscale place like this.

The facts of his pathetic situation were straightforward. He was thirty-two years old, single, living in a rented flat. He had no savings, no security, and his ten-year-old Toyota Corolla needed a major brake job. He'd been up in Canada for six years now, and every time he went back home to Philadelphia his friends were wealthier than the time before. He kept getting poorer.

What did he have to show for the last six years? Eighty-eight pages of his thesis. Before he came here, he'd been warned: the PhD program at McGill is tough. But he was a top student, Phi Beta Kappa in the linguistics department at Cornell. Montreal had sounded like an exotic adventure. Against everyone's advice, he thumbed his nose at UCLA and MIT grad schools and headed to La Belle Province. He'd figured that in four, maybe five years, he would have his doctorate and the world of academia would be at his feet.

It hadn't worked out that way. His first advisor was an abusive jerk with whom he'd fought for two years. It took a year to get permission to switch advisors, and while the new professor was great, he had a different view of Larkin's thesis. So he spent another year redoing his research. When he was close to finishing, a bicyclist ran over his advisor. Massive brain injuries. It took McGill another six months to get him someone new, a woman this time. She was fine, but she wanted more research done, a different angle explored. A year later she took an appointment at Harvard.

By now six years had ticked away and the grant money had run out. Even the meager teaching jobs were beginning to dry up. He was no longer the young, bright light of the department. New faces had arrived to carry that mantle. People were beginning to whisper about him. He could imagine what they were saying: "That American Larkin, is he still doing research? We thought he was a real talent when he first came. How many years has he been working on his thesis?"

None of it was his fault, but in the petty world of academia that didn't matter. If he was going to finish his doctorate, he'd need to start with a fourth advisor. If he was lucky, he might be ready to defend it in two years. He'd be on the job market, a thirty-three-year-old who took eight years to get his PhD. And why did he do it in Canada? It was over. Time to move out of his turret and back into the real world.

An hour earlier, when he'd driven up to the valet parking stand, the

Italian kid with slicked-back hair who took his car keys laughed out loud when he saw Larkin's Toyota. The doorman at the bar looked at his plaid shirt and baggy pants and hid Larkin away in this booth near the kitchen. The waitress grudgingly took his order, a Heineken, and delivered it on the run as she scurried off to more lucrative customers.

That's why nothing could have surprised him more than the sound of a female voice asking: "Do you mind if I sit here for a minute?"

It was her. The woman from the bar.

"Well, sure." Larkin shifted over to make room.

"There's a former hockey player up there who's getting drunk and I want to stay out of his way," she said in a voice that sounded flat. One thing about being a linguistic student, Larkin could usually place people's accents easily. Not this one. It was neutral, like that "from Nowhere USA accent" actors used on TV.

The waitress instantly appeared at the table, with an obsequious smile. "Can I get you another drink, sir?" she asked him, all friendly now. "And your friend?"

"A Perrier, if you don't mind," the woman said.

Still smiling, the waitress stared at Larkin with a "Let's see what you're made of, buddy" look.

"I'll have another Heineken." He watched the waitress's smile turn down.

Once she was gone, Larkin wasn't sure what to say. The woman hardly seemed to notice he was there. He picked up the empty Heineken and tried hard not to peel the label off of it. He felt like coughing, but stifled the urge.

At last the waitress returned. Larkin gave her a twenty-dollar bill, and she slowly went through the motions of making change. He looked up at her and waved off the tip. That brought the smile back to her face.

The woman poured her Perrier. It took a while until she looked over at Larkin. "I'm sorry to bother you." She squeezed a wedge of lemon into her glass. "I'm sure you were much happier to be left alone."

"You're welcome to sit for as long as you like."

"I bet you're waiting for a friend, and I don't want to get in the way."

"Well, no, I'm here on my own," he said. Oh no, he thought, that sounded pathetic. "I don't usually come to bars, especially bars like this. I mean alone and all." He heard his voice trail off. The more he talked the worse it got. He figured another thirty seconds and she'd be gone. But she turned back to him, and even touched his arm for a second.

"I'm not a barfly myself. I was supposed to meet a girlfriend here. She's late, and sitting at the bar waiting for her, I've been hit on more times than a camper without mosquito repellent."

They both laughed. Then there was silence again. Larkin poured his beer and, despite himself, started picking off the label. He had to say something.

"I'm a graduate student in linguistics, and I have to say that your accent baffles me."

She chuckled. "Lots of people say that."

Larkin waited for her to offer a further explanation, but she touched his arm again. This time her hand lingered longer. The feel of her sent a jolt through him. It was as if he were being awakened from a long and lonely sleep.

"I was thinking of taking a linguistics course next year. What's it like?"

The conversation moved easily from there. Before he knew it, Larkin was telling her his life story: how he'd wasted all these years trying to finish his doctorate; how badly the department had treated him; how he was going back home with his tail between his legs. Talking to this woman made him feel better. Was it because she was so attractive, or because she seemed so interested?

He saw her sneak a look at her watch and stifle a yawn. He was horrified. "I'm sorry, I must be boring you to tears with all this academic drivel."

"No, it's not that at all. You're much more interesting than the vice president of the farm implements company or the insurance salesmen up there at the bar. When I called my friend's family at their cottage, they told me her car broke down. She won't make it into town until tomorrow. So I'm, you know, kind of stranded."

Larkin was paralyzed with fear. Should he offer her a lift? Give her cab money? He couldn't ask where she was staying, that would sound awful.

"I'm sorry that I bothered you." Her hand came down on the table, next to his.

"Well, I'd be happy to offer you a lift." Larkin couldn't believe what he was saying. Why are you doing this? he asked himself. She'll say no and you'll feel even worse. Instead, her hand drifted over on top of his and gave it a short squeeze.

"If you wouldn't mind, that would be nice of you."

Larkin practically leapt out of the booth. In a minute they were outside, and when he was standing with her on the curb, the most amazing thing happened. She put her arm around his neck and kissed him on the cheek.

The Italian kid drove up in the Toyota and gave Larkin a quizzical look.

He was shocked that this woman was leaving the bar with a nerdy guy driving a beat-up old vehicle, Larkin thought, as he put his car in gear and prayed he wouldn't pop the clutch like some nervous first-time driver.

MARINA

64 HOURS MORE

"SEX. DON'T BE AFRAID of it. Use it," Alisander had said. "Men love beautiful women, but even more, they love women who love sex. If a man thinks you want it more than he does, he'll do anything for you. Anything."

Marina thought about Alisander's lessons as she swung her long legs into Alan Larkin's old car and lifted her knees up high. Larkin got in the driver's seat and fumbled with his seat belt. She could see he was nervous. That was good.

Marina remembered how Alisander had touched her: "Lie like this. Move your legs up like this. Open your mouth like this. Close your eyes, tilt your head back, exhale. Move your hands down your body until . . . "

"Do you want me to do up my seat belt too?" she asked Larkin.

"Uh, well. It's up to you."

She reached back and pulled the belt on. "I don't want to make you feel uncomfortable."

"Uncomfortable?" He laughed. The car jumped as he put it in gear.

She touched his right arm. "Can we go somewhere quiet for a few minutes? That bar was so noisy."

"Sure. Where would you like to go?"

"How about Mount Royal? I've never been up there, but I hear there's a beautiful view."

Larkin drove in silence.

Marina saw him steal the occasional glance at her. As they started to climb the big hill, she touched his arm again. This time she left her hand there. "Why don't you go this way?" she whispered, pointing to a road that cut into the woods.

He pulled into a lookout over the city, put the car in park, and started to fidget with his hands. She stretched across and turned the engine off. Then she flicked off the headlights. Now it was dark and quiet inside.

She faced him and whispered, "Let's go for a walk."

Outside the car, she took his hand and pulled him toward the woods. "Over here," she said. "Quick."

They walked for a minute in the moist night air. Soon they were deep in the forest. She put her back against a tree and in one motion pulled her sweater over her head.

He seemed paralyzed.

"Don't be afraid," she whispered as she drew him to her. She opened her legs and swung her arms around his shoulders. He wrapped his arms around her.

It took a few seconds for her to find the spot she was looking for on his neck.

It took a few more seconds for his grip on her to loosen. His knees buckled. A moment later he was prone on his back, a look of fear and confusion in his eyes. Then they went blank.

GREENE

64 HOURS MORE

THERE WAS NO ALARM clock in his hotel room, so Greene had wisely asked the front desk for a wake-up call. A few hours earlier, the fatigue had hit him as he'd walked into the hotel, and he didn't trust himself to wake up in time to catch the overnight train.

It was nine o'clock when the hotel phone rang.

"Yes, I mean *oui*. *Merci* for the call," he answered.

He stumbled out of bed, went to the washroom, splashed cold water on his face, and drank a large glass of water.

Back in his room, he thought about calling Meredith. She'd headed up north to the cottage early for the long weekend and was spending the week there. She'd been disappointed when he told her he couldn't come with her. Chief Keon had sworn Greene and Bering to secrecy about this assignment. He'd been forced to tell Meredith—and his father and mother—that he'd been put on a last-minute traffic duty because of the upcoming G7 summit and that they wouldn't hear from him for a few days.

Instead he rang the front desk again and had them put in a call to Bering.

"I hope you're sitting down," she said.

"I just woke up. But now I'm standing. What's happening?"

"A lot," she said. "First, the FBI found out that a professor on holiday in northern Vermont died of an apparent heart attack. He was on a road about a mile away from the border where you were at the parade. It turns out he and the two bodies in Quebec were all injected with the same poison that stopped their heart within seconds."

"So he's killing people by some kind of injection," Greene said, glad he wasn't sitting down. He started pacing as far as the phone cord would let him go.

"Probably not a he," Bering said.

"What?"

"The RCMP interviewed everyone they could find at the parade and found two boys, twins, who say they saw someone walking out of the backyard. It was a woman wearing what one of the boys says was a fat backpack. She was heading east, that's the direction of the bus depot."

Greene stopped pacing. Sat on the bed.

"Did they give any more details about her description?"

"They said they couldn't see her face because she was wearing sunglasses and a baseball cap," Bering said. "The report you faxed to me, you list on the first bus a young woman sitting alone in an aisle seat. Did she have a backpack?"

"She did. It was on the seat beside her. And," Greene said, "she was wearing sunglasses and a baseball cap. Did they by any chance see what kind of baseball cap it was?"

He waited, rubbing the scar on his arm, as he heard Bering shuffle through her notes.

"They did," she said. "Turns out they play Little League baseball, so they remembered. It was a Montreal Expos cap."

Greene practically dropped the phone.

"Your notes don't say what kind of baseball cap she was wearing. Do you remember?" Bering asked him.

"I do," he said. "Same. It was a Montreal Expos cap."

MARINA

63 HOURS MORE

IT CAN BE SO sweet on a warm summer evening in Montreal. The wind drifts off the St. Lawrence River and blows the worst of the day's humidity up Mount Royal, leaving the city deliciously cool. The streets fill up with people of all ages out for an evening stroll. The sidewalk cafés bubble with conversations in French and English, and around every corner a different kind of jazz seems to flow effortlessly into the sweet night.

As she drove Alan Larkin's old car down into the city, Marina lowered the driver's-side window and took it all in. The moist air caressed her skin. The lights promised an excitement she'd never known before.

Alisander had warned her she'd feel this way. "When your mission begins, you'll be twenty-two years old. You've been in training since you were a child. You've never been in a northern climate, you've never been in a city, and you've never been to North America. And you've never been alone."

She was four years old on the night of the fire. That terrible evening when everything burned. The house. Her bed. Her hair. Her left eye, burning. When Alisander saved her. When she awoke, she was in the compound. Alisander nursed her back to health. Started her training. Made her forget the old language. The old songs.

And he taught her to hate. "Remember always," he said, "it was the Russians who bombed you. Who killed your parents."

She worked hard. Developed extreme physical strength, sensory awareness, and tolerance for pain. She learned to use every conceivable weapon. How to kill in an instant. She lived exclusively inside the compound. "The world thinks you died in the fire," Alisander said. "You must remain unknown. For all your training, for all your strength, for all your beauty, your greatest asset is your anonymity."

She brought the Toyota to a stop at a red light at the bottom of Mount Royal and slid her bare elbow out the window. She felt a hint of a breeze as it slid up her arm, down under her shirt.

A car pulled up in the lane beside her, and a handsome man with blond hair combed straight back glanced over. He smiled at her. She returned the smile.

She broke off eye contact and looked at the traffic light and watched it turn green. She glanced back at the blond man beside her. They both hesitated. He cocked his head as if to say: "I'm turning left, want to join me?"

Tempting, she thought. But instead, she flashed him one more smile, turned right, and followed a series of side roads, heading west out of Montreal.

For the next half hour, she drove carefully, staying within the speed limit. She had to be ultra-cautious now. With the death of the American border guard, the police, the RCMP, the FBI, and the Secret Service would be all over Montreal watching the airport, the main train station, the bus station, and the highway to Toronto.

That's why she was taking this back-roads route that led to the parking lot of a suburban train station west of Montreal. She didn't want to risk driving all the way to Toronto, especially in a car with Quebec license plates. She knew from her preparation all about the schedule of trains to Toronto. Her plan was to board the overnight train and sleep for a few hours. Sleep, that would be lovely.

This station was used by executives who commuted regularly to Toronto to work for a few days. That meant there would be nothing unusual about a car sitting on the far edge of the parking lot for three or four days. Even if they found Larkin's body and went looking for his car, it would take time to find it, and by then she'd be long gone.

She got out of the car, pulled her backpack from the trunk, and locked the car before slipping into the nearby woods, where she changed into a new outfit. Now she wore a stylish blue jacket, cuffed grey pants, a silk blouse, and a string of fake pearls. No more sunglasses. No more baseball cap.

She reached into her backpack and pulled on two hidden internal handles. In this way she flipped it inside out and turned it into a standard-looking suitcase. Another one of Alisander's inventions.

Looking carefully to see that no one was around, she left the woods and went directly to the station. An older man wearing a red cap, leaning on his pull cart, lifted his head and looked at her. He seemed to be about to say something, so she gave him her haughtiest stare and strode past.

"Talk to as few people as possible," Alisander had told her hundreds of times.

She didn't want the man to touch her suitcase and feel how light it was, because the only thing inside was her knapsack filled with a change of clothes, cash, and her weapons. Otherwise, it was empty.

Everything was going well so far. There was only one loose end. The Toronto police officer who had jumped on then off the bus.

Where was he now?

GREENE

63 HOURS MORE

THE TRAIN STATION IN downtown Montreal was one of the last
bastions of Anglo supremacy in a province that had spent decades rooting
out most traces of the once-dominant English culture. Tall stone pillars
held up a dull marble ceiling. Names of battles fought in the Great War
were chiseled into the hard limestone walls. And the no-longer-elegant
waiting room was lined with fading black-and-white photographs of former railway commissioners, men with English names such as Scott and
Johnson and Wilson. The LeClairs and Denaults appeared in the more
recent colour shots.

Throughout the station, cheap modern signs covered the dusty old
English-language script carved into the stone walls. Yet, try as the Quebec
government might to make the station French Canadian, nothing could
erase the essential Waspiness built into its bones, Greene thought as he
made his way to the ticket counter.

He scanned the faces of his fellow passengers, recording them in his
mind as he went. No sign of the woman in the flowery dress he'd seen
on the bus.

A few minutes later, he was taking his seat on one of the middle cars of the train. It was mostly empty. There was a folded blanket provided on his seat, and he was tempted to unfold it, pull it over himself, and fall asleep. Instead, when they started to move he walked to the first car, turned, and went all the way to the back, memorizing every face. He knew that this was a milk run and there'd be two stops before the train pulled over for the night. That meant more people would be getting on.

He finished going through the cars, returned to his seat, and decided to unfold the blanket and slide under it. The motion of the train was so soothing that he had to struggle to keep awake. Twenty minutes later, they made their first stop in a Montreal suburb. He stared out the window. The night was dark and he could barely make out the shapes, never mind their faces, but he did count eight people coming aboard.

He dragged himself out of his seat and re-catalogued every face. There was no sign of the woman.

Back in his seat, the motion of the car was seductive. He had to fight sleep. Another twenty minutes and the train stopped again farther west of Montreal. He stared out the window. This station was even darker, but he made out three faceless bodies getting on board.

Once the train started again, he knew he had an hour before it pulled over for the night. At last he allowed himself to close his eyes and drifted into a light sleep.

Wait, he told himself. He couldn't sleep for long. He could feel the train was slowing down. He checked his watch. He'd been out for fifty minutes.

As tired as he was, like a sleep-deprived intern prowling the halls of a hospital ward, he got up for one last set of rounds.

By the time he got to the second-to-last car, he'd counted two of the three new passengers on the train. He knew from his last count that there should be five people in this car. An elderly white-haired lady, a mother and her baby, and a middle-aged couple, who were playing cribbage. They were all clustered in seats near the front of the car.

This really is futile, Greene thought as he counted them easily in the flickering light.

The train kept slowing while he made his way through the rest of the car. As he expected, all the seats were empty, until he got to the last row.

There was a young woman lying down, pulling a blanket up over her head. Just as she covered herself, the train passed by an illuminated road sign.

For a split second, the light caught her eyes. Eyes he'd seen before. It was her. The woman on the bus whose sunglasses had fallen off when he was looking at the passengers. They were memorable. So very dark, and one eye, the left, off-centre.

MARINA

61.5 HOURS MORE

MARINA WAS TRYING NOT to panic. It was the Toronto police officer, the same man she'd seen during the parade, on the bus, and now he was on the train. How had he found her? Who had blown her cover?

For the last few minutes, she'd felt the train slowing down. Now she knew why. He'd contacted the local police, and they were going to surround the train. She'd have no way to escape. She used her tongue to remove the cyanide pill. The train kept slowing.

All at once, the train veered sharply to the right.

Wait.

Then she remembered a detail about the train schedule. This overnight train pulled off to the siding for a few hours so the passengers could sleep and get to Toronto at breakfast time. Alisander was right about all those years of training—knowing these details could make all the difference.

Wait. Maybe the police officer hadn't seen her, she thought, using her tongue to slide the pill into its hiding place again and flicking the cap back onto her tooth.

She heard the back door of the car open. She pulled down the blanket enough so she could peek over it in time to see him close the door behind himself and walk into the last car.

Better not take any chances. She had to move fast. She slunk down out of her seat, keeping low to the floor. She narrowed her eyes and listened hard for footsteps. Nothing.

She slithered like a snake out into the aisle, close to the floor. She had a clear view in both directions. There wasn't a soul in sight. She concentrated on the back door, about twenty feet away. This was the danger point. At any moment, he could come back through it.

She heard the door rattle hard on its hinges, and the safety chains on the outside railing between the cars jangled louder as the train continued to slow. But she didn't hear footsteps or someone trying to turn the door handle.

Her eyes travelled back along the floor to the curtained luggage rack. She'd sat in the last seat in the car so she would be close to it. It was about six feet away. She took one look back up the car again. The coast was clear.

It would take her four, maybe five seconds to get behind that luggage rack curtain. If he walked in while she was out in the open, she'd be exposed. She had to move. Now.

She flew across the floor, unfurling her athletic body, yet keeping herself well below the window on the door. She dove through the curtain. She was almost inside when she felt something catch.

Oh no. The cuff of her pant leg had caught on a bent piece of metal on the outer shelving. Instinctively she tugged at it to get inside, but that embedded the material even more. She was half hidden, but her legs were strewn across the centre aisle like two baby whales stranded on a beach.

From the other side of the door she heard the unmistakable sound of footsteps, then a hand on the metal handle, jiggling it.

He was opening the door.

She tugged with all her might but couldn't free herself.

She tried to pull her leg up. Maybe in the darkness he wouldn't see them. She felt absurd and vulnerable, like a hooked fish flopping around on the bottom of a boat. She heard the latch in the door disengage.

Come on, come on, she prayed. With one last tug, she tried to get her leg out of the way. But she was stuck.

GREENE

61.5 HOURS MORE

AS GREENE EXPECTED, THERE was no one new in the final car. He checked it out quickly and rushed back to take another look at the woman under the blanket. Was she really the same woman as he'd seen on the bus? What were the chances?

At the front door of the car, he put his hand on the slick metal handle and started to slide it open. The train halted for a long moment, then lurched forward. He tried to plant his feet to steady himself, but he lost his grip. He stumbled backward. The heavy door slammed shut with a loud bang.

"Damn," he cursed.

He regained his balance, stepped back to the door, grasped the handle again, tugged the door open, and walked cautiously into the car. The aisle was dark and empty. In a few steps he was beside the woman's seat. She wasn't there. The blanket she'd been under had been tossed to the side and there was no sign of her anywhere. No luggage on the overhead rack. No books, magazines, food wrappers. She'd vanished.

Was he wrong about this woman? After all, he'd only seen her twice, both times just for a moment. Had she simply gone to the washroom or taken a walk toward the front of the train? Or, and this seemed far-fetched, had she recognized him and hidden somewhere?

He looked around. This part of the train car was deserted. There was no washroom back here, just empty seats and the luggage rack. He went over to the rack and pulled the curtain aside. Nothing there but a piece of luggage. He slid the curtain back in place.

His instincts were screaming at him: something wasn't adding up. Why had this woman left her seat after he saw her? Was she really the killer the twin boys in Stanstead had seen walking out of the backyard and going toward the bus station?

His attention was drawn to someone moving through the car. He looked up and saw it was the conductor checking people's tickets, coming down the aisle toward him. She was a big woman with a warm smile.

Greene waited patiently. He'd have to ask her for some favours. He'd learned that in an emergency the best way to make things happen was to keep calm. He felt his heart begin to beat a faster. Take a breath, he told himself. Breathe.

MARINA

61.5 HOURS MORE

THE TRAIN JERKED AND Marina's body careened uncontrollably into the aisle. She was out in the open. The train sputtered to a stop for a split second, and she could feel her pants had come unstuck. She scrambled back behind the curtain and pulled it shut. She felt her way to her luggage. It had taken Alisander a year to perfect the design of this mobile hiding place, and she'd learned to assemble it in less than ten seconds.

The fake piece of luggage had vertical hinges running down the sides. Silently, she opened it and, turning her back to the open space, wound her body into a ball and slid inside. Two pieces of string hung down and she used them to pull the panels back up into position. Now she was completely enclosed.

The train tumbled forward. She heard the back door open and listened for the man's footsteps. She was hoping he would walk back up the car. But he didn't. She could sense he was right outside the curtain. She heard him take a few steps, then stop. She could tell he was looking at her now-empty seat. He'd see the blanket she'd been under, and now he'd see that she was gone.

She held her breath. Come on, walk away, she said to herself, again using her tongue to ready her back tooth. Instead, she heard a few more steps. Getting closer. She heard a swooshing sound. He'd pulled open the curtain and was looking in the luggage compartment.

She willed herself to remain still, willed her breathing to cease, her heart to stop.

Another swoosh and she heard the curtain close. She let herself breathe.

She heard footsteps. Was he leaving? No, the steps were approaching from the other end of the car. Had someone seen her hapless dash across the aisle? Was she about to be surrounded?

"Can I help you with anything, young man?" she heard a new, female voice say.

"Yes, you can." It was him. The Toronto cop.

"I'll need your ticket."

"Here it is."

"Are you looking for something?"

"Yes. No. I mean, I'm looking for some*one*, not something."

"And who would that some*one* be? I doubt anyone's riding in the luggage rack."

"My name is Officer Ari Greene . . . "

His voice had dropped down to a whisper. In the pitch darkness, Marina listened with laser-like concentration. She had to strain to make out his words over the clamber of the still-moving train.

"Here's my badge. I'm on a special assignment and it's important I get to a radio, immediately."

"Police. From Brockville, are you?" The woman didn't bother to whisper.

"No, from Toronto. Can you take me up to the engineer? Is there a radio there?"

"Come along . . . "

The footsteps were moving away and the voices faded.

She'd heard enough. Officer Ari Greene. That was his name. In a few minutes the police would be swarming all over the train. Her hiding place wouldn't hold up. She had to get off. Fast.

She pulled herself out of the fake luggage and poked her head out from behind the curtain. The aisle was empty. The few people sleeping at the other end of the car hadn't stirred. This was her chance. She ducked back inside, pulled out her small backpack with all her essential gear in it, and clipped the fake luggage back into its original shape. When Greene started looking for her, her hiding place here would not be obvious. It might buy her more time.

She peeked out into the car again. Coast was clear still. She shoved her knapsack out, jumped up into the aisle, and walked calmly through the back door.

The cool night air felt refreshing on the landing between the cars. The train continued to slow, but it was still moving quite fast. She went to the north side and peered into the deep darkness. The night was cloudy and warm, and a misty rain was falling. Hoping her eyes would adjust to the darkness, she scanned the blackness for a hint of light. But she couldn't see what lay below.

She wanted to let the train slow more, but she couldn't take the chance of waiting a second longer. She climbed up on the chain railing between the cars and brought the backpack up to her chest.

She leaned out. The rush of air whipped her hair wildly across her face, like a renegade kite dancing in the wind. Concentrate, she told herself, but her mind kept drifting back to the conversation she'd overheard.

Ari Greene, she thought. Now I know your name. She replayed his voice in her mind. She liked the way he half whispered. She remembered his blue-green eyes. His dark hair.

Nice to meet you, Officer Greene. Too bad I couldn't stay longer, she thought as she squeezed her knapsack tight. Then, the same way she did as a little girl clutching a flutterboard to her chest before jumping into an oncoming ocean wave, she took a deep breath, closed her eyes, and flung herself into the night.

GREENE

61.5 HOURS MORE

GREENE HUSTLED THE CONDUCTOR through the train, scanning the seats and the aisles, praying he'd see the woman sitting somewhere reading her book. But he could feel she was gone. How had she gotten off the train without him seeing her?

At the front, Greene was introduced to the engineer, a short stocky man with a shock of white hair. Greene explained who he was and what he needed.

"You're a lucky one, son." The engineer had a thick Scottish accent. He handed a headset to Greene. "We received this new technology about a month ago. You ring the operator, and she can hook you up to any phone number you want. Amazing."

He felt anything but lucky right now, Greene thought as he took the set. He dialed the operator, a French Canadian woman who he could tell spoke English as a second language. He recited Bering's number slowly in English. A few seconds later the phone started to ring. It rang five, ten, twenty times. Where the hell could Bering be?

"Could you please hang up and try the number again?" he asked after the twenty-fifth ring. Maybe she'd dialed the wrong number. This time he gave the number in French.

"Yes, I understood the first time. Those are the same numbers I used."

The phone was ringing again. On the first ring, it was answered.

"Greene?" It was Bering. "Sorry. I was dead asleep. Where are you?"

"In the conductor's cabin on the train. Listen." He told her what had happened.

"You did the right thing," she said.

"But I should have—"

"What? Challenge her and get killed or cause an incident with an innocent passenger? Stop the 'I should haves.' Waste of time and energy. You have to stop the train."

"Good timing," he said as he felt the train come to a halt. "We just stopped at the overnight turnoff."

He asked the engineer for their location and passed it on to Bering. For the next few minutes, they made a priority to-do list. Greene could hear her making notes.

"Hold on for a second," she said.

Greene looked out the window at the deep darkness. He avoided the eyes of the engineer. Bering came back on the line.

"I had the chief install a second phone for me. I've got the local police, the OPP, and the Mounties on the way. Any minute now you're going to have a corral full of squad cars. We got lucky. Some patrols were in the area."

"There must be a twenty-four-hour donut shop nearby," Greene said.

Bering didn't laugh. They were both too tired and anxious to banter.

"I'll stay on the line until someone arrives," Bering said. There was an awkward silence again. Phones are for talking, Greene thought.

In a few minutes, he saw a pair of headlights moving through the pine trees. Then a second pair.

"I see them. Thanks, I've got to go."

"Call as soon as you have something."

"Sure," Greene said, watching the headlights round into the parking lot. The cavalry had arrived, he thought, but was it too late?

GABRIEL

61.25 HOURS MORE

JESUS, THERE MUST BE twenty cars here in the middle of the friggin' night, Ontario Provincial Police officer Brian Gabriel thought as he inched his cruiser into the rail yard parking lot. It was filled with local cops from Brockville and Presquille, other OPP cruisers from as far away as Cornwall, and even a couple of RCMP from Napanee. When the horsemen show up, you know something major is cooking.

Gabriel pulled over beside one of the Mounties. Look at their cruiser. Being a horseman. That's the job Gabriel had wanted. If you were a Mountie you could go out west, up to the Northwest Territories or to the Yukon. Yeah, you would *really* need to speak French in the Yukon, Gabriel cursed bitterly, remembering how not being bilingual had been fatal to his job application.

He threw his cruiser into park, straightened his tie, and smoothed out his uniform. He scooped his OPP cap from its perch on the passenger seat and tugged it firmly over his close-cropped hair, while with his other hand he patted down his blond moustache.

A second later he popped out of his seat, closed the door and, with his chest pulled tight, walked over to the RCMP cruiser.

"Hi, Brian Gabriel, OPP Brockville." He extended his right hand.

"*Oh, oui, 'ello*," the Mountie in the driver's seat said. He gave Gabriel a long look, then a soft handshake.

"What's going on? Any idea why they dragged every cop for a hundred miles out of bed?" Gabriel asked, speaking rapidly.

"Well, I guess, we are not sure." The Mountie smiled weakly, his French Canadian accent evident. He was a skinny type, still in his twenties probably. Although Gabriel was thirty-three years old, he felt as if he were from another generation.

Hmmm. Let's see how bilingual *you* are, Gabriel thought. He threw out a torrent of questions: "What's the drill? Do we sit tight? Move out? Wait for more troops to arrive? Or check in with some big cheese at the putt-putt over there?" Gabriel waved vaguely off in the distance with his right arm toward the stationary train, smiled beatifically down at the Mountie.

"I'm not certain, um, you said, cheese?" The Mountie instinctively pulled back. He looked nervously over at his partner for clarification, but Mr. Passenger Seat shrugged. The bewildered Mountie looked quizzically back at Gabriel.

"Don't worry." Gabriel slapped him on the shoulder, straightened up, and started toward the train. "If you guys mess up, we'll save your bacon."

Gabriel had his best laugh of the night at that one.

Soon there was nothing much left to chuckle about. Gabriel stood among a crowd of chattering cops near the back of the train. No one had any idea what was going on.

Finally, a man came out. He wasn't in uniform.

The crowd quieted right down while the man stood patiently on the back platform of the last car. He looked like a politician making a whistle-stop speech, minus the bands and the bunting.

"Hi," he said simply, "I'm Officer Ari Greene. Apologies for pulling you out here tonight."

That was odd, Gabriel thought. He didn't say where he was from. What's the big secret? Look at his shoes—check the shoes first. That was one of his rules. This guy is from Toronto, clear as day. No way he got that classy footwear out here.

"I wish I could tell you I have a clear or simple assignment." The cop named Greene paused and rubbed his right hand across the underside of his left arm. This looked like an old nervous habit, the kind of thing Gabriel always watched for when he interviewed suspects.

"We believe that a woman—a young woman—jumped off the train four to five miles back and that she's extremely dangerous. It's vitally important that we find her. Vitally important."

He didn't have the usual arrogance you'd expect from a Toronto cop, Gabriel thought. He wasn't pushy. He was almost shy. He wasn't being overdramatic—cops hated that. But to Gabriel the cadence of his speech was off. Cadence. It was a trick an old court constable taught Gabriel when he first started.

"I never listen to what witnesses say," the constable told Gabriel during a break in one of his first cases. "The words don't really matter. Everyone is up there lying their pants off, we all know that. I listen to the cadence. The rhythm. When a witness pauses too long, when they think too hard, or even when they talk too fast, that's when you know they're holding something back."

Gabriel replayed in his mind what Greene had said. "We *believe* a young woman jumped off the train . . . she's extremely dangerous . . . " File it, he thought.

"What's the suspect's description?" an officer called out.

Gabriel saw Greene frown. "That's where it gets dicey. All we really know is that, uh, that she's, well, young, attractive."

That really narrows the field out here in six-toe country, Gabriel muttered to himself. He thought of the sparse female pickings he'd found the last two years since he'd been posted to Brockville. Sparse was being generous.

"Height, weight, hair colour?" someone up near the front piped in.

"Don't really have that either," Greene said. He seemed unsure of himself.

"How dangerous?" someone else shouted from the left side.

Gabriel watched how Greene looked straight at his questioner. "Very," he said in no uncertain terms.

"How attractive?" someone else asked, breaking the tension and sending a chuckle through the crowd.

Greene started to rub his left arm again. He broke into an open smile. "Very." The crowd laughed. Everyone was warming to him.

"Sounds like she's drop-dead beautiful?" someone called out from the back, and Gabriel watched Greene laugh. He could take a joke. That was a good sign.

"I understand there is dense bush on both sides of these tracks," Greene said once the laughter died down. "Either she'll go north to Highway 401 or south to old Highway 2. The tracker dogs should be here soon. I'll need a few officers to go with them and me. The rest of you, we'll split up into two sets of cars and patrol the highways and side roads north and south of the tracks."

Gabriel felt the mood in the crowd change. The fun was over. They were professionals and it was work time. Even though this was important, Greene was so calm you'd think he was a division sergeant parading his officers before a regular shift.

"Any more questions?"

Gabriel saw his opening. Cadence, he thought. "Are you certain this attractive woman is off the train?"

The question seemed to catch the crowd, and Greene, off guard. So did Greene's answer.

"Well . . . " he said. He paused.

Gotcha, Gabriel thought. He's not 100 percent sure.

"I'm going to check the train again, and once the dogs arrive we'll bring them in to get her scent." He looked directly at Gabriel. "I need a backup. I wasn't quite sure how to ask for a volunteer. You interested?"

MARINA

61.25 HOURS MORE

MARINA WASN'T ACCUSTOMED TO humidity. Alisander had warned that it would make her feel slow, and sleepy. Until three days ago, she'd lived her whole life in the desert. Now she felt it. But as she pulled herself up from the hard gravel stones by the rail line where she had landed, the moist air felt good on her scraped legs and elbows.

She watched the slowing train rumble ahead into the darkness as she checked to make sure nothing was broken. A lifetime of stretching and practicing falls from great heights had saved her. She was okay.

She had to get going. The train would stop in another few minutes and soon there would be a search party out looking for her. She smoothed the stones on her landing spot, stripped out of her business suit, changed quickly into a T-shirt and shorts, and started to run, heading back east, away from the direction of the train. The bush was so thick that the tracks were the only way to put some distance between herself and the train. She knew they could get her scent from the seat and the blanket for tracker dogs. But she kept tripping on the oddly spaced railway ties, so started to walk as fast as she could.

There must be a path through the bush.

The sky was beginning to brighten. She looked back. Behind her the clouds in the west were catching the sun's first rays and turning a hard red. Which way to go? Alisander had made sure she knew every inch of the terrain between Montreal and Toronto.

If she turned left and headed north, she'd eventually get to Highway 401, the divided highway between Montreal and Toronto. Once she crossed it, her scent would be lost. But the road was busy, even this early in the morning.

If she turned right and headed south, she'd reach Highway 2, the old Toronto-to-Montreal route. It was a quiet two-lane highway, much easier to cross without being seen, nearer to the town of Brockville and close to the St. Lawrence River.

She had to get off the track. Time to try a diversion. She turned north and clawed her way through the bush, her arms and legs getting scratched at every turn. After about a hundred yards, she turned east again and kept going parallel to the railway tracks. This time she went farther, maybe half a mile. It was hard, tiring work.

Finally, she cut back to her right and made her way south to the tracks. She looked behind her and saw nothing. She shut her eyes and listened. Didn't hear any footsteps or any tracker dogs. They'd be here soon. She couldn't linger on the tracks. She could move faster than a group of police officers following their dogs, and the more bush she dragged them through the better.

She headed south, barging her way through the underbrush, cutting and scraping her legs and arms until she was bloody all over. Her energy began to wane. The warm air felt less like a warm blanket and more like a wet towel dragging her down.

Except for the noise of her footsteps and the cracking of branches, the bush was startlingly quiet. She stopped whenever she dared to, and listened for the sound of other voices or dogs barking. But she heard nothing.

The dawn came quickly. Soon the sky was growing redder, the cumulus clouds thick as a sand dune. She stopped again. She heard something up ahead. It was too faint to make out what it was. She moved toward the sound. After two minutes she stopped again. It was louder. She tore at the branches, moving faster than she thought possible. Rushing toward the sound.

Her heart beating hard, she pulled away the last branch and saw a delicious sight: a river, about ten feet wide, tumbling past. Perfect. She knew that if she walked through the water for a while, her scent would be irretrievably lost.

The skin on her arms and legs had hundreds of cuts, and she was hot and sweaty from the bushwhacking. She dropped her knapsack on the riverbank and plunged into the water. It was cool and wonderful, even though the cuts stung. She dunked down and put her whole head under. She opened her eyes, but in the darkness—she couldn't see anything. The sensation was mysterious.

She needed air. Pushing her feet down onto the rocky river bottom, she kicked hard and popped out. Her T-shirt and shorts clung closely to her skin like a protective wrap. She reached back to the shore, grabbed her knapsack, and held it well above her head as she hiked down the centre of the river.

After about fifteen minutes she found a rock sticking out in the water and stopped. Turning around, she slid her back against a flat spot, worn down by water passing over it for hundreds of years. The rock had retained some of the heat from the day before—like the rocks in the desert.

The water was particularly deep at this point. Blood was caked on her arms, her hair filled with sweat and bugs. She put her knapsack on top of the rock and, letting her body relax, bent her knees and dunked down again into the water. It felt like the most luxurious bath she'd ever had. She came up for air and did it again before burrowing back into the warm rock.

She pulled off her T-shirt and bra and flung them on the rock behind her. She unzipped her shorts, stepped out of them, and threw them on the rock too.

She looked straight up at the thick jumble of clouds directly overhead.

The sky was a deep red. Somewhere in all her training she remembered a phrase: "Red sky in the morning, sailor take warning."

There was a shuddering sound in the trees, and a torrent of warm rain burst upon her. She opened her mouth wide and tasted the water on her tongue. The soft rain tickled her naked breasts. The rushing river felt smooth against her thighs. Her mind drifted back to the night before: the men in the bar in Montreal lusting after her; Alan Larkin so eager in his darkened Toyota.

The water rolling up her legs was so soothing. The rock behind her was so warm. She remembered Alisander at night coming to her room.

She thought about Greene, the policeman she'd last seen on the train. His dark hair. His blue-green eyes. She lowered her hand and let the pleasure fill her body. Handsome eyes, she thought as her tongue licked the warm mixture of rainwater and sweat from her upper lip. Yes, such handsome eyes.

GREENE

61.25 HOURS MORE

TECHNICALLY, THE OPP OFFICER had "volunteered" to search the train with him, but Greene knew no cop wanted to say no to an assignment in front of his fellow officers. He probably wasn't happy about this.

Greene watched the big man hop up onto the train platform, where there was just enough room for the two of them. He was nimble for someone his size.

"Ari Greene, Metro Toronto Police. Nice to meet you," Greene said as he opened the door behind him to let the cop into the train before he followed him inside.

"Brian Gabriel, Brockville OPP." The man put his hand out and gave Greene a firm handshake.

Greene gave him a quick rundown of what had happened. "We have a train full of sleeping people," he explained. "My authority to search this train is marginal at best. We could turn on the lights, wake everyone up, and cause a scene—but I'm not inclined to do that—at least not yet."

"She might be hiding somewhere, even in that car?" Gabriel asked in a half whisper. "I assume you checked the washrooms."

"Every washroom, every seat. No sign of her. Even though my gut tells me that she got off, I have to prove it to myself."

Greene proposed he go into each car first and Gabriel, who was in uniform, would be backup. They'd remain in visual contact at all times.

They started with the last car. She wasn't there. They went through the passageway to the door to the next car. This was the one where Greene had seen the woman. He looked back at Gabriel, nodded, opened the heavy door quietly.

Nothing seemed to have changed. He approached the seat the woman had been in. His heart was pounding. He could feel the circulation in his fingertips.

It was still empty. Nothing there but the blanket she'd been under. He looked back. Gabriel was inside the door now.

Lifting his arms and turning his palms out, Greene signaled for him to wait.

Then, almost furtively, Greene slipped into her seat. He wanted to sit where she'd been. He pulled up the blanket she'd slept under, put it to his nose and inhaled. He thought he could smell a whiff of perfume—or maybe he was fooling himself.

He looked below the seats. Not even a child could fit underneath. He stood up and signaled for Gabriel to come forward.

"This is where she sat," Greene said in a half whisper.

Gabriel looked around, taking everything in. Greene was impressed by how thorough he was. Don't underestimate the local police force, Greene thought.

Gabriel walked quietly to the back door, still looking around. He motioned his head toward the luggage racks and raised his eyebrows inquiringly.

"I looked in there," Greene said. "Nothing."

Gabriel nodded.

But Greene didn't feel as if he was listening to him.

Gabriel bent his knees and, with a clean swift action, pulled aside the curtain covering the luggage rack. The same bag of luggage was there as when Greene had checked it a few minutes ago.

"See, luggage." Greene's voice grew louder.

Gabriel shook his head.

He sure is a quiet cop, Greene thought.

Gabriel pulled the piece of luggage into the aisle. He lifted it, looked at Greene. Turned it around and ran his hand around the outside.

"Feel how light this is," he said, not bothering to whisper. He pointed out a hole in the luggage. "Let's open it up."

It was Greene's turn to be silent. He watched as Gabriel unlatched the luggage. It was empty. Gabriel took his flashlight out and began to examine the inside. There were two clasps on one of the inside panels. He flicked them and the panel folded open.

"Perfect hiding place," Gabriel said. "Open these inside panels, and there would be room to slip inside."

"I saw the luggage," Greene said, pounding his fist against the wall beside him, "and walked out of the car."

"All she has to do," Gabriel said, "is zip over to the back door . . . "

"And with the train slowing down," Greene said, "jump off."

TUESDAY

JULY 5, 1988

OSGOODE

52 HOURS MORE

FRANK OSGOODE KNEW HE was late for court. But fuck it. Judge Henry fucking Humphrey Jacobs and his dumb three names would have to wait on his pernickety fat ass for a few minutes. Too damn bad. Blame it on the bloody Essex County Judicial Committee. They're the ones who gave Jacobs the stupid judicial appointment that should have been his.

Maybe it was just as well, Osgoode thought as he jammed the cigarette lighter into the dashboard of his beat-up Camaro and hit the gas. If they'd picked him to be a judge, like his father and grandfather had been, he'd have to be there in the courthouse, all prim and proper, every single morning by 8:30 and stay until 4:30, even on a good sailing day.

To hell with it. There was more to life than a pension and a paycheck. Osgoode kept his left hand on the steering wheel as he used his right hand to reach over to the glove compartment and fumble around for the bottle of Bufferin he was pretty sure he'd stashed there. And besides, a paycheck was legal tender his ex-wives could garnish, he reasoned as he found the bottle, clawed it open with his teeth, and swallowed three pills whole. They can't touch the cash my clients slip me on the courthouse steps, he thought as he leaned forward and wiped the inside of the windshield with the sleeve of his twelve-year-old sports jacket.

This rain was no help. He could hardly see ten feet ahead. That's it: he'd tell old Judge Three Last Names that his car slid out in the downpour and that's why he was late. And that's why he looked like such a wreck. Ha.

The lighter popped and Osgoode tugged it out between his baby and ring fingers. His hand searched the passenger seat for his pack of Player's. He yanked out a cigarette and brought it to his mouth and was lighting it when he saw something up ahead on the road. Oh my. A woman hitch-hiker. Here on a desolate stretch of old Highway 2. And would you look at that, Osgoode thought as he pumped the Camaro's creaky brakes and pulled over. I'll bet the King's Highway hasn't seen such a cute ass in years.

"Thanks a lot, man," the woman said as she pulled the door open.

Osgoode winced as he heard the hinge creak. She was gorgeous. He flashed her his best Steve McQueen grin. He might be pushing fifty, twice divorced, twenty pounds overweight, and grey in more places than his temples, but he still had the baby-blue eyes and high cheekbones that had once made him the biggest high school idol this town had ever seen.

"No problem. What's a pretty young thing like you doing out here in the rain?" Osgoode shook his head. Just yesterday he was Brockville's most eligible bachelor, now he sounded like an old fart.

"Freezing my ass off, what do you think?" she said, tossing her knapsack into the back seat.

Well, she had spunk. He put the Camaro in gear and pulled back out onto the empty road.

"It's a long story that I'm sure you could live without hearing," she said, turning around and looking through the back window of the car.

"Try me. I listen to people's stories for a living."

"How about," she said, turning back to him, "my boyfriend and I were camping, had a fight, so I took off in the dark and ended up getting soaked right down to my panties hoping someone would pick me up, and here I am, blabbing away about my wet underwear with a total stranger."

"What did you fight about?" Osgoode hoped he'd hear more about her wet panties.

"The thing everyone fights about."

"Money?"

"No, stupid, something more personal, if you know what I mean." She pulled her sweater over her head in one quick motion and shook out her hair. She looked around and out the back window again. "It's pretty deserted out here."

"During the week. On the weekend it fills up with tourists."

"Do you mind if I curl up on this seat? I'm kind of tired." Without waiting for his reply, she rolled herself into a ball, her head resting inches from his lap.

Jesus, she looked about the same age as his daughter, Bev. "Fine with me," he said.

The car hit a bump and he felt her head touch his leg. Boy was he ever a has-been. He'd spent last night seducing an overweight forty-eight-year-old divorcée, and this morning this sweet beauty comes into his car and he's still hung over from the red wine and . . .

"I hope you don't mind," she purred.

"Not at all."

Her head moved closer, right up to his thigh.

"I kind of need a place to crash. I wouldn't want to bug you or anything."

"Well, I was going to court this morning."

She ran a hand through her hair and her fingers brushed against the outside of his knee. "I guess you could drop me downtown somewhere. I can sleep in a park."

"My daughter, Bev, is about your age, and she'd never forgive me if I made you do that. This court appearance is not a big deal, and I could always phone in and be a few minutes late."

"I'd really appreciate it." She yawned and stretched like a cat. "I'm really cold."

"I'm not much of a cook, but I can make you some hot tea," Osgoode said, shaking his head at his good fortune.

He banked the Camaro onto the soft shoulder and pulled a wide U-turn. Looks like His Honour will have to sit on his fat ass a little longer, Osgoode thought with a playful smirk as he gunned the car back down the highway.

A few seconds later he saw his friend Brian Gabriel's OPP cruiser driving toward him. There was someone in the front seat with him, and Gabriel looked like he was in a hurry. Probably a witness. Gabe must be late for court, which wasn't like him at all.

Osgoode tapped his horn and gave his buddy a winsome smile. Ha, if only he could see the gorgeous woman lying here just below his sight line, Osgoode thought, his Cheshire cat grin growing as he felt her slide her hand onto his thigh and snuggle in beside him.

Then he burst out laughing as a thought occurred to him: Thank the good lord they never made him a judge!

GREENE

49 HOURS MORE

WHEN GREENE AND MEREDITH were up at her cottage, on rainy days they'd tour different nearby towns and usually end up in the local diner for lunch. The menus, which Meredith called the All-Canadian Small-Town breakfast, were as predictable, he liked to joke, as the Toronto Maple Leafs playing a hockey game against the Montreal Canadiens on a Saturday night. They all had the same greasy fare, the same as the food selection he was reading about on the plastic-covered menu at the Thousand Islands Diner that Brian Gabriel had brought him to.

"The luncheon special today is hot hamburger plate," said the thin blond waitress, who'd approached their table as soon as they'd come in. Her treble voice grated like an AM station on a cheap transistor radio. "Comes with your choice of chicken noodle soup or chef's salad or potatoes—fried, mashed, or baked."

"I'll have a tea with milk and a salad. What kind of dressing do you have?" Greene asked absentmindedly. He regretted the question as soon as he asked it, since he knew what the answer would be.

"Blue cheese, Ranch, French, Thousand Island," she said in a sharp, clipped twang.

"When in Rome," Greene said with a laugh, looking across the linoleum table at Gabriel. "I'll have the Thousand Island dressing."

They all chuckled.

"I'll bring you the dressing tray and you can help yourself, hun." She touched his shoulder as she took back his menu. "How's 'bout you, Brian?" She turned to the beefy OPP officer.

"Grilled cheese and my usual drink, Sally," Gabriel said, leaning hard on the second syllable of her name. Greene noticed he'd acquired a bit of a twang—local talk.

Sally lingered for an instant before she left. Greene caught a hint of an exchange between her and Gabriel. He watched her as she walked away. She had the hard look of a small-town girl who had quit school at sixteen, had three kids by the time she was twenty-one, and was divorced and smoking a pack of cigarettes a day by twenty-nine. Still, there was something endearing about her. Greene noticed Gabriel didn't have a ring on his finger. Those winter nights out here must get pretty lonely.

Greene looked squarely at Gabriel. It was almost noon. In the few hours they'd worked together, they'd transformed themselves from strangers to partners.

After they'd searched the train and found the empty luggage, the dogs arrived and they followed them back up the railway tracks and into the bush. The scent took them north, and Greene used Gabriel's handheld radio to send most of the squad cars up to Highway 401. After half an hour the trail turned south, and twenty minutes later they were back at the railway tracks, with the dogs yelping at the scent on the south side.

Greene realized the woman had done this elaborate maneuver to throw them off. He got back on his radio and split his deployment, keeping half his cars on the 401, the other half south of the tracks to Highway 2. He sent the officers with the dogs on ahead and kept Gabriel back with him.

"Looks like you're my designated driver," he said as the dogs headed eagerly back off into the bush.

"Anything beats this bushwhacking," Gabriel replied.

"How long will it take to drive back to Highway 2?"

"Fifteen, maybe twenty minutes. Once we get to my cruiser, that is."

They ran back on the railway tracks as fast as they could. The skies opened up and it began to rain, making everything slipperier and slower. By the time they got to Gabriel's cruiser, Greene was chewing up the inside of his lip in frustration.

As Gabriel drove along Highway 2, Greene radioed the cars he'd deployed there. One by one they reported in with no news. The officers with the dogs radioed in from the bush. More bad news: they'd come across a river and had lost the scent.

She's playing me for a fool, Greene thought, his anger at himself growing as he stared out the windshield.

Every time a car passed coming from the other direction on the two-lane highway, Gabriel waved as if each driver was his best friend or first cousin.

"Is there anyone here you don't know?" Greene asked him after the fourth or fifth car passed them.

"Small town," he said. "Everyone knows the local cop."

Greene knew he couldn't tie up the entire police force for the whole morning. He got back on the radio and released the other cars and thanked the officers for their help.

Gabriel drove him into Brockville. It took all of ten minutes to tour the town, another ten to meet the chief of police. Greene used the phone there to call Bering and update her again.

"I had a thought," Greene told her. "This woman didn't get on the train in Montreal, but in a suburban station west of it, where it was dark and no one would recognize her, including me. Question: How did she get there? I saw a bunch of cars in the parking lot."

"You think she stole a car and drove out there?"

"Worth checking out."

"Good idea. I'm on it."

Greene turned to Gabriel, who'd been listening to his part of the conversation.

"Sounds as if she's a lone wolf," Gabriel said. "That makes her harder to find."

"I think so," Greene said. "She came well prepared."

They left the police station and drove to the courthouse to see if anything unusual was happening. Again Gabriel seemed to know everyone. Then they headed here to Gabriel's favourite restaurant for something to eat.

Sally brought over Greene's tea and Gabriel's usual drink, which turned out to be a large glass of milk. She said their food would be ready in a minute. Greene stared absently at the plastic place mat as he stirred some milk into his tea. It had a map of the Thousand Islands and a list of "Ten things you didn't know" about the historic area, including that there were: "1,864 islands."

"How long have you been stationed here?" he asked Gabriel once Sally was out of earshot.

"Coming to the end of my second year," Gabriel said. "It was fun at first, but, well, this is a pretty small town."

Greene let the thought linger. It was a smart answer. Open enough to allow for a more personal query, but closed enough that he could pass over it without insult. He watched Gabriel take a sip of his milk. It painted a faint white patina on his neatly clipped moustache.

"I'd guess," Greene said, lowering his voice, "this town doesn't have the most exciting social life."

"There's an understatement, but some people like it that way." Gabriel picked up his knife and cleaned it off with the thin napkin that was part of the standard place setting. "The lawyer we saw this morning, Frank Osgoode? His father and grandfather were all famous judges. He's a character. Twice divorced, we call him the local stickman. He'll go after practically anything female that moves."

Greene nodded, half listening. The television above the counter was running a promotion for summer reruns of *Starsky & Hutch*. He was dumb enough to be on that show, he thought. How did he miss her in the luggage rack?

Greene looked back at Gabriel. There was a moment of silence. Greene realized Gabriel was waiting for his response to what he'd said. More out of courtesy than curiosity, he lobbed back a rote question.

"Which trial was Osgoode doing at the courthouse today?"

"No, no," Gabriel corrected him. "He was late and not in court. A high court trial, jury and all. Remember I joked with the other lawyers about Osgoode having his usual Friday morning hangover and it isn't even Friday? He's the guy we passed on Highway 2 this morning with the big grin on his face."

Greene dropped his spoon and it landed with a loud clank into his empty mug of tea.

"In the old Camaro?"

"Yeah. I told you he must have been heading home from one of his girlfriends. Remember, I said he was driving the wrong way and he'd be late for court again, and the judge, who he's always feuding with, was going to be pissed off?"

"Wait," Greene said. "Did he show up in the courthouse?"

"Not when we were there. The court clerk called Yvonne, his secretary, and she didn't know where he was. That's unusual for Osgoode. Yvonne runs his life and usually knows who he's shacking up with on which day of the week. But I didn't think anything of it . . . "

"You said he was on Highway 2," Greene said, standing up. "Driving away from town. Does he live near there?"

"Just south of the highway. It's a fifteen-minute drive from here, tops."

Greene kicked his chair into the table.

Gabriel stood and took a gulp from his glass of milk.

"Let's go," Greene said. He threw down a twenty-dollar bill and rushed to the door.

Gabriel grabbed his jacket and scooted after Greene.

"Sally," he yelled across the restaurant as he paused at the front door, "hold the grilled cheese."

BERING

49 HOURS MORE

THERE WAS A SHARP but tentative knock at Bering's hotel door. She looked up from the desk, where she was working.

"Yes," she said impatiently.

"Officer Bering," Mudhar said. "There's a FedEx package for you."

Bering was on her feet before he finished his sentence. In a flash her hand was on the door handle.

"Thanks," she said, and took the package. The return address was the Sûreté du Québec.

Bering sat down again and put the unopened package on her desk. She turned her attention back to a map she'd been studying. It was really two maps that Bering had taped together and pasted onto a piece of cardboard. One was of the New England states. The other was of Eastern Canada. To her annoyance, she couldn't find a map that covered both the United States and Canada, so she'd had to make her own.

She'd circled the town of Stanstead, Quebec, twice in red. A few miles south, just inside the border, she'd drawn a circle with a question mark inside it. She'd drawn a circle around downtown Montreal, where the bus station was located, and another around the suburban train station west of Montreal, where the woman had boarded the train.

She ripped open the package. Inside was a ten-page report from the Bureau des détectives de Montréal. The title page read: GREYHOUND BUS NUMBER 856, STANSTEAD, QUEBEC, TO MONTREAL, QUEBEC, MONDAY, JULY 4, 1988—results of interviews with all parties available at this time. It was dated Tuesday, July 5, 1988, 6:00 a.m. Someone had worked all night to turn this around fast.

As Bering read, her face became more and more flushed. Her heart began to pound, and she could feel the pressure build up in her temples. By the time she finished her hands were cold and clammy, the way they felt before she testified in court.

She put the report down. The bus driver had followed this mysterious woman and watched her make a phone call saying only one word: "Montreal." That could mean only one thing: this killer was reporting her progress back to someone.

This was no lone wolf. She was highly trained and prepared for her deadly mission. And Greene was chasing her.

"Oh no," Bering whispered. She felt a tendril of cold tension winnow up her spine. She shook her head ever so slightly. Ari, she thought, even though she never called him by his first name.

In the silence of the room, she wasn't sure if she had said his name out loud or if she was hearing the frightened voice inside her head.

GREENE

48.75 HOURS MORE

THERE WERE MOMENTS WHEN Greene wished he could, by sheer force of will, make time stand still. Now he was trying to stare down the digital clock on the dashboard of the OPP cruiser, which read: 12:15. He willed the numbers to remain constant as he pushed down on the accelerator. Seconds earlier, Gabriel had thrown his keys to Greene as they'd rushed to the cruiser.

"You drive, I'll work the radio and give you directions," Gabriel shouted at Greene. "That will be quicker."

It wasn't humanly possible to drive faster. The siren was blaring as they flew through town. When they arrived at Highway 2, he gunned the powerful engine. He had a sickening feeling about what they were about to find. He shot an accusing look at the clock. It was 12:16.

The next few minutes were painfully slow, even though they were moving fast. "Tell me when we're within about a mile," Greene said. "I'll kill the siren. No need to announce our arrival."

Gabriel nodded. "Okay, the turn is coming up after the next bend in the road."

Greene cut the siren and hit the brakes. The noise dissipated and the cruiser became eerily quiet. Neither man spoke. Gabriel pointed to a turnoff, and Greene swung onto a dirt road that meandered across a flat, treed field.

At the end of the road, an old wood-frame house with a caved-in front porch squatted contentedly on an overgrown lawn filled with clover. On the south side it looked as if someone had once tried to put in a perennial garden. The few remaining plants had grown leggy and were losing their battle for sunlight to a persistent crowd of weeds.

Gabriel pointed. "There's Osgoode's car."

Parked carelessly to the side of the house was a late-model Camaro. The driver's-side door had a deep dent in it, which Greene could tell even from a distance hadn't been repaired for a few winters because the rust was beginning to take over.

During their manic drive, Greene and Gabriel had devised a simple plan to approach the house. That was one of the nice things about being a cop, he thought as his shoes hit the mushy ground. Meet a good police officer from anywhere and within a few minutes you could work together as if you'd been doing it for years.

Gabriel leapt from the cruiser and pulled out his gun. Greene walked over to the Camaro and ran his hand across the hood. He looked at Gabriel and mouthed the words: "Still warm."

Gabriel frowned.

Greene nodded, and as they'd agreed, began to count: one one-thousand, two one-thousand, while he walked around the house. When he got to the back door he was at eleven one-thousand. He kept counting: twelve, thirteen, fourteen. At fifteen one-thousand, he put his shoulder to the doorframe, and in an instant he was inside. His gun out, pointed in front of him.

The house was a predictable mess. And quiet. Bad quiet, as he'd feared. Greene walked up a small flight of linoleum-covered stairs into the kitchen.

Gabriel burst through the flimsy wooden front door at the other end of a narrow hallway. They didn't say a word, but their eyes confirmed each other's worst suspicion: this wasn't good.

Despite the grim situation, Greene had to stop himself from smiling. Gabriel's "usual drink" had left a white milk moustache on his upper lip.

Greene pointed his gun to his right, indicating that Gabriel should check out the room on that side of the hall. He moved to the one on his left and cracked the door open. What he saw made him feel ill.

A naked middle-aged man was sprawled across the bed, pornographic magazines spread all around him and his hands down around his shriveled-up penis. Across his lower stomach, a smattering of semen lay like spilt yogurt.

He'd drawn the short straw, Greene thought as he creaked the door all the way open, gun at the ready. It took a few seconds to determine there was no one else there.

Oh, how the mighty have fallen, Greene thought as he left the room, closing the door behind him. He went to get Gabriel.

The big officer was in the other room, looking through a small messy study. He looked up when Greene came in. He could read the bad news on Greene's face.

"It's ugly," Greene said to him in a near whisper. "You might want to spare yourself."

In their hearts, they had both known this was coming. But that didn't make it any easier. Greene saw the pain etch deep into Gabriel's face as the news sunk in.

"Why didn't I think of this when we passed Osgoode on the road this morning?" Gabriel said. "None of this would have happened."

"You don't know that," Greene said. He put his left hand on Gabriel's beefy shoulder. The tears of the clown, Greene thought as Gabriel's eyes welled up and his white moustache turned sad.

"I'll be back in a minute," Gabriel said.

With heavy footsteps, he walked down the hall. In a few seconds

Greene heard the bedroom door creak open. Greene didn't move. Finally, he heard Gabriel say, "Shit." In stark contrast to the word, his voice was mournfully soft.

Greene went out into the hall. Gabriel had opened the bedroom door, but he hadn't gone inside. Greene approached, reached around him, shut the door with a gentle tug, and directed him back to the study.

"I need to call this in," Gabriel said, picking up his radio.

"Not the radio," Greene said, stopping him and pointing to the phone on the desk. "Use this."

He found a neglected rag sitting on the bookshelf and used it to cradle the phone's handle.

He did this knowing that there probably wasn't any point in worrying about fingerprints. This woman was too well trained to slip up.

He passed the phone to Gabriel, who made the necessary calls. Then Greene called Bering and gave her a precise update and finished by saying: "The top forensic OPP guy in the area is on his way and so is the coroner."

"What about the press?"

"We did it all by phone and instructed everyone: no police radios. We'll be able to keep this quiet for a few hours."

"No sign of the woman?" Bering asked.

"No. But the lawyer's car is parked outside. It's still fairly warm. I'd guess it was turned off less than two hours ago. She can't be too far. She's tried buses, cars, and trains, maybe it'll be an airplane next."

Gabriel looked up at him, his eyes wide. He mouthed the words "Wait a minute" and rushed down the hall.

"This keeps getting worse," Bering said.

Seconds later, Gabriel came back clutching something in his hand. He looked triumphant. "It occurred to me as I heard you talking to your partner about trains and planes," he said. "Osgoode's boat."

"He's got a boat?"

"A fast one."

"Where?"

"At the marina down the road. Everyone knows his boat key. Typical Frank. It's got a half-naked mermaid on it. And look." Gabriel opened his hand and revealed a key chain. "It's missing."

KRUPP

48.75 HOURS MORE

WAYNE KRUPP LIKED TO work the day after the July 4 regatta. The marina was always quiet, and all he had to do was pile some wet clothes into the lost-and-found box and deal with the odd club member who came by to take their boat out. Easy.

Today was quieter than usual. It was just after noon and not a single boat was on the water. That suited Krupp just fine because all he wanted to do was think about his big day coming up in a little more than a week: July 14. He shook his head and smiled at the thought. Jennifer. Beautiful Jennifer North was going to marry him—fat and friendly Wayne Krupp.

Unbelievable.

What had he done to deserve her? Oh sure, he'd been her best friend since they were in grade three together. He'd been her shoulder to cry on when her mom and dad split, when things went wrong with her hockey-star boyfriend, when her modeling career in Toronto was a bust and she had to take the bus back home embarrassed and alone.

Now it was nine days until their wedding day. And he had nine more pounds to lose, he thought as he looked across the small office at the entreating lights of the candy bar vending machine. Shaking his head, he pulled himself up off his stool to go outside for a walk.

As he opened the door he saw a woman walking onto the pier. She wore a red short-sleeved shirt, tight blue shorts, and old-fashioned white running shoes. A knapsack was slung over her shoulder. Krupp was no ladies' man, but even he could see she was extremely attractive.

"Ah, excuse me," he said as he let the screen door go and the heavy metal springs swung it closed with a familiar clank. "Can I help you?"

"Hi. I'm a friend of Bev Osgoode," she said in a friendly tone. "We came down last night from Kingston and were hoping to go for a boat ride today. This morning she got a call from her professor at Queen's all in a panic about some research he wanted her to do. She'll be stuck inside all day."

"Oh, I see," Krupp said. Old man Osgoode must have been happy Bev brought home such an attractive classmate. He knew Osgoode's reputation with the ladies all too well. The scumbag even tried to put the moves on Jennifer after she and Krupp announced their engagement in the *Recorder and Times*. The guy was out of control.

"Where's Mr. Osgoode?" Krupp asked.

"He's in court on some case. He keeps complaining about the judge, a guy with three first names or something."

Krupp smiled. That would be Justice Henry Humphrey Jacobs. Or "Henry fucking Humphrey Jacobs," as Osgoode liked to call him.

The woman swung her knapsack down from her shoulder, swiveled her hips, and smiled at him. "Mr. Osgoode gave me the key and said to come down to see if anyone could take me out."

There's no use flirting with me, Krupp thought as he watched her twirl the key in her hand. But he had nothing to do all day but stare at the candy machine, and Osgoode would tip him well for helping his daughter's friend. He could use the cash to help him make another payment on the wedding ring.

"You picked a slow day and I'm the only one here," Krupp said, returning her friendly smile. "Let me lock up and I can take you on the river for, say, half an hour. Mr. Osgoode's boat is to the right on the last pier."

"He said it was called *Wind Bag*, which I thought was pretty cute."

"That's Mr. Osgoode," Krupp said. The boat was misnamed, he thought. It should be called *Sleaze Bag*.

Typical of the guy, Osgoode had a souped-up powerboat. A Donzi. A brand-new Z-33 Crossfire, with twin 454 big-block engines painted red on the side, white on top, with a red stripe down the middle. Like Osgoode, it stood out in a crowd.

Krupp slipped back into the office, tore the top off of an old cardboard box, and wrote: "Out on the River. Back by 1:00, Wayne." He stuck it on the door, scooped up his blue canvas sail bag, tossed in his three-generation-old Thousand Islands map that he always took with him, and ambled down the dock.

"My name is Wayne, by the way. Wayne Krupp." He put out his hand to shake hers.

"Hi, I'm Linda McClelland," she said, taking his hand and holding on to it for an extra few seconds. "Everyone calls me Lindy."

"Okay, Lindy, get ready to hold on," he said as he helped her on board, and sat down in the driver's chair behind the heavy oak steering wheel. "This boat really moves. Be prepared."

"Cool," she said, smiling. She slung her knapsack off her shoulder and clipped it onto a hook on the side of the windscreen. "Let's rocket."

"Which way?"

Lindy said she wanted to head west.

Krupp took out his map and put it in front of him, gunned the engines, and headed upriver. He maneuvered easily through a complex maze of islands. It didn't take long until they had lost sight of the shore. The *Wind Bag* made good speed against the powerful current.

She said she was interested in the geography of the river, so he told her how the great glacier had formed the whole region, gouging out the lakes and rivers and creating the islands. He gave the map to her.

"Don't you need to look at it?" Lindy asked him.

Krupp laughed. "Not yet. I grew up on the river. I took my first boat trip when I was six weeks old. That's twenty-five years ago. My granddad, then my dad, used to run the club before me. The map has been passed down through three generations. It's kind of a local legend in town."

"Amazing," Lindy said. "You must know every nook and cranny."

"Almost," Krupp said. "But even I get lost sometimes. No one knows all the Thousand Islands. In fact there are 1,864 islands. That's why I never, ever go out on the river without my map."

Lindy picked it up and studied it carefully before she gave it back to him. She flashed him a smile. "I've got to use the washroom," she said, and went down the stairs to the cabin below.

Krupp scanned the sky. Dark clouds were billowing on the eastern horizon. They looked much worse on the river than what he'd seen from shore. He checked the telltales, long thin pieces of plastic tied to the radio aerial. They were flapping in the wind that was blowing in hard from the east. Not good. The air was hot and humid, even on the water. He knew how a major storm from the east could move in with frightening speed. One minute you were sunbathing, the next you were running for cover from the sheets of rain and hail.

He might have to cut this tour short, but at least it would keep him away from food for a while.

Lindy came back up to the main deck. "It's really getting warm." As she spoke, she pulled her T-shirt over her head. She wore a thin lacy bra, which barely covered her breasts.

"I hope you don't mind. I didn't bring a bathing suit."

"No, it doesn't matter to me," he said. It was the truth.

With one quick tug, she pulled off her shorts. All she had on now was her underwear.

Krupp thought of Jennifer. Just his luck. For his whole life, no woman would even look at him. Now he was about to marry Jen, and this beautiful woman was practically stripping right in front of him. Oh, sleazebag Osgoode would love to be here right now.

She sat cross-legged a few feet from him. As if she were doing no more than reaching for a glass of water, she slid her hand in between her breasts, unclasped the bra, and let it drop idly onto the deck.

Krupp gulped. He was getting nervous. He didn't know what to say. He tried not to look, but he snuck a peek. She had a terrific body.

A minute passed. Then two.

"Does that radio work?" she asked.

"Sure," Krupp said. His mouth was dry. He turned the radio on. Bryan Adams was singing "Cuts Like a Knife."

"I love this song," Lindy squealed. She jumped up and began to sway to the music. Her breasts swayed too as she threw her arms up in the air, singing along with the lyrics, dancing away.

"Do you have any sunscreen?" she asked as casually as if she were asking to borrow a pencil. She was moving closer to him.

Krupp swallowed hard. "Yep," he said, pulling a bottle out of his bag. His hand shook as he passed it to her.

"Look," he said, pointing to the sky. "Bad weather on the horizon. We'll have to head back soon."

"Not too soon, I hope," she said as she spread the sunscreen all over her neck and arms. When she got to her breasts, she stopped, poured out more liquid on her hand before she rubbed it in.

She moaned.

Watch for the rocks, Krupp told himself, averting his eyes and making himself stare off into the distance.

She lay down right in front of him. Despite himself, Krupp snuck another peek at her. She was outrageously good-looking. He had to admit it. She had incredible dark eyes, though her left one was a bit odd. Still, that overpriced modeling course in Toronto that had flunked out Jennifer would have taken Lindy in an instant.

"I hope I'm not embarrassing you," she said, "but the truth is that I've been locked up in a library for months and, well, you know . . . "

Krupp was breathing hard. He tried to look away, but those breasts.

"Look," Krupp said, struggling to keep his voice even. "You're really nice-looking and everything, and I can't believe someone like you would be at all interested in me, but you see . . . "

She didn't seem to hear him. Her eyes were unfocused. She slid her tongue out and licked her lips. She slipped her thumb under the band of her panties, and in one jerk twirled them over her legs and tucked them into a side pocket of her knapsack. Now she was totally naked.

Krupp didn't know what to do.

She swung her legs around, stood up, and came over to him. Because he was sitting down, her breasts were right in front of his face.

"Please, give me a rub," she said dreamily.

"Well, you see," Krupp stuttered, "I'm getting married in nine days, and I couldn't do it to Jennifer."

She seemed to be in some kind of trance. She reached across his body and took his right hand and pulled it to her. He resisted slightly, but she was strong. She moaned again.

"Just for a minute," she whispered.

Krupp tried to pull his hand back gently. She wouldn't let go, so he pulled back harder. "Listen, I'm sorry," he said, "but I can't—"

Before he could finish his sentence, her grip tightened on his wrist. She pulled his arm over the top of the steering wheel and slammed it down with full force.

He pulled back with all his might, but she had the advantage of surprise. Before he could brace himself, she kicked him square in the chest. He could feel the wind go out of him. Her knee crashed into his head. He tried to raise his arm to protect himself, but she still had it in her grip.

She smashed his arm down again on the wheel.

She's trying to break my arm, Krupp realized.

Smash. She slammed it down a third time.

Recovering from the shock of the attack, he leaned forward and groped at her with his free left hand. His fingers found her right breast and he squeezed it hard. She slammed his arm down again. He yelled out in pain.

He tightened his hand on her breast as tight as he could. He could feel he was hurting her. He had to try to make her release him.

She slammed his arm down a fifth time, and this time he heard the bone crack.

Incredible pain raced through his body. He had to let go of her. She pulled her fist up and smashed him in the face, sending him reeling back into his seat. He was in agony. She took a rope out of her bag and began tying him down. He couldn't resist.

His arm hurt so badly that he could hardly see. In seconds, he was immobilized. He began to feel faint.

He wanted to cry.

But even more than that, he wanted to see Jennifer.

GREENE

48.75 HOURS MORE

"OSGOODE'S BOAT CLUB IS down by the river," Gabriel yelled as he ran out of the house with Greene.

"How far?"

"Five minutes." Gabriel pointed toward a clump of overgrown pine trees. "There's the path over there."

They got to the 1001 Islands Yacht Club in just over three minutes. As it came into view, Gabriel began to shout: "Wayne! Wayne, are you here?"

"Who's Wayne?" Greene said, slowing down, gasping hard for air.

"He runs the club." Gabriel ran up to the boat office and snatched a cardboard sign, which was hanging innocently on the screen door. "Oh no," he hissed under his breath, and passed the sign to Greene.

Gabriel started to run onto the dock. Greene took off after him.

"Osgoode's boat, it's on the last pier," Gabriel yelled over his shoulder.

The dock was long and wide. But with two men running at full speed, it started to bounce wildly up and down.

"Damn!" Gabriel swore as he reached the end and turned to his right. "His boat's gone."

Greene saw a gaping hole on the pier running south off the main dock.

Gabriel stopped to catch his breath, but Greene kept going. He had to get to the spot where she would have stood. Trace her steps. He got to the empty mooring. Nothing was there except the painfully open space.

He looked down and saw a white plaque with the classic image of a blindfolded woman holding up the scales of justice. But instead of wearing white robes, she had on a sexy bikini. On one of the scales there was a boat and on the other there was a bottle of beer.

Greene shook his head and looked up. The swiftly flowing St. Lawrence River was wide and powerful. Everywhere he saw water. And islands.

He looked down again, as if the ground the assassin had so recently walked on might yield a clue. All he saw were neatly tied-up ropes and some mooring clips. He spotted a small stone embedded between two of the wooden boards. The space between them was tight, and he got a splinter in his finger as he pried the stone out. He raised his hand to his eyes to study it. Blood started running down onto his palm.

He lowered his hand and watched the blood change direction and trickle back down to the tips of his fingers.

The only sound was the lapping of waves against the dock. Greene took one last look at the stone in his hand. He raised his head and gazed out at the seemingly endless St. Lawrence. All those islands. He counted the ones nearby and in seconds he was up to more than thirty.

"One thousand eight hundred and sixty-four fucking islands." He yelled so loud that some pigeons three piers away took flight. He drew his arm back and hurled the stone as hard and as far as he could.

KRUPP

48.5 HOURS MORE

"FAT BOY, WAKE UP!"

A woman was screaming at Krupp. It wasn't Jennifer. She'd never yell at him like that. Why was the woman yelling?

He felt a torrent of cold water hit his face. He felt the horrible pain in his arm. And he remembered.

Lindy. The woman who said she was Bev Osgoode's friend. She was standing beside him, his 1001 Islands Yacht Club pail in her hands. She was still naked. She went to the side of the boat, filled the pail again, came back, and threw more water on him.

"Wake up," she yelled, "if you want to see Jennifer again!"

Krupp felt his body jerk. He looked down and saw his arm. It was misshapen. "What do you want? Why did you break my arm?" he moaned.

"You're going to drive this boat as fast as you can and drop me at the most deserted beach you know on the north shore." She wasn't yelling anymore.

He bit his lip to hold in the pain. He tried to move but realized she'd tied him in place. "Then what?" he asked, squealing.

"Do what I tell you to do, or you'll never see your Jennifer again." Her pleasant voice had turned deep and dark. "Understand?"

Krupp nodded. The pain made it hard for him to keep his eyes open. He tested the ropes on his legs—they were tight. He had to think fast, but it was hard to think because he was in so much pain.

"Wayne, keep awake or I'll break your other arm. Do you hear me?"

"I need my map," he said through gritted teeth. "Get it and hold it up for me to see."

The truth was, Krupp didn't need the map. He knew exactly where he was and where he wanted to go. But with his arm broken and his body tied to the wheel, he needed to get some measure of control over the situation.

She hesitated.

"The map. Hurry and get it before we crash on those rocks up ahead," he said.

She turned and saw the pile of boulders in their path. "Okay," she said. She turned her back on him to retrieve it.

Good, he thought. Let her think she could take her eyes off him for a few seconds. It would make her less cautious. He started to loosen his right leg from the ropes before she brought the map out and held it to her chest.

"Hold it up where I can see," he ordered her, lowering his voice. She did as he asked. The map obscured her view of his leg. He moved it, loosening the rope more. He had to keep her distracted for a few more minutes. He tilted forward, pretending to study the map.

"I can't reach the throttle," he yelled at her through the sound of the engines. "Those boulders are coming up fast. If we don't slow down, we'll smash into a rock and kill the prop."

She was facing him, so her back was to the bow. She turned to see where they were going. To get around the rock pile, they had to take one of two channels.

"We have to go to the right," he shouted, showing her the direction with his chin.

"Why? That channel looks narrow."

"Because it's so narrow it's also deep, that means there's less chance of hitting a rock. It's the quickest way to shore."

She regarded him skeptically. She pulled the map back and looked at it. He kept talking. He had to convince her.

"Why don't we head this way?" She pointed to the channel to the left. "Look at these tight contour lines. It's deep."

She's smart, Krupp thought, and she knows how to read a map. If they went that way, all would be lost.

"The current through there makes it hard to handle the boat," he lied. "And there's a summer camp at the other end. I don't think you'd want to pass it undressed the way you are."

She looked uncertain.

"Listen, if we smash up on those rocks, that's it." He put some anger in his voice. "Especially at this speed. You've got about ten seconds to decide."

She pulled out a knife from behind the map. She must have picked it up when she went downstairs. She put the blade right behind his left ear.

"Okay," she said. "We'll go your way. No tricks or you lose your ear."

She eased the rope on his right hand enough so he could touch the throttle and the wheel.

He lightened up on the gas and the boat slowed as he entered the channel. It became quieter on board. They rode in silence. Krupp slowly increased the gas while he ever so gradually tilted the motors up. Easy, easy, he had to make sure she didn't see it.

They were halfway through. Krupp could feel his heart pounding as they rounded a tall granite rock face. In a few seconds he'd be able to see the end of the channel and be seen by the people at the resort that was there. He hoped there wouldn't be any sailboats, kayaks, or canoes coming around the corner.

He had to distract her.

"Show me the map again." He tried to make it sound like a command.

She gave it to him and pulled her knife back away from his ear. He held the map tight in his left hand and held it up. Under it, he began to work his right arm loose.

"It'll take about another five minutes to get through," he shouted as loud as he could, hoping to mask the increased noise of the engines, which he was tilting even higher. This way he could speed up the boat and make it less stable.

Five minutes, it'll be about thirty more seconds, he thought. "It's deep through here, so we can speed up." He gave the engines more gas.

Looking over her naked shoulder, Krupp saw the resort's famous big sign come into view. SAND ISLAND: A FAMILY PLACE it said in bold block letters. She'd see it as soon as she turned around. He needed to get closer and keep her attention away from the bow. The faster he went, the more unstable the boat became. He increased the speed again. The boat started to teeter from side to side. She braced herself with her hands to keep her balance.

"Don't think I didn't find you attractive," he said, trying to stop her from turning around for a few more seconds. He tilted the motors up another notch. The boat sped up even more. "You have a great . . . "

She wasn't listening. Her body stiffened. She turned to look.

Now! Krupp slammed the throttle forward all the way. At the same time, he lifted the motors to full tilt to destabilize the boat and pulled hard on the wheel, throwing the boat sharply to the left.

The force of the turn sent her careening across the deck and smashing into the starboard gunwales. The knife flew out of her hand and skittered across the deck.

Krupp dropped the motors, cut the speed, turned the wheel full to the right, and accelerated with maximum force.

The torque of the quick turn threw her back across the boat, headfirst, smashing her into the port gunwales. Blood spurted from her eye and splashed across her body. He rammed the wheel back to the left. She was whipped back onto the starboard gunwales again, like a rag doll rocked from side to side by an angry child.

Go overboard! Go overboard! Krupp prayed.

But she didn't.

He swung the boat back around. The resort was up ahead, its wide dock stretching far out into the water. He aimed right at it, weaving wildly to keep her off-kilter.

She pulled herself off the railing, bloody and angry. She dived at him and grabbed hold of the steering wheel. He jammed the boat to the right, but he couldn't throw her off. She had remarkable balance. He had to crash into the dock. It was drawing closer and closer. He needed to keep control of the boat.

With one hand, she tried to pry his hand off the wheel. He was amazed by how strong she was. She began to pull his fingers free one at a time and tried to turn the wheel and the boat away from the dock.

With her other hand, she reached back into her bag and pulled something out.

Oh no, Krupp thought when he saw what it was. With a last burst of his waning strength, he pulled the wheel back and pointed the boat directly at the wooden pier. It was so near. People were jumping up and beginning to scatter.

He had to hit the dock.

He felt her stab him hard in his chest, but it didn't seem to hurt.

Up ahead, he could see people racing off the dock. Others were diving into the water. Please, God, let me get there, he thought.

But something was happening. His legs felt lax. His arms felt numb. He was losing his sight, his strength. The boat was turning away from the dock.

He had to hold on to the wheel. He was holding the map, but he had to hold on to the wheel, were Krupp's last thoughts as he felt his hands fall away and saw, before his eyes closed for the last time, the boat veer back out into the open water.

KEON

48 HOURS MORE

KEON WAS OUT WALKING again. He needed time to think. He headed south of the Danforth and wandered through his childhood neighbourhood. As he strolled down the sidewalk, a baseball rolled across the street. He bent down to get it, and threw it back to an athletic-looking Asian girl with an oversized baseball glove.

His mind slipped back to hot, muggy nights when there would be soccer games in the park and people would sleep in their unfinished basements—the only cool place in the house. His parents cursed the heat, but Keon loved it. Sleeping downstairs was a big adventure. Often there would be a spontaneous sleepover. A whole bunch of kids from the street would end up in someone's basement, too excited to get any rest.

Those soccer game–sleepover nights were the only times that the Protestants and Catholics on the street played together. They went to different schools and different churches, and were pretty much kept apart.

For Keon—a Catholic kid and the only "Mick" who didn't go to Catholic schools—it was unusual to have other Catholic kids around. His parents had had enormous fights about which school he should go to. Not surprisingly, Mother won and Keon joined the Protestants across the park.

He could still hear his teacher's voice every February. "Now, Charles, you'll be missing class next Wednesday, so I'll give you a special assignment to take home." He could still see the snickers on the faces of the meaner boys as they marked up their foreheads with black markers to mock him.

That was probably why he became good friends with his oddball neighbour, Aubrey Talbot. The two outsiders: Keon, the big Catholic kid, and Talbot, the boy who liked reading books and threw a baseball like a girl. At school, Keon became Talbot's schoolyard protector, while at home Talbot gave Keon books his mother had brought from the library downtown where she worked.

On weekends in the spring they went fishing down in the Don River. One day Keon snagged his line on a piece of driftwood, which was wedged between two rocks. For a few frustrating minutes he tried to liberate his hook—loosen, tighten, pull up hard, nothing worked. In frustration, he waded into the swollen river.

It had been a snowy winter, and the spring runoff was high. He didn't realize how deep the river was, or how quickly the bottom dropped off. Everything happened so fast. His foot slipped on a mossy rock, and in an instant he was in the cold water. The current was hard and fast, and soon he was in over his head and struggling. He barely had time to call out, "Aubrey," when his body gyrated sideways and his head smacked a rock.

The next thing he remembered was being on the shore, Talbot's soaking-wet face looking anxiously over him.

"You okay?" Talbot asked.

"Sure." Keon felt his head. There was a large gash on the back of it. "I was going down, wasn't I?"

Talbot didn't say anything.

"Lucky you're a good swimmer. How did you carry me out all by yourself?"

Talbot blushed. "Maybe I'm not such a weakling after all."

"You saved my life," Keon said as the true measure of what had happened sunk in.

"Let's keep it a secret. That's what real friends do. Besides, if your mother ever found out, that would be it for fishing."

Who would ever have expected, Keon thought, feeling for the spot on the back of his head that had hit the rock so many years ago, that he would end up as chief of police and Aubrey Talbot the warden of Hart House? And in two days the two of them would be there with the G7 leaders for their final luncheon. Out there on the patio while the presidents and prime ministers had their final photo op.

It looked as if the pair of misfits turned out okay, Keon thought as a boy and girl on skateboards, both of them wearing black T-shirts that said KISS: THE FAREWELL TOUR, rumbled down the sidewalk and Keon skipped out of their way. He turned to watch them roll past, smiled, and pulled out his clunky portable phone.

"Miss Rose," he said when she answered, "with this fancy new contraption, can you put me through to Hart House so I can talk to Aubrey to congratulate him?"

GREENE

48 HOURS MORE

GREENE TOOK OFF HIS headphones and motioned for Gabriel to do the same. Trying to make himself heard above the whir of the helicopter, he shouted: "Do any of those boats look familiar?"

"There are a bunch of cigarette boats on the river, and they all look the same," Gabriel yelled back, pulling the binoculars from his eyes. "Wayne's a big man. I'm trying to find someone as large as he is, but from what I can see all these fat cats deserve their names. Each guy seems fatter than the next."

Greene smiled. He was glad Gabriel was able to crack a joke.

"Osgoode's boat has a white top and a big red stripe down the middle. It's difficult to spot from so far away, but look out for that," Gabriel said.

"Will do," Greene said. They both looked down at the river again through their binoculars.

Ten minutes earlier, after seeing Osgoode's boat was gone, they'd run back to Krupp's office at the marina. Greene called Bering from the phone there.

"I'm going to need a helicopter ASAP," he told her.

"One is on the way," Bering said.

Keon had been smart to station Bering as his backup, Greene thought. How lucky had he been to meet her the very first day of police college and have her as his partner ever since. Bering had an extra gear. She was tireless, always thinking ahead, never leaving a stone unturned.

The helicopter arrived minutes after their call, and Greene and Gabriel had been airborne for about ten minutes, flying back and forth across the river from the north to the south shore, hoping to spot the boat.

No luck.

Greene looked down at the mass of boats and islands spread out before them, stretching all the way to the horizon. He pulled the map off the dashboard. It was encased in a plastic holder with a three-inch ruler attached to it by a string.

"Let's assume she got an hour head start on us," he said. "Figure they were going at a high speed, say twenty knots. How far could they have gone by now?"

Gabriel inched closer and looked over Greene's shoulder.

"I used maps like this when I was in the reserves. They started here." He took the map from Greene and put one end of the ruler on the 1001 Islands Yacht Club. "Assume they cut over to the centre of the river." He angled the ruler across the map and marked a spot in the river with his right pointer finger. "That would have taken fifteen minutes. Say they turned due west"—he rotated the ruler around his finger—"and went for another forty-five minutes." He moved the ruler down the map three times. "Right now, they'd be about right here. Mallorytown Beach."

"Ever been there?" Greene asked.

"Yep. It's a beach not many people know about. Great sand, but locals avoid it because there's a strong, dangerous current."

Greene took the map and shifted forward to speak to the pilot. "If we stopped crisscrossing the river and flew straight there, how long would it take to get there?" he yelled.

The pilot glanced at the map. "About ten minutes as the crow flies." He spoke in a normal voice that was unexpectedly audible. "Look out back.

A storm is coming in fast. It could knock us out of the air at any time. Got to keep my eye on those easterlies."

Greene turned and saw a wall of black clouds rumbling in. He looked down at the river. It was tempting to fly straight to this Mallorytown Beach. If she was that far ahead, it was their best chance to catch her. But if they overshot her now, there would be no way to double back and find her.

It was too risky.

Greene put the map down and picked up his binoculars again. "Keep crossing the river," he told the pilot.

For the next few minutes, it took all of Greene's self-control to remain quiet while they flew from shore to shore. He let the binoculars drop around his neck and checked his watch. His right fingers began to rub unconsciously at the scar on his left arm.

He was going to give it five more minutes, he swore to himself. Then they'd fly straight to— He never finished the thought. A voice crackled through on his headphones.

"Officer Greene." The voice sounded strained.

"Greene here."

"We just got an urgent call. A boat almost smashed into a dock at a resort upriver from your position. It went through a crowd of swimmers at a high rate of speed, then took off heading west. Numerous injuries. Ten-four?"

Greene met Gabriel's eyes. They registered the shock he felt.

"Where?" Greene yelled into his headphones. "Where? Where's the resort?" he shouted. What was wrong with the radio?

Gabriel looked at him and mouthed the words "Ten-four."

"Ten-four. Ten-four!" Greene shouted.

"Sand Island Resort." The voice seemed to grow calmer in direct proportion to Greene's impatience.

"That's about four minutes from here," another, even calmer voice said. It was the pilot.

"Go, go. Straight there," Greene ordered the pilot, trying hard to moderate his tone. "As fast as this thing can fly."

Greene turned his attention back to the voice on the radio. "Do you have any description of the boat? Ten-four?"

"Info is pouring in," the voice said, speaking slowly. He's reading while he's talking, Greene thought as he waited to hear more. "It was one of those cigarette boats. White top with a red stripe. Two people were seen on board. Descriptions: driver, white male, mid-twenties. Passenger, female . . . Wait a second."

Greene's heart was pounding. The helicopter did a steep turn and sped straight upriver.

"What?" Greene jumped in. "Ten-four!" he yelled.

"A boater west of the resort radioed in. They say they saw a woman swinging an ax at the driver of a cigarette boat. The boat sped away heading northwest, toward the small boat channel. Ten-four."

Greene looked over to Gabriel. Oh no, he thought, the poor man has just lost another friend.

"There's one strange thing," the voice said, "in this report from the boater, ten-four."

"What? Ten-four."

"It says the woman with the ax was naked."

The cockpit grew quiet. The image of this woman, buck naked on the boat, wielding an ax over her latest victim, dazed them into silence.

The voice on the other end of the radio was stunned too. He'd forgotten to ten-four Greene back.

MARINA

48 HOURS MORE

HER RIGHT EYE WAS bleeding, badly. Her left shoulder hurt like hell. Her knees were scraped and stiff. Her left breast was horribly bruised and sore. She was covered in blood. And she was stark naked.

Those were the least of Marina's problems.

The boat had created a disaster at the resort. Boats near the dock were overturned. People were scrambling to fish others out of the water. She heard frantic screams for help.

But it got much worse.

She was standing facing the steering wheel, her back toward the bow. At least the fat boy was dead. But he was slumped over the throttle, and it was shoved to full speed.

She turned to see where the boat was headed. That was the worst part of all—the islands and channels were coming up fast. She had to get off the boat. But which way should she go? She'd spent hours studying maps of the Thousand Islands, but even Alisander had agreed that it would be impossible to memorize every island and every channel between them.

"You can't know everything, Marina. Your best training is to be resourceful enough to get out of any situation."

Jumping down from the foredeck, she cut off the ropes holding Krupp and tried to pull his body off the driver's seat. She was strong, but he was too heavy to move. She looked up. A small rocky island was coming right up. At this speed, they'd smash into it in about a minute.

The throttle. She had to slow the boat down, but Krupp's hand was wrapped around it, and all his weight was on his hand.

She scoured the deck for something to pry him off with. But there was nothing. She remembered something she'd seen down below. The island was getting nearer by the second. There might be just enough time.

She raced below deck and pulled an ax off the wall. She flew back up the stairs. The island was not very far away.

Breathing hard now, she lifted the ax over her head and brought it down on Krupp's arm. Blood splattered everywhere. But the arm still held. She raised the ax and chopped again, this time hitting bone. The arm bent, but it didn't break. She struck a third time.

Bits of skin and blood and hair flew up at her in the wind and stuck to her naked body. But his hand was still on the throttle. She looked up. The rocks were jutting out so close to the boat.

She was in a frenzy now. "Break, break, break," she shrieked as she brought the ax down on his arm again and again. Finally, the bone cracked. She raised the ax back up, gasping for air.

"Break!" she screamed, and slammed the ax down with all her might. The blade sliced through the arm and hit the deck below. Krupp's hand was still frozen around the throttle.

It didn't matter. She dropped the ax, seized the severed hand, and pulled back the throttle. The boat slowed, yards from shore.

She turned to look behind her. The resort was now a small dot on the horizon. She steered the boat to the left and navigated around the island. Anyone from the resort who was watching would think that she'd headed south, to the American side.

Once she was around the island and into the shelter of the channel, she put the engines in neutral. Her situation was desperate. She had to get to the north shore, back to Canada. She had to get rid of the boat.

She had a waterproof sack inside her knapsack. She filled it with clothes, a sealed container with ten thousand dollars in Canadian bills, and her weapons, then tossed the knapsack overboard. She quickly got into the bathing suit.

She put the throttle back in gear and searched the sky for the first sign of the airplanes or helicopters she knew would be coming. There was nothing there yet, except dark clouds she saw gathering behind her. She gunned the engines to full speed. The boat charged forward. It was risky to go this fast with the river being so shallow in places, but she had no choice.

She weaved randomly in and out of a series of islands. She could hear the thud as the bottom of the boat scraped against the rocks and the loud ping when the rotor blades hit them. She pushed on.

Soon the river opened up. She scanned the north shore for a place to land. There were houses along the lakefront with a busy road behind them and farmland across the road. Too many people. She looked behind her, still no boats following her. She checked the sky again. No planes or helicopters were out yet, but the clouds were rolling in fast. She had to get off the water.

She pressed on. Up ahead the green landscape turned a light brown colour. A spit of land was sticking out into the lake. As she drew nearer, she saw the whole area was one gigantic sandbar. She looked for protection, a place to hide on shore. There were only a few trees scattered about, but they'd have to do.

Throwing the boat into neutral, she took the ax and rushed down below. She was going to chop a hole in the boat and hope it would sink fast, before it was seen from the air. She swung the ax. It hit the wall and bounced right back at her. The hull was solid fiberglass. She smashed the same spot three more times. At last, she opened up a small crack and a trickle of water began to come in. She took one more swing, but the hole seemed no larger. It would take forever to bash a hole that was big enough.

She ran back above deck and looked around. There were other boats farther out in the river. She walked back over to the dead body, engaged the motors, and turned the boat so it headed south to the American side. She eased back on the throttle as much as she dared without stalling the engines, then used the ax handle to pry Krupp's body until it slumped over the steering wheel, fixing it in place. She found pieces of rope lying on the deck and tied the wheel into position to ensure that it stayed on course.

She looked back to the receding Canadian shore. With her injured shoulder and the strong current, it would be a hard swim. There was no other option. She found more rope, tied the waterproof bag around her waist, took a deep breath, and plunged into the river.

GREENE

48 HOURS MORE

IT ALL SEEMED UNREAL. The islands, the boats, and the widening blue river stretching out before Greene looked like a child's miniature play set. So beautiful. Hard to believe that at this very moment people were gravely injured, maybe dying or already dead.

The helicopter hurtled forward, pushed by the strong tailwind that had come up behind them. "The resort is up ahead at two o'clock," the pilot said in his flat, hard voice. "I'll come in low to give you a better look."

Greene's stomach climbed to the top of his chest as the pilot cut into a steep descent. A few seconds later, the tiny figures on the ground looked all too real. People were madly scrambling about. Some carried bleeding bodies from the water onto the shore. Higher up the beach, three or four white sheets were laid out.

The pilot touched Greene's arm and pointed out the window. Three medical helicopters were charging toward the island.

Greene grabbed his radio. "This is Greene. This is urgent. Ten-four."

"Yes, Greene, go ahead. Ten-four."

"We're above the resort. It's a mess. Numerous serious injuries and possibly as many as four fatalities. Three medical helicopters approaching.

Are we required to land and assist? Ten-four." He wasn't going to forget to ten-four his transmissions now.

"Negative. More help is on the way. Continue on your mission. Good luck. Ten-four."

Greene took his binoculars and looked down at the carnage below. On the beach, he saw a thin brunette woman kneeling in the sand. She was crying hysterically. Beside her there was a white sheet, much smaller than the others.

"Greene. Ten-four?" the voice rang out in his headset.

He lowered his binoculars, embarrassed that he'd inadvertently trespassed on the poor woman's moment of horror.

"Yes. We are continuing," Greene said. "We will find her. Over and out."

Greene pulled his binoculars back up and scanned the blue water to the west, searching for the woman, the killer, the assassin.

"Look at that boat." It was Gabriel.

"The one at, call it ten thirty. There, headed across the river, moving south. See, it's going in a straight line. Every other boat is zigzagging or moving around one way or the other."

Gabriel was right. There was something different about the way the boat moved. It was subtle, but once you knew what to look for, it stood out.

"What does it mean if it's going perfectly straight?" Greene asked. But as the words left his mouth the answer popped into his brain. "Oh, I see," he said. "You think that the steering wheel is fixed in place."

Gabriel peered through his binoculars again. "That's it. I see the red stripe on the bow."

He was interrupted by a loud crack of thunder. Even though the sky was still blue in the west, a few raindrops began to fall on the massive windshield. Greene looked behind him. The eastern sky had turned even darker and more foreboding. A storm was coming in fast, like a dark blanket draped over a corpse.

Gabriel waited for the thunder to pass. "I fear our lady friend is long gone."

The pilot tried to drop down to get closer to the boat, but the eastern tailwind buffeted the helicopter. It bounced and shook in the turbulence like an out-of-control amusement park ride. The storm clouds were moving in faster than Greene thought possible, and soon the whole sky had turned an ominous grey. A light rain began to fall. The pilot flicked on the windshield wipers and their flapping sound added to the dissonance produced by the motor, the wings, the thunder, and the wind.

"I warned you about those easterlies," the pilot growled, focusing his attention on the dashboard, where the meters were dancing up and down like a conductor's baton. "It's much worse dealing with a tailwind. We're going to have to get downwind and circle back up. It'll take a few minutes."

"How low will you be able to get?" Greene asked.

"We won't know that until we fly back upwind, will we?"

The pilot banked the helicopter and circled back around through the headwind until they were on top of the boat. Greene focused his binoculars on the deck. He could see the back of a man draped over the steering wheel. He wasn't moving.

Greene didn't say a word. He peered over at Gabriel, who was looking down with his binoculars.

"That must be Wayne," Gabriel said finally.

"I'm afraid so."

"He's not moving."

"No, he isn't."

Greene's mind was thinking about the direction of the boat. The woman must have set it on this course and jumped off. That meant she swam to the north shore directly across from here. A few miles away now. Every second we lose counts, he thought. But he waited for Gabriel.

Gabriel let out a great sigh. "He might still be alive."

Greene had been afraid Gabriel would say that. "We can radio in our position and they can send a rescue team out right away," he said.

"No time," Gabriel said. "Wayne might be bleeding to death right now. Every moment matters."

"In this wind, it'll be difficult to lower someone," the pilot said.

"I'll take the risk," Gabriel said. "I've lost one friend today and I'll do everything I can to save another."

There was a tense silence in the cabin.

"Pardon me for asking," the pilot said at last, "but how much do you weigh, Officer Gabriel?"

Gabriel looked at Greene as the obvious import of the question sunk in.

"Maybe two thirty, if I'm lucky."

"And you, Officer Greene?"

Greene looked down at the choppy water. Torrents of rain were lashing the ship's deck. "Maybe one seventy, soaking wet."

No one spoke as the pilot maneuvered lower, getting closer to the boat. A gust of wind caught them, and the whole helicopter bobbed up and down like an abandoned surfboard in heavy waves.

"Listen. Straight up," the pilot said. "You want to try to rescue a dead man, I don't want to go down in the drink with you. With this storm blowing in and Baby Huey down there, every pound, every ounce, will make a difference. I'm sorry, Officer Gabriel. Officer Greene, you go or it's no dice."

Greene didn't need to look up to see Gabriel's eyes were on him. Besides the obvious danger, there was another reason for him not to go. The time they'd lose could be fatal to their pursuit of this killer woman.

He stared at Gabriel. "I've lost one friend today." The words rang in Greene's ears.

He looked back down at the boat.

"Officer Greene," the pilot said, his voice taking on an edge. "I can only hold this position for another few seconds."

Greene knew that if he went down to the boat instead of continuing his pursuit of the woman, he'd be debriefed afterward by the higher-ups.

"So let us get this straight," they'd say. "You chose to try to rescue a man who was most likely dead, instead of pursuing an assassin who had killed four people? And who planned to kill the seven leaders of the free world? That was the decision you made?"

He turned back to Gabriel.

All traces of the milk moustache had worn away.

Greene tapped the pilot on the shoulder and asked, "Where's the harness?"

MARINA

47 HOURS MORE

MARINA KNEW SHE WAS alive because she could feel the sand in her mouth. It tasted gritty and horrible. Other than that, she felt dead. It had been hours since she'd slept. The struggle on the boat had been much worse than anything she'd ever endured in training. She was bashed and bruised all over. After she jumped in the St. Lawrence, the swim against the current had been terrifyingly difficult. Every part of her body ached.

She lay at the edge of the water and closed her eyes. Rest for a second, she told herself. A short rest. The cool, comforting waves washed over her. She felt sleep crawling up her legs, up her body. The bright blue sky was turning dark. She was losing track of time. Was night coming in?

"Fight sleep. Fight it," Alisander had demanded. "Sleep will kill you!"

In training, she'd stayed awake for three, four, once even five days at a time. Sleep. She could hardly remember what it was like to sleep.

Using every bit of willpower, she lifted her head up and looked down the long beach, hoping it would be deserted. At the far end, she saw two girls playing in the water. They looked as if they were about five years old. Both had their black hair tied into matching braids.

Marina sat up and looked around. There was no one else on the beach.

No one seemed to be with the girls. She was transfixed as she watched them run into the water, splashing each other and laughing. Even from this distance, she could see they were identical twins.

Marina's mind began to drift back to a time so long ago. She was a little girl. On a beach. The water was salty, the sun was hot. Playing. Water poured in fun over her head.

"Don't think back. There is nothing to remember," Alisander made her repeat every morning and every night.

But this time she couldn't stop her mind. They were laughing and talking. Speaking the old language.

"Forget that language, only speak English and French," Alisander insisted. "The old language for you is dead. You must never use it. Forget it."

She could hear the old words. The language sounded so distant, yet so near. Everything was red. And hot, burning hot. Voices were screaming. The pain hit her left eye. A man took her in his arms.

"Help, help!"

Marina shook her head and refocused down the beach. One of the girls was screaming. Where was the other one? Where were the parents?

"Don't ever help anyone. People who help are noticed!" Alisander had made her repeat a thousand times.

There was no one else on the beach but Marina.

"Help, please someone help!" The girl's voice rang out at her across the sand.

Don't interfere, don't interfere! Alisander's voice was screaming in her ear.

"My sister!" the girl cried.

Marina sprang to her feet. "Stay still," she shouted at the girl and began to run.

The girl turned to her in terror. "My sister is gone," she cried.

"Don't move," Marina yelled as she approached the scared child. "I'll get her. Stay right here."

Marina dove in. The water was murky and she could hardly see. She thrust her arm down and stretched out her fingers. Nothing. She kept searching. Where was the girl?

Marina was out of breath but kept flailing her arms in the dark water. Exhausted. Still nothing. She had to come up to breathe.

Bursting through the water, she gulped in the fresh air. She looked back at the beach. The other girl was still there, in the same spot. She was crying: "My sister, I want Bethy." There were still no adults anywhere.

"Stay still," Marina yelled. She took three more deep breaths, swallowing as much air as she could, and dove back down. There must be some sort of undertow, she thought as she swam farther out. She could hardly see. She reached down as deep as she could. She felt something. It was a toe, a foot. She yanked it up.

The child was surprisingly heavy. Marina pulled with all her might and got a hold of her body. But she couldn't get her up to the surface.

What was happening? It was the undertow. It had taken the child. Now Marina was caught in it. They were being pulled down, like a horse in a harness forced to kneel.

She struggled to pull her own head up above the water. But with the child weighing her down she couldn't get to the air. She needed to breathe. She had to let the child go or they'd both drown.

There was one other thing she could try. It was a gamble, but the only hope. Stop fighting the undertow and drift. Eventually it would deliver them to calmer waters. But would it be too late?

Did it matter? She was so tired. She so needed sleep. She stopped fighting. She let herself float underwater. She managed to roll over onto her back and pull the child up onto her stomach. Cradle her the way she used to cradle her handsewn doll when she was a girl, before it was burned in the fire.

Now she could drift. Drift. Drift away.

But then. Magically. She felt her body rush faster and faster in the water like a leaf in a culvert during spring runoff.

Air. Air. Her lungs were screaming for air.

Sleep. Her mind was crying to sleep. The water felt so smooth.

Air, air. Sleep, sleep.

She felt her body begin to slow down. She went limp. Something scratched her left foot. Instinctively, she pulled her leg up to avoid the pain. Yet a voice from the deep recess of her mind was calling out. What was it saying?

Touch it.

Hold on to it.

Grab it.

She pushed her foot back down and it touched the hard thing. It was a rock. A huge granite rock. She slammed both feet onto it. Her mind was coming back, waking up. Fighting again.

Air, air, she wanted air. She needed air.

She bent her knees, marshalled her last bit of strength, and gave one final push.

She hit the surface with such force she felt as if she'd stuck her head out of a window of a speeding train. Her lungs were screaming for oxygen. She breathed in so hard her mouth hurt. She looked down at her arms. The slight girl lay there motionless. Marina pulled her face up and began to breathe into her tiny mouth. Not too hard or you'll burst her lungs, she thought, trying to remember where she'd learned that. Be patient, keep breathing, steady.

She heard a voice behind her on shore.

"Oh no, that's Bethy!"

It was a woman. Must be her mother, Marina thought, but there was no time to turn and look. Keep breathing. Come on, Bethy. Come on.

Marina felt it. A shudder in the girl's body. Followed by a much bigger one. Bethy's arms started to flap, and her stomach heaved. Marina kept breathing little breaths into the girl's little lungs, waiting until the last moment. When she felt the convulsions, she turned Bethy's head away from her and pulled her hair by the braids.

The child threw up a horrid combination of water and vomit. Her lungs kicked in. She was breathing. Short but satisfying gulps of air were raising and lowering her small chest. But her eyes were still closed. Then they fluttered. And opened.

Her eyes were a brilliant blue against her warm skin. She looked up at Marina, threw her small arms around Marina's neck, and hugged her with all her might.

GREENE

47 HOURS MORE

GREENE WAS TIED INTO the harness and ready to go.

"Take a close look," the pilot said, his tone more concerned now. "That boat is starting to list. I'll bet it's taking on water."

Greene looked down. He was right. The boat was swaying dangerously to one side.

"And Officer Greene," the pilot said, "you see that tanker, upriver?"

"What about it?"

"The current is strong and it's moving faster than you realize. A minute or two after the tanker passes, it's going to send out some gigantic waves, so be careful. That boat down there doesn't have much time left. Whatever happens, don't untie yourself. If things get wonky, we're taking off. If you aren't tied up, you're on your own. We'll give you three tugs as a signal. Tug back three times and I'm hoovering you out of there."

"Sounds like a plan." Greene tightened the rope around his chest. He met Gabriel's eyes.

"Thanks, Ari," Gabriel said.

Greene smiled back and slid out into the void.

Once cleared of the helicopter, he dangled like a puppet with a broken string. The draft from the rotors pushed him down while the east wind nudged him sideways.

As he got closer, Greene saw the boat was rolling toward him. If he missed landing on the deck, he could be smashed to death in an instant on the side of the boat.

The winch lowered him nearer and nearer. The chop of the sea was growing higher and wilder. He could see the man's back. He wasn't moving. The rest of the boat looked empty.

The deck was right below him, rolling to and fro like a teeter-totter.

He pulled himself up on the rope, climbing higher to collect some slack on the drop line. He had to wait for the right moment. He had a few seconds before the boat would slip away.

Now!

He loosened the rope, felt it slide through his hands as he tried to swing himself onto the boat. But at that moment, a big wave hit the boat and it lurched away from him. In an instant he was plunging straight toward broiling water below. He tried to struggle back toward the boat, but he was helpless to direct his fall.

As he was about to hit the water, a wave from the other direction smashed into the boat and swung it back at him. Now he was lower than the ship's deck and right in line to get hit dead-on. If he didn't climb higher, it would crash into him. The pilot must have seen the danger Greene was in, because he felt the rope begin to pull him upward.

He had to get above the deck and throw a leg over it to gain purchase on board. The boat was moving fast. The helicopter wouldn't be able to lift him soon enough.

Desperate now, Greene climbed up, pulling as hard as he could on the slippery wet line. The rain was pelting down on him. The boat was so big it made him feel small, like when he was a skinny kid climbing rope in his huge grade school gym. Fatigue gripped his body. Was it worth it? If he stopped now, the boat would hit him and . . .

With one last heave, he pulled himself up as high as he could and flung his legs up wildly into the air, praying they would land over the railing.

MARINA

47 HOURS MORE

"MY BABY, MY BABY!"

A big woman with long, unkempt hair plunged into the water, charging toward Marina like a mother bear after her cub.

"I just went to the washroom for a minute! Damn stomach! My baby, my baby, my baby," she said as she tore through the water, her arms outstretched for her child.

"She's breathing, she's going to be all right," Marina yelled into the wind.

"Mummy, Mummy, Mummy," the girl cried as her mother splashed through the water to them.

"Thank you," the woman shrieked a moment later as she enveloped both of them in her thick arms.

"Thank you, thank you," she said to Marina.

"Mummy," Bethy sobbed. "It was so dark."

"It's okay, darling," her mother cooed. "You're safe now."

"I was so scared."

"I know, baby, but you're okay. It will never be dark again. I promise."

The child loosened her grip on Marina's shoulders and slid into her mother's arms. Standing on her own, Marina became unsteady. The sleep deprivation, the injuries, the lack of oxygen. The wind picked up and she felt as if it would blow her over. Her knees started to buckle. She couldn't keep her eyes open. She was falling.

"Wow, I got you, honey," she heard the woman say, though her voice sounded distant. "Hold on to Mama Bear. Let's get you both out of this killer water."

Marina felt light raindrops on her shoulders. She opened her eyes. She had lost track of time. How long had her eyes been shut? Where was she? She reached out below her and felt sand—she was on a beach. She bolted upright. She had to run. Where was her knapsack?

"Slow down, buttercup, there's nothing to worry about," the woman beside her said, stroking her hair. "Mama Bear pulled you out of the water just like you saved my Bethy. I wish I could say we were even, but, darling, I owe you my life and more."

Marina looked around. There was no one else on the beach except for Mama Bear and the girls. The two sisters were sitting together. Marina had been right, they were identical twins. So similar she couldn't tell which one was Bethy.

She smiled at them, turned to Mama Bear. "How long have I . . . ?"

"Only a few minutes, sweetie. Don't worry, there's nobody here but us chickens."

"And your daughter?"

"Amazing. Like it never happened." She shook her head. "I made them promise me they wouldn't go into the water. I had to run to that stinking washroom back near the parking lot. Thank my lucky stars you showed up."

"I . . . I have to get going."

"Get going? You saved my daughter's life. You don't look in the best shape yourself. Someone put a pretty bad licking on you, and it wasn't my Bethy." Mama Bear rubbed her hands over Marina's badly bruised thigh.

Marina pulled her leg back. "It's a long story," she said, looking down the beach. She peeked up at the sky. Bulbous black clouds were moving in, covering the blue, but she didn't see any planes or helicopters. They'd be there any minute. She had to get to the trees for cover.

"I must go. The storm is moving in fast."

"Well, my little beauty queen, I don't know where you're going, but you'll need this." Mama Bear pulled out Marina's knapsack and placed it in her hands.

"Where did you find it?"

"While you were out, I checked the beach for you. It was the least I could do. You don't have to say anything if you don't want to, but I took a pretty good look at those bruises, and there's only one explanation for them."

"What?" Marina tensed and made a fist with her powerful right hand behind her back.

"I know what happened," Mama Bear said.

Marina got ready to spring into action. Had this Mama Bear woman heard about the boat almost crashing into the resort? The dead man on the boat? Even though she was much bigger than Marina, Marina would have the advantage of surprise. With one punch, she could knock her out.

"Men. They'll hit anyone. But how some man could touch someone as beautiful as you I'll never understand. To think some dumb fool would abuse you. It makes me want to vomit."

Marina unclenched her hand. She was wounded, exposed, and without transportation. Mama Bear was her last hope.

She hung her head. "He's so strong, and he won't let go. I try to get away and look," she said, her sad voice a faint whisper as she motioned toward the gash in her right leg with her hand and shook her head. Tears began to stream down her cheeks.

Then she heard the sound. It was a long way off, but it was there. *Thump. Thump.* The steady drone of helicopter wings. In a few seconds, Mama Bear would hear them too.

"He knows everyone," Marina said. "He's so powerful. How can I ever get away? See what happens when I try? He'll have the whole police force out looking for me. I know it."

Mama Bear turned. She'd heard the helicopters. Marina looked up and pretended she'd just heard them too. Her faced lined with fear. "I have to hide somewhere, please help me." She clutched Mama Bear's massive forearm.

"Help? Hell, I'm going to get you out of here. Come on, Bethy, Barbie, let's go. Pronto."

They ran up the beach to the parking lot in the trees. "Welcome to our summer home," Mama Bear said, opening the side panel of her red Dodge van.

The inside looked like a house on wheels. The main piece of furniture was a built-in wood-frame bed in the back covered with a thick mattress. Towels and clothes and books were all neatly stacked in built-in shelves. It was spotless.

"I built this so we can take off and sleep wherever we want. The girls love it."

The twins crawled inside and scrambled up on the bed to play as the sky opened up. A pounding rat-a-tat sound echoed through the van. It was hail, coming down in golf ball–sized chunks as the sound of the helicopters grew louder.

Marina stepped inside the van. She was shaking.

"Now, don't worry, sweet pea, Mama Bear's got a foolproof place for you to hide." She shooed the twins off the bed. She pushed the mattress against the wall of the van. The wood frame underneath it was on a hinge.

"This is my secret hideaway." Mama Bear proudly pulled the top up, exposing a storage unit filled with clothes and toys. "Now, sister, you slip your skinny body into here. I'll put this mattress back on top and the girls will play on it and no one will find you in a million years."

WHITECASTLE

47 HOURS MORE

"THIS IS THE BBC News on the hour," said the haughty woman's voice, with her plumy Oxbridge accent. Whitecastle paused at his potting table to listen and savor the moment.

This was the place where he felt most at home: alone in his greenhouse, pressing newly pruned geraniums into clay pots, listening to his favourite newscast on the radio. It was the summer news doldrums, so there wasn't much to report. The newsreader led with an item about farmers in the Midlands complaining there hadn't been enough rain. The next item was about the revival of tourism in Britain, and then there was the inevitable report from Northern Ireland about plans for a Protestant parade and an IRA bomb threat.

At last there came the report he'd been waiting for.

"And finally in the news, we have photos of the prime minister, who is attending the G7 summit in Toronto, Canada, in discussion with Russian president Mikhail Gorbachev, who has been granted special observer status. For more on this development, we turn to Edward Constant, professor of international studies at Norwich."

Whitecastle clicked off the radio, smiled, and imagined the scene two days from now. In the 1970s, he'd visited the Cambridge-style, fine-stone building at the University of Toronto, so he could picture the Hart House quadrangle. At precisely 1:00 p.m. local time, the world leaders would stroll out onto the stone patio. One o'clock in Toronto was six o'clock in London, perfect for the supper-hour news shows.

Whitecastle didn't know what would happen next. Alisander had made certain of that. "Professor, trust me," he had said three years earlier when they agreed that the assassinations were necessary. Especially that of the Russian leader. "I'll tell you where and when it will happen so you can be prepared. But you must never know any of the details. That would be too dangerous for you."

Whitecastle marveled that their years of planning were about to come to fruition. It had all started twenty years earlier when, despite Whitecastle's impassioned pleas, Alisander insisted he must bring his family home.

The consequences were even more catastrophic than Whitecastle had feared. The country was convulsed in a horrific civil war, and to make matters worse, the Russians secretly sided with Alisander's enemies.

For months Whitecastle, an unknown history professor at the time, tried to get news of his prized student. Late one night an old Cambridge classmate who was at the Home Office called.

"Angus, there is no time for pleasantries. Get dressed and be downstairs in two minutes."

"Certainly. But what does this concern?"

"Let's say one of your prized students has finished his field studies."

Whitecastle got dressed and rushed out to find a waiting black car, which whisked him to a military airport north of London. He was escorted to a small room with a smattering of steel chairs and a desk bolted to the floor. Sitting in the corner, his head buried in his arms, was Alisander. Whitecastle approached and touched his arm gently.

"Alisander, it's me, Professor Whitecastle . . . "

Alisander looked up. His face was gaunt and sallow, his hands trembled, and his usually fierce blue eyes looked bruised and vacant.

Whitecastle was shocked.

"Sherani was pregnant with our second child," Alisander said. "The Russians tied her to a chair and cut her hands off. They waited until she bled to death. And my daughter . . . "

Whitecastle kneeled down and put his arm around his former student. He was so thin Whitecastle thought he might bruise him by touching him.

"Promise me, Professor."

"Anything."

"The Russians. You'll help me stop the Russians."

Alisander threw himself into devising his revenge. When the puppet government the Russians had tried to install in Afghanistan was overthrown, he was ready. He returned home with his plan in place.

Back in London, Whitecastle shocked his colleagues by resigning from the university and entering politics. Much to the surprise of the pundits, he was a remarkable success. There was something about him—his courtly manners, his old-fashioned dress, his precise diction—that struck a chord with the British public.

With each succeeding cabinet post, he gained more influence and independence. And ways to funnel funds to his former protégé. Alisander set up his compound, which, unseen, became an elite training ground for terror and assassination.

When the Soviets began to "open up," Whitecastle and Alisander were not fooled. They could see the Russian Bear was playing nice so the West would become soft. Margaret Thatcher said she "liked Mr. Gorbachev," and that they could "do business together."

Whitecastle and Alisander knew better.

The phone rang in the greenhouse, pulling him out of his reverie. "Whitecastle here," he said.

"Bonjour, Monsieur Prime Minister."

Whitecastle gripped the phone.

It was Francis Verault, the former Canadian prime minister. The two men had met many times at various G7 summits while they were both leaders and had remained fast friends. Verault, who resigned at the peak of his power, still had a string of contacts at all levels of government. He missed "the game" more than he let on, and these days revelled in having the inside scoop and gossip.

They'd both had to adjust to being out of politics with all its perks. But one thing they agreed upon: they were glad they weren't in America, where ex-presidents were dogged by twenty-four-hour security. In Canada and England, once out of power, thankfully, you were left alone.

"Bonjour, Monsieur Prime Minister," Whitecastle replied in his terrible French accent. "I'm most pleased you telephoned."

Whitecastle struggled to keep his voice even. A few weeks earlier, he'd called Verault on the pretext that he and his wife were thinking about doing a trip to the Canadian North—a part of the country that Verault loved. During their casual conversation, Whitecastle had mentioned the upcoming G7 summit in Toronto and said, "Do let me know if you hear anything interesting. For old times' sake."

Today their phone call was brief but to the point. According to Verault's source, the Toronto police had received an anonymous tip about a potential assassin, and had sent a local police officer to the US border, where he'd found an American border guard dead on the Canadian side.

"All hush-hush," Verault said, "but there's lots of panic going on behind the smiles and waving to the press."

"This is terrible news." Whitecastle had tried to sound shocked and concerned, but his mind was reeling.

"Apparently the Americans originally thought this tip was nonsense. Now no one is quite sure what to make of it," Verault said.

"Well, you know the Yanks. I'm certain they'll pull out all the stops to get him," Whitecastle said, thinking, How had this happened? Had there been a leak?

"I'm afraid, my friend, it is not a him," Verault said, clearly relishing the top secret gossip he was about to pass along, "but a her."

"Her?"

"Apparently it is a woman."

Whitecastle nodded to himself. He'd wondered about that. Yesterday when he'd received the "Montreal" call, the caller's voice had sounded odd. Said only the one word, but he had wondered if it was a man or a woman.

"And," Verault added, "apparently they've lost track of her, but are trying desperately to find her in time."

Whitecastle begged off the phone call. Working frantically now, he wrote a note on a small piece of white paper, finished potting his plants, and rushed out to the wall.

Once there he arranged the pots with the top of the triangle of the middle pot pointed back toward his backyard, the signal that he had urgent news. He looked up the road. No one was there. Good. Alisander had made it clear that Whitecastle was never to see the motorcyclist. The less he knew the better.

From somewhere nearby a voice shattered the stillness of the garden.

"That's a nice design, dear."

Whitecastle practically jumped out of his skin. Grasping his hands together, he turned. "Darling, you gave me a shock," he said to his wife. "I thought you were in the sunroom with your book."

"I'm halfway through a silly Agatha Christie novel. I thought I'd spy on you a bit."

"You surprised me. Shall we go in for dinner?"

"Yes, but dear, you put one of those pots backwards. Here, let me line it up with the other two." She moved deftly toward the wall.

"No, no, darling." Whitecastle tried to block her. He could hear the motorcycle getting closer. Alisander had warned him that if the driver saw anyone he would drive past. "You see, darling, I place this one in reverse to get more sun on its backside."

"Don't be ridiculous. It looks all wrong." She was at the wall now, and beginning to move the pot.

Whitecastle looked up the road. The sound of the motorcycle was just around the bend.

He had to stop his wife. "Debs," he yelled. "Be careful, don't touch the pots."

She turned to him in shock. "Really, Angus. What is the problem?"

"The spray. There is root rot and I've had to spray them. The whole pot. The stuff is a real mess if you so much as touch it."

She shook her head at him. Some people might not believe this odd man in his odd white hat had been the prime minister of England. She still loved him dearly, even after all they'd been through: the long election campaigns, the winning, the losing, the boring meetings, the endless receptions and piles of thank-you notes to write. Now all he had to do with his time was putter around with his plants. He looked so helpless. Men, they aren't made for retirement, she thought.

Back on the night of his election defeat, she'd created a stir in the press with one simple quip to a reporter. "Oh, I don't really mind that he lost," she said with her usual candor, "so long as he doesn't expect me to make him lunch every day."

Deborah pulled her hands away from the pots and gave him a warm smile. "You and your geraniums." She pressed his ancient floppy hat down onto his head.

Whitecastle, playing along, flailed his arms out in her direction. He lifted her with ease. All those years of working outdoors had kept him strong.

"My lady, your gardener is at your service," he said, walking her down the path, putting distance between them and the wall.

"My. The lady of the manor cavorting with the gardener. What would the people in the village say?" she said with a laugh.

Whitecastle nuzzled her neck as he stepped up the pace. "They would say if she doesn't allow him in the dining room at lunchtime, what's she doing with him up in her bedroom after dinner?"

"Oh, let them gossip," she said.

Whitecastle grunted animal sounds in her ear as he raced her back inside, carrying her over the threshold with the enthusiasm of a new groom.

Thank goodness he could still fulfill his marital vows, he thought, safe in the knowledge that his wife wouldn't hear the motorcycle down the lane.

GREENE

47 HOURS MORE

IT WAS HARD FOR Greene to tell what hurt more. His knee, which he'd hooked onto the railing, his right shoulder, which had slammed into the wall of the cabin when he stumbled blindly onto the boat, or his head, which had smashed onto the hard wooden deck.

He lay on his back for a few moments, too tired and stunned to move. The rain was coming down in cold sheets. He stood up and, steadying himself with the rescue rope tied to his waist, walked gingerly across the deck like an oversized marionette.

The man was in the driver's seat. Motionless. By the time Greene got to him, he knew Krupp was dead. In his five years on the force, he'd seen enough dead bodies: winos, old folks in nursing homes, car accident victims, even a few murders. You got to the point where you could feel death.

Still, Greene had to confirm Krupp had no vital signs. He put his hand on the man's massive shoulder, no response. He touched the skin of his left hand. It was cold. He felt for a pulse among the folds of skin. Nothing. He put his cheek to the man's mouth. No breath.

He stood back and took in the killer's handiwork. She had the steering wheel held firmly in place by two ropes, one tied to the central mast, the other to the starboard side railing. Krupp had been tied to the steering wheel for insurance.

How had she kept the boat at a steady speed? He spotted the severed right arm tied to the throttle. It must have been broken in an incredibly violent way. Blood was everywhere. The poor man was right here bleeding to death, Greene thought, while we were searching downriver.

Something hit his head. He heard a loud pinging noise all around him. It was hail. Rock-hard pieces were pelting the deck. He covered his eyes. Suddenly a gigantic wave broadsided the boat. Greene soared across the deck and smashed into the port gunwale. He picked himself up and waited for the boat to right itself.

The blood, Greene thought. Krupp had put up a real fight. Some of the blood might be hers. As his side of the boat began to rise, he scampered across the deck. But the boat moved faster than he'd anticipated and he was hurled on top of the dead man.

The boat was at such a sharp angle that Greene could hardly pull himself off the body. He felt three tugs on the harness rope, the pilot's signal for him to come up. All he had to do was pull on the rope three times and he'd be off this ship of death.

But he wanted her blood. He looked at the reddened shirt on the mangled arm. All he needed, Greene thought, was a simple Swiss Army knife. But he didn't have a knife, or anything sharp he could use.

Fighting the steep angle of the ship, he maneuvered around Krupp's motionless body and got his hand on the bloody sleeve. Just rip it off, Greene thought. He tried to pull it apart. It was impossible.

The waves of hail were pelting the deck like a rapid-fire machine gun. Another huge wave rocked the boat, and it began to list back in the other direction. In a few seconds he'd be flung across the deck again.

What else could he take? He scanned the dead man's body. Then he saw it. An old map of the Thousand Islands in the man's far hand. The map was splattered with blood. But could he reach it?

The boat was almost back to level. Greene braced his legs to try to keep his balance. His shoe caught on a loose nail in one of the floorboards, ripping a hole in the sole.

He heard a mighty crack. The boat began to swing madly away from him. It was at such an extreme angle that to keep his precarious perch he had to hold on to the man's body and launch himself down toward the map.

He needed to get it. He touched it. He tugged at it. But it was stuck between Krupp's fingers.

A new, more horrible smell filled his nostrils—the stench of the dead man's skin. And blood.

There was an even louder crack from the other side of the boat. Greene looked up and saw it had reached critical mass. If it flipped over, taking him down, the helicopter would have to cut him loose. He'd be sucked down with the boat, too deep to survive.

He gave the map one last tug. It came free in his hand. He stood back up. He pulled the rope one time.

The pilot and Gabriel must have seen the danger he was in, because before Greene could do a second pull, the rope tightened around his waist. In an instant the boat was falling away underneath him as he was scooped up off the deck.

Looking down, he couldn't take his eyes off the dead man, about to enter his watery grave. The sweet, clean air brushed across Greene's face. The helicopter whisked him upward as he slid the bloody map inside his breast pocket.

He took one last look down. The dead man on the dead boat was being swallowed up by the water.

The rope around Greene squeezed his chest even tighter like an anxious lover's embrace. He lolled his head back and gazed up to the living sky.

COBALT

47 HOURS MORE

OPP CONSTABLE SCOTT COBALT loved to do the math. It was six weeks until his retirement date. Thirty-five hours a week times six weeks equals 210 hours left on the job. Now 210 times 60 makes 12,600 minutes. Times 60, that's 756,000 seconds.

That meant 756,000 seconds until he was at their remote cottage full-time with Denise, his wife of forty-six years. He'd take his granddaughter, Rachel, rock bass fishing and teach her how to tread water. No phones up there, just wilderness and peace. And he'd never again have to worry about getting some vague assignment like this one, a roadblock right on Highway 2 and orders to search every vehicle for a young woman who appeared to be "out of place, in distress."

Not that he was complaining, mind you. Today was like hitting the bingo in five calls. Not just overtime, but holiday overtime plus emergency and short-notice overtime. Every hour counted as four. This eight-hour shift he was doing would lop off thirty-two hours. That's 1,920 minutes, that's 115,200 seconds gone.

Cobalt straightened up and closed the trunk of a white Mercedes four-door sedan he'd just searched. The passengers were two immaculately dressed Asian couples. Hong Kong money, he assumed. Boy, were they smug, sitting contentedly in air-conditioned comfort while he was out in the pouring rain.

He pulled out his notebook and, as he'd done for more than thirty-four years, meticulously recorded every relevant detail he'd observed. Early in his career, a senior cop had lectured him on the importance of good note-taking: "Decide right from the start if you're going to be a professional or not. Ninety-five percent of the things you investigate will never go to trial. Most of your best work no one will ever see. But the other five percent will go to court months or years later. When you are on the witness stand at the trial, your notes will be all you have. If they're not good, some defence lawyer will carve you a new asshole right up there on the stand. Either take pride in your work or get another job."

He waved the Mercedes on and looked up at the line of roadblocked cars, trucks, and vans that stretched as far as the eye could see down the highway. The hot sun had been blackened by this easterlies storm, and the whole scene looked helpless. Who in their right mind would cut off the Highway 2 on the July 4 weekend? Some dingbat from Toronto. He was sure they had never even considered how close Mallorytown was to the border, or that more than half the cars on this highway were American tourists.

A beat-up-looking red Dodge van pulled up next. The driver was an overweight woman with pasty skin and long, stringy hair. She wore a scowl that could intimidate a lion. Her windows were open—presumably she didn't have air-conditioning. Cobalt knew this one was going to be trouble even before he leaned in the open passenger-side window. In the back of the van he saw two cute twin girls jumping up and down on a homemade bed.

These folks sure didn't fit the description of the suspect he was supposed to be searching for, Cobalt thought, remembering the call he received a few hours earlier from his friend Sergeant Austin Klatt. "Look for a young woman, beautiful, and she may be injured." There had been a pause over the phone line while Cobalt waited for the usual description: height, weight, hair colour, distinctive features, clothing, etc. None came.

"And the rest of the description?" Cobalt asked finally.

"That's it," Klatt said.

"You've got to be kidding."

"Wish I was, Scotty," the sergeant said, his voice flat as a pancake. "But you're the tenth officer I've had to reel in for this and I've got a dozen more to go."

"What's this all about?" Cobalt said.

"Damned if I know. Rumor is some big-shot Toronto cop is pulling strings all over the province. These have to be the goofiest orders I've ever given and you can quote me on that," Klatt said with a friendly chuckle, "after you retire."

"I'm down to my last two hundred ten hours and counting," Cobalt bantered back. Good old Austin, he's a real straight shooter. Friends like him were the part of the job he was going to miss.

"Take your time. Note down every license plate, make of car, number of occupants. Take a look around and find out where they're coming from. Keep an eye out for maps, brochures, food wrappers, you know the drill. That way we'll have something to show the folks from Hogtown for our overtime charges. And give my love to Denise and that granddaughter of yours. She's lucky to have the two of you to raise her."

The van would be his twentieth car this hour. Cobalt looked behind him and saw an officer walking up the hill, coming to give him a coffee break. He could have left the van to the cop, but the mantra he'd followed for thirty-four years still held, retirement coming up or not. Be a professional.

"Hello, ma'am," Cobalt said to the driver. "Sorry for the inconvenience—"

"Don't you 'hello, ma'am' me, pops. What the hell's going on here?" she retorted before he could finish his sentence.

"Well, ma'am—"

"Quit with the ma'am stuff. Can't you see I've got two starving kids back here and no rich man's air-conditioning like you've got in your cruiser."

"Mummy, Mummy, we're so hot. Mummy, Mummy, we need something to drink," the kids shouted out.

They were bouncing around like rubber balls at the arcade. Typical single mother, Cobalt thought. Mooching off welfare and working under the table. Like Cobalt's drug-addicted daughter. He and his wife had spent four years and remortgaged their house to pay the lawyers to finally get their granddaughter away from her.

"I'm sorry, ma . . . I'm sorry, but we'll have to search your van. We're doing it to every car on this highway."

"What are you looking for? The girls' missing Hot Looks dolls?"

"No ma . . . no. We are looking for someone," Cobalt said as he opened the side panel door. Christ, what a mess. Sleeping bags, towels, clothes, books, you name it, were strewn all over the place.

"Maybe you want to play with their newest toys?" she asked. "Real cute dolls called Smoothies. Fun to squeeze."

"No, thank you," Cobalt said as he looked around the squalid scene. "Where are you coming from?"

"From our mission to the Arctic Circle. What do you think?" she replied, not letting up on the sarcasm for an instant.

Cobalt couldn't blame her for being hot under the collar, he thought, as he gasped for air in the stifling van.

With his right hand, so the mother couldn't see what he was doing, he felt for one of the towels. It was damp. He peeked under it and saw two child's bathing suits scrunched up there. He touched them. They were wet.

The twins kept bouncing on the bed. He peered in to see if he could look under it. There was a side panel that closed by a nifty latch.

"I'll have to check in here, ma'am—" Cobalt said.

"Watch that ma'am stuff, pops. Be my guest if you want to poke your nose in our storage. And let me know if you find those dolls."

Cobalt undid the latch and opened the panel. A handy piece of carpentry, he thought as he peered in. There was enough room to reach in with both arms. It would be almost impossible for anyone to climb in here.

He could see what their mother meant about the lost dolls. Piled in under the bed there were pots and pans and packs and sleeping bags and foam bedrolls. There wasn't an inch to spare.

"Looks like you've been camping," Cobalt said, pulling his head back out. Keep them talking—you never know where a conversation will lead. Another trick he'd learned over time. The young cops watched too much TV. They thought everything happened in a minute.

"We camp every night."

"Where did you camp last night?" It was Basic Interrogation 101. Go from the general to the specific, then try to pin them down to details.

"Last night?" she said with a laugh. "We didn't camp anywhere last night. We stayed with my sister in Montreal."

"Been anywhere else today?"

"Just this traffic-jammed highway. We planned to be home in Toronto for a swim before the city pool closes. But thanks to this stupid traffic jam you cops created, we'll probably miss that. And you wonder why my kids are going rangy."

Cobalt shook his head. They hadn't been in Montreal, they'd been at the beach. This was what he'd been taught at police college so many years ago: about 15 percent of the population hate the police and will lie to them for no reason at all.

He pulled his head out from the van. The cop who was taking over was now standing, waiting, a few feet away. Cobalt was hot and wet. He thought about letting the new guy finish off the search, but that wasn't his style.

Do every job as if the whole world is watching. That's how he'd always lived, and that's what he was teaching Rachel.

He unclipped the expandable baton from his belt. With a practiced, swift flick of the wrist, he opened it to its full length. He was going to poke around under the bed to make sure no one was hiding in there. He wiped the sweat off his brow with his arm.

"What are you doing now?" the mother yelled at him. She'd come out of the van and was marching toward him.

"This will only take a minute or two," he said as he started poking his long pole under the bed.

Then he smiled.

Hey, another minute, that will knock off another sixty seconds. Two minutes would be 120!

GREENE

46.5 HOURS MORE

GREENE COULDN'T LOOK DOWN. An hour ago he'd been amazed at seeing the wondrous Thousand Islands from the air stretching out before him like a constellation of stars on a clear night. Now he hoped he never saw the St. Lawrence River again.

As soon as he'd been pulled into the helicopter, Gabriel had wrapped a blanket around him, but it wasn't helping much. Greene was shivering badly. He didn't know if it was because he was so wet or if he was shaken from everything that happened in the last ten minutes or both.

The bad weather was fully upon them, and the helicopter was bobbing about like an abandoned life raft in a storm. Even the cool-and-calm pilot was no longer dispassionate.

"Look," he said the moment Greene was inside the helicopter and slammed the door shut behind him, "to get out of this storm I've got to fly straight up. It's going to get cold in here. Officer Gabriel, your friend Greene is turning blue. You better give him a Dick Butkus bear hug because he's going to need every ounce of heat to keep him from going into shock. This is going to be a bumpy ride."

Greene felt Gabriel's arm wrap around him, his head collapsing onto the big man's shoulder. He didn't remember much of what happened after that.

"Greene, can you hear me?" A voice was saying: "This is hot, try to drink."

He opened his eyes. It was Gabriel. Holding a mug up to Greene's face. Steam rising over the rim.

Greene looked around. They were still in the chopper, but it wasn't moving. They were on the ground.

He took the mug and drank it greedily. His body felt light and tingly, and the warmth of the liquid seemed to spread to every pore. He didn't know what he was drinking and he didn't care. So long as it was warm.

"Where are we?" he said, coughing out the words.

"At the RCAF Trenton base," Gabriel said. "You've been asleep for about forty minutes. The storm has passed. I've talked to your partner, Bering, in Toronto. She's up to speed."

Greene cradled the warm drink in his hands. Three or four blankets were wrapped around him, and a few people, who looked like medical personnel, were standing outside the helicopter.

"Forty minutes," he said. "And no word?"

"About what?"

"Her."

"No," Gabriel admitted, like a doctor holding back bad news until his patient was ready to hear it.

"I'm okay." Greene started to pull off the blankets. "Let's go back up."

Gabriel shook his head. Regretful, as if he was still that doctor with even worse news he had to deliver. "Bering told me to call her when you came around. She warned me you would want to keep searching. I'm supposed to tell you there are more than twenty helicopters combing the river and the beaches and they've thrown up roadblocks on both Highway 2 and the 401. That's a first."

Greene gritted his teeth so hard his jaw started to tremble. "Get her on the line," he said.

A few seconds later he was talking to Bering.

"Greene, you okay?"

Greene waited until he was sure his teeth stopped chattering. "I'm fine," he said. "I'm going back up."

"No," she said. "They're pulling you off the search."

"What?"

"Not my idea."

"I don't care whose idea it is. And I don't care how many cops and choppers are out there. I'm the only one who's seen her."

"Yes, I know. There's a higher priority."

"What could be higher priority than finding this killer?"

He took a large gulp of the liquid. His sense of taste was returning and he could tell it was tea. His other senses were returning too. He felt the sock in one of his shoes was wet, and remembered stepping on a nail on the boat.

"Direct orders. Your pilot will fly you straight to the Toronto Islands airport. You're going to meet with the chief—"

"You must be kidding," he said, handing the now-empty mug back to Gabriel and mouthing the words: "Thanks, more please." "I'm being pulled out of the field to attend a meeting? That's the most ridiculous—"

"And," Bering cut back in, "the whole central command unit, top cops from all eight countries who run security. They're waiting for you."

"What do they want me for?" he said, and curled his shoe to look at the damage to the sole.

He had what he knew was a ridiculous thought. When his father was in a concentration camp, he had told the Nazi in the lineup that he knew how to repair shoes. It was a lie that had saved his life. He learned fast, and when he came to Toronto, it was natural that he'd start his own shoe repair shop. He'd be appalled at the state of his son's shoes—no matter that Greene was trying to catch an assassin.

"They're talking about postponing the summit," Bering said. "The decision depends on your report."

Greene ran his finger along the sole of his shoe. The hole was wider and deeper than he'd thought.

"Listen. The biggest manhunt in Canadian history is happening right now," Bering said. "Every bush will be looked under, every house will be searched, and every car will be stopped. She'll be found, unless she's at the bottom of the river. And, if she is, they'll drag every inch of the St. Lawrence. We couldn't keep all this out of the press."

"What does the chief say?" Greene asked her, sticking his finger right inside the hole and feeling his sock.

"He wants you back," Bering said. He heard her take a deep breath, and then she added, "I think he's right."

"Okay," Greene said. If they were sending him back to Toronto, he had to go see his father at his shop, ASAP, or there'd be hell to pay. "I'm on my way. I'll have to drop in to visit my dad. Don't worry, I won't say a thing. I need him to fix my shoe. One of them got ripped up on the boat."

Bering laughed. She knew all about Greene's father and how important it was to him that his only son have proper shoes.

"I'll come see you next," he said. "I have an idea. I'm the only one who's still alive who has seen her. Line up a composite artist."

MARINA

46 HOURS MORE

EVERY PART OF MARINA'S body still hurt. Even her mind. All she wanted to do was sleep. But in another part of her brain, the message was even stronger.

You must not sleep. Wake up, wake up, or you'll die. Your mission is to stay awake.

She opened her eyes. She was in a room. On a bed. Alone. It was comfortable. She closed her eyes, listened intently. She could make out the sounds of a radio playing the song "Girls Just Want to Have Fun." It made her smile. Then she heard the voices of the twins. Talking. Arguing. Playing.

She remembered hiding under the bed in the van. The sound of the police officer opening the vehicle's sliding side door. Him talking to the girls, asking them to move out of the way. The latch to her hiding place under the bed snapping open. Scant light coming in. Then a thin metal rod poking in near her face.

She didn't dare move. Breathe. Holding her weapon in her hand.

All at once, the twins erupting. Yelling. Arguing.

"Give me my Care Bear!" one of them cried. Marina couldn't tell which one it was.

"No, it's mine," the other twin retorted.

Mama Bear screaming at the officer. "I've had it. We don't have the fancy air-conditioned cars like the other rich folks on this highway. We've been sitting here for two f'ing hours, my kids are hotter than fried eggs. You want to poke anything, poke me. I'm fatter than the Pillsbury Dough-boy."

"Well, ma'am," the man's voice said. The metal rod wavered. "It's just—"

"For the last time, pops, cut the ma'am stuff. I'm about to call and complain about unjust imprisonment, and I'll have your badge, buddy. Then you can retire to some trailer park in Timmins, if you can afford it."

"Okay, okay, calm down," Marina heard him say. He sounded older.

The rod pulled back and away from her. The door to her hiding place swung shut and she was enclosed in darkness again. Sweet darkness. She let herself breathe.

"Here, see, I'm putting my baton away," the man was saying. "Happy? You can be on your way . . . "

Marina remembered the relief of hearing the van door slide shut. A second later they started to move. Marina had tried to keep her eyes open, but soon the rocking of the van and the purring of the engine lulled her to sleep.

The bed Marina was in now was firm and warm. She slid out from under the covers and went over to the window. The girls were in a small square backyard, running through a water sprinkler, while Mama Bear was sitting at a picnic table sorting through a box of photos.

Marina lay back on the bed and reviewed her options. She could get away right now. Slip out the front door. That would be easy. But that wasn't how she'd been trained.

"Killing is not just for adults," Alisander had told her. "Old people, young people, children, it does not matter. You make contact, you kill. Contact. Kill. You must follow that rule. No exceptions. Ever."

There was a loud sound of doors slamming in the hallway and little feet running inside. "I had that first, give it back."

Marina recognized the voice. It was Bethy, the girl she had saved.

"Nah, nah, you can't get it." It was her sister, Barbie, running through the hallway toward Marina's bedroom.

"Yes, I can, I've got it. Let go!"

"No, I had it first."

"No, you didn't!"

The children's voices got louder and closer as their argument rushed toward its inevitable conclusion. It didn't take long.

"Let go, now!"

"No, I won't!"

Marina heard a loud rip. Whatever it was they were fighting over had been torn. The argument turned to wailing and tears.

"You, you, you ripped it." It was Barbie, crying hysterically.

"No, you did," Bethy retorted, equally upset.

Marina heard Mama Bear come on the scene.

"Shh. Shh. Girls. It's only a photograph. We have to be quiet. Our special visitor is still asleep. I told you two how important it was not to make noise. Both of you, give me a big Mama Bear hug."

"I, I wanted to show her our picture," Bethy said, gasping for breath between sobs. "I wanted to thank her for, for saving me."

Marina smiled. She popped out of bed, silently cracked the door open, and peeked into the hallway. Mama Bear and her two daughters were down on the floor, their backs to her, wrapped in a tight embrace.

"Don't worry, Mama Bear, I'm up," she said.

The twins turned, squealed with delight, and ran up to her. Bethy jumped into her arms.

"Look." She was holding up half of a ripped photograph. It was a picture of Bethy. "We wanted to give this to you, before it got ripped, that is."

Marina took the half of the photograph from Bethy, and Barbie handed her the other half. Carefully, she pieced them back together.

"It's our favourite picture, until she ripped it," Bethy said.

"I didn't, you ripped it," Barbie wailed.

"Don't worry," Marina found herself saying, "I can put this back together."

"I know you can," Bethy said, snuggling into her neck. "You're magic. You can do anything."

GREENE

46 HOURS MORE

THE SKYLINE OF TORONTO seemed to emerge all of a sudden from the surrounding flat farmland as the helicopter flew into the city low and fast. Greene saw the clutch of sleek modern skyscrapers huddled by Lake Ontario, punctuated by the soaring needle of the CN Tower.

From the air it was easy to see why the early British settlers chose Toronto as a town site. The waterfront was a lagoon, sheltered by three islands strung out across it like a string of pearls, forming a perfect natural harbour.

On the farthest island, the airport soon came into view. Two paved runways formed an off-kilter *V*. At the point where they met there were a few aluminum-sided buildings, a small glassed-in radio tower, and an airplane hangar.

The helicopter touched down at the far end of the south runway. On another runway, Greene saw a collection of black limousines. As he exited the chopper, two beefy men in dark suits and sunglasses appeared and hustled him into a small transport bus.

Greene hadn't shaved and his clothes were a dirty, blood-spattered mess. He was shaking slightly, still recovering from the near-hypothermic state he'd been in when Gabriel rolled him into the helicopter. It was hard to believe that yesterday morning he'd thought he'd been sent on a wild-goose chase.

When the vehicle stopped, Greene got out and made his way with his two escorts to the highly guarded airplane hangar. Instinctively, he slid his right hand into his inner left breast pocket to make sure the map he'd pulled from the dead man's hand was still there. He wasn't quite sure why, but he hadn't told anyone about it yet. Not Gabriel. Not even Bering.

Greene walked slowly into the airplane hangar. The change from the bright sunlight to the deep dark interior was startling. He stumbled as his pupils dilated to adjust.

The two men escorted him to the farthest corner of the high-ceilinged building. Chief Keon and some half dozen people he'd never met before sat on metal chairs around a rectangular table. Waves of tension emanated from the group like the heat from a cheap electric space heater.

His escorts directed Greene to an empty seat on the far side. Take your time, he told himself, walking with a deliberate slowness. They're waiting for you. Greene knew that slowness, like silence, could be a powerful weapon.

He lowered himself into the chair. He didn't even glance at the chief. It was a technique he'd learned as a police witness in court: Never look at the prosecutor when an aggressive defence lawyer is cross-examining you. It gives the impression that you are looking for the answer, as if you have something to hide.

There was a long pause until the man seated directly across from him spoke. "Thank you for coming on such short notice, Officer Greene."

He was a thin man, dressed in a blue blazer over a blue-and-red broad-striped shirt and a pretentious-looking yellow-and-green polka-dotted bow tie. His wavy blond hair was combed straight back. His voice was high-pitched and harsh, not silky smooth as Greene expected from such a preppy-looking dresser.

Greene looked him in the eye. He'd learned that in court too: Always look right at the lawyer who was cross-examining you. Use your silence. Let him fill the dead air.

Rarely did Greene dislike someone on first sight. But he didn't like this guy. When he didn't like someone, he let his mind run wild imagining the person's story. He could picture this man's story: Childhood of wealth and privilege. Probably grew up on the American East Coast, in private school from grade one, an Ivy League college his father and grandfather attended, summers on the Cape, winter holidays at their ski chalet in France.

"Allow me to introduce myself," Mr. Bow Tie said at last. "My name is James Jameson, I'm the head of this, the G7 security committee. You know Chief Keon. Let me introduce everyone else."

In short order, Jameson named seven security chiefs, one from each G7 country. The eighth was Russian.

"Officer Greene," Jameson said, "we're ready to hear your story."

All eyes were on him. Greene waited. Inhaled. "It's not a story," he said.

"Yes, I mean we want to know what happened today." Jameson made a show of shooting his left wrist out from under his gold-cuff-linked shirt.

Greene listened intently. Jameson's accent was posh, but not really British. More like an American who spent a year at graduate school in Britain and affected a mild English accent.

Greene nodded, clasped his hands together, and began. "Three days ago, Chief Keon gave me and Officer Bering an assignment." He gazed at Keon for an instant, then stared laser-like at Jameson. In a succinct narrative, he recounted everything that had happened from the moment he went to the Quebec–Vermont border until now. Something told him not to tell them about the map in his inside pocket.

He concluded by saying: "About half an hour ago I was pulled off the search for the killer and flown directly here to attend this meeting. Last I heard, this woman hadn't been caught. I hope I'm wrong."

Silence filled the oversized room. Greene kept his eyes fixed on Jameson.

"Thank you, Officer Greene." Jameson didn't meet his eyes. His obsequious tone turned nasty. "I have some questions. According to your narrative, you're the only police officer who has seen this woman."

"It appears so."

"You're an experienced police officer. But your description of this woman, you'll agree, is vague."

Greene had been cross-examined enough times to know the best way to answer a leading question was to keep your answer simple. Otherwise, you start arguing. Still, he had to make his point.

"When I first saw the woman on the bus, I had no reason to suspect her. I saw her for less than ten seconds that time. She was wearing sunglasses, except for when they slipped off her face, as I've told you. On the train I saw her for even less time. Most people don't realize that the English language has few good descriptive words for the human face. My description is vague, but that wouldn't surprise a professional investigator." Greene leaned hard on the word "professional."

Jameson mumbled a "Hmm."

Greene thought his answer had been too long.

"Officer, you were the first one to see the bodies of the American border guard and the old French Canadian woman, correct?"

"No," Greene said.

"Well, who else?"

"The killer."

"Yes, the killer. But you were the first one, *after* the killer, to see them both dead."

"As far as I know."

"And you didn't report it to the authorities."

"No."

"And you were the first one to see the lawyer, Mr. Osgoode, dead as well—except for the killer."

"Officer Gabriel saw him a few seconds later."

"Yes, this time there was a police officer on scene."

"This time there was *another* police officer on scene," Greene corrected him.

"As you told us a few minutes ago, you encouraged Officer Gabriel to not look at Osgoode's body."

Greene saw where this was going. It wasn't a question, so he didn't reply.

Jameson dove into his leather attaché case. He extracted a number of manila files.

"An autopsy was performed on US customs border guard Agent Hickey. Cause of death: heart attack. The gentleman was known to suffer from chronically high blood pressure." Jameson let the folder fall on the table with a bang. The sound echoed through the rafters.

He picked up another folder and waved it at Greene.

"Autopsy on Madame Isabel Rousseau, the old lady on the porch. Cause of death: heart attack. Ninety-four years old, she'd suffered two previous heart attacks."

Bang. Jameson dropped the second file. Another echo. Picked up a third.

"Frank Osgoode. Diabetic who chronically mismanaged his condition. Long history of heart disease in his family, and he was an alcoholic. We're still awaiting the autopsy results, but it will almost certainly show cause of death to be a heart attack."

Jameson let the third file fall. Bang and echo again.

"Heart attacks are the number one cause of death of adults in North America."

Greene never moved his eyes away from Jameson. Wait for it, Greene told himself. Don't rush. He took a deep breath. He took a second one.

"How about death by having your arm hacked off with an ax and bleeding to death on a boat in the St. Lawrence River. Is that the number two cause?"

He glanced over to Chief Keon again and saw him grin.

He looked back at Jameson, who seem unfazed.

"Officer Greene," he said, "Wayne Krupp is still listed as missing at this time, as is Osgoode's boat."

Greene looked back at the chief. Now he looked angry.

What was going on here? Greene wondered. Then the penny dropped. He nodded to his boss, his way of saying, "I get it."

This guy Jameson and all these big shots were pissed off because a couple of Toronto cops did some good police work and were about to show them up. This whole thing was one giant turf war, and he was the ball being kicked around.

"How much longer will the 401 roadblock remain in place?" Greene asked.

Jameson looked at his watch. "I ordered it taken down twenty minutes ago." He fished back into his briefcase and pulled out a typewritten piece of paper. "One thousand two hundred cars were searched. Three people have been charged with driving while impaired, four with having open beer bottles. And two with committing an indecent act in public. Apparently it was too long a wait in a hot car for one couple."

There was a soft chuckle around the circle. Greene didn't laugh.

"Everyone here wants to thank you for your effort. The committee will take over all matters of security going forward," Jameson said, looking around the table at the others, a contented smile on all of their faces. "Officer Greene, you may attend any of the G7 events—I've ensured you and your partner, Officer Bering, have full clearance. But your continued participation in this investigation is no longer required."

He said it all with a smile that was dangerously close to a smirk, Greene thought. A smirk that he'd love to wipe off that smug face. Now he saw Jameson's game. He was glad the woman hadn't been found in the roadblock. This way, if they caught her now, this committee would take all the credit. If they couldn't find her and she pulled the trigger on the G7, they would blame the Toronto cops. Especially the chief, since he was the one who chose Greene for this assignment, and Greene, because he had gotten so close to the assassin and kept letting her slip through his fingers.

Greene looked back at Jameson and waited until their eyes locked, then he stood up slowly. He was more exhausted than he'd realized. As he got to his feet, he was hit by an overwhelming sense of vertigo. He stumbled for a second and grasped the back of the chair.

Maybe it was good that he was off the case. Let Jameson and his gang worry about this now. The wild twists and turns of the last few days had left him exhausted. He wanted his life back. He missed Meredith. He could try to call her. They had an old phone up at the cottage that they rarely answered. She had been campaigning with her parents to put in an answering machine, but they were resistant to new technology. He could drive up there and surprise her, get in their canoe, go to their favourite beach.

He regained his footing and straightened up. "If you have no other questions, I'm going to go home to get some sleep."

In fact, he was going to go see Bering at the hotel room, where Keon had put her up. Their own war room.

And before that he was going to go see his parents at his father's shoe repair shop. He hadn't talked to them for two days and he knew they'd be worried. And the sole of his shoe needed to be repaired. His dad would be appalled if he didn't get it fixed.

But Greene wasn't going to tell Jameson his plans.

Jameson still had a smile across his smooth-skinned face.

Greene would have loved to slap him. Real hard. He felt vindicated by his decision to dislike this guy right from the get-go. Call it hate at first sight. Instead, he chuckled to himself as he thought of how much fun it was going to be one day to tell his father, who hated pretentions of any kind, about this Jameson and his polka-dotted bow tie.

"There is nothing perfect in life, Ari," his dad liked to say about anyone he felt was putting on airs, "except a perfect asshole."

MARINA

46 HOURS MORE

MAMA BEAR INSISTED MARINA go back to bed. "Let me make you some food," she said.

Marina smiled and told her what she wanted to eat. Then she asked, "But how did I get into this bed?"

"Ha, easy peasy," Mama Bear said, and made a muscle with her arm. "You're so thin, I could have carried two of you."

Marina crawled back into bed, and soon Mama Bear brought in a tray of mint tea, toast, and jam, and laid it down on the covers.

"This is all you are going to eat?" Mama Bear said, fluffing up the pillows. "I'm the fat one here, not you, hun."

Marina bit into the toast. The bread was thick and warm and it tasted delicious.

"I've got something for you," Mama Bear said. "I'll be right back."

Marina watched her exit the room. She poured herself some tea and sat back against the pillows. She cupped her hands all the way around the teacup and felt the warmth radiate out to her fingertips.

Mama Bear returned armed with another tray. On it was a washcloth, a bowl of warm water, and a hairbrush. She sat on the corner of the bed and Marina felt her weight tilt the mattress.

She dipped the cloth in the water and began washing the cut above Marina's eye. She moved to a gash on Marina's cheek. She picked up the comb and began to comb Marina's hair.

Neither spoke. The house was quiet and still.

"I sent the girls over to our neighbours to play with their friends so you could get some sleep," Mama Bear said.

"Thanks," Marina whispered.

She noticed the ceiling fan above the bed. It purred like a cat, feeding a steady stream of smooth, cool air down on her sore skin.

Gradually, like a ship appearing in the mist, a new thought came to Marina. Something that had never been remotely on the horizon of her consciousness. And here it was. She could almost touch it. She let herself imagine.

Disappear.

I can disappear. No one knows who I am. No more of the Mission. No more running. No more fighting. No more killing. And sleep. Just sleep for as long as she wanted to.

Mama Bear slid her hands over Marina's hands and guided the cup of tea up to her mouth. "Take another sip. It'll warm you. Sleep. Let Mama Bear take care of you."

Yes, Marina thought as she felt her eyes drift shut, let Mama Bear take care of me.

TALBOT

46 HOURS MORE

AUBREY TALBOT LOOKED OUT the leaded windows of his office as warden of Hart House, the stone building at the heart of the University of Toronto, built in 1919 by the legendary Massey family in the style of the stone buildings at Oxford or Cambridge. Talbot believed it was the finest piece of university architecture, with its great hall and picturesque quadrangle, in Canada. And right there, on the flagstone patio, was the spot where the seven world leaders would stand. Eight if you included the Russian president. And Talbot would be there too. Right with them.

Centre stage.

He felt as excited as a young boy checking off days before Christmas on his Advent calendar as he opened his leather-bound datebook, picked up his initialed Cross fountain pen, and erased another day with a single confident stroke.

The world leaders were in Toronto, and there were two more days to go until journalists, photographers, and television crews from all over the world would be right there outside his window to record the final event of the G7 summit. It was all timed down to the minute. Lunch in Hart House's Great Hall at noon, at 12:45 they'd release their final joint communiqué, and at precisely one o'clock, just as the Hart House clock tower bell rung out the hour, he'd lead the most powerful people in the world out onto the patio for their last and most important photo opportunity. The picture would be beamed all around the world and memorialize this moment for all time.

Talbot had been warden of Hart House for more than twelve years. Five years ago, when it was an open secret that Toronto was slated to host the next G7 summit, he began his political manipulation to beat out the other local contenders—the art gallery, the museum, the science centre—to get the final leaders' luncheon here.

He aggressively courted the then prime minister, Francis Verault. Each time the man was in Toronto—a city he claimed privately to loath, like all those Montreal snobs—Talbot invited him to a book reading in the library or a debate in the East Common Room or a Sunday night piano recital played on Hart House's Steinway.

One summer night Verault came to a special oboe recital by an internationally known Canadian musician—who also happened to be a most beautiful woman. Over a glass of sherry, the deal was sealed. Talbot told Verault about three little-known guest rooms on the west side of the building. Situated on the top floor, they overlooked the quadrangle. The rooms, Talbot explained to the prime minister, were rarely used and *totally* private.

The next time Verault was in Toronto, which "happened" to coincide with the oboe player doing another Hart House concert, discreet arrangements were made. The three upstairs rooms were vacated, and a room key was left under a certain loose granite flagstone. Talbot knew Verault would like that touch. A month later, a hand-delivered note invited Talbot to Ottawa to finalize plans for Hart House to host the final G7 summit luncheon.

Talbot smiled at the memory, and let his gaze linger for another moment. Five years of scheming and two more days to go. This morning the RCMP and the American Secret Service had debriefed him for two hours. And, boy, were they thorough.

They had checked out his wife, his brothers, even his doctor, for goodness' sake. When they saw on his résumé that he was an Oxford graduate, he knew they thought they had him: Ah-huh! Oxford, postwar, isn't that where all those English men turned into Russian spies?

"And what did you study at Oxford?" the snotty fellow named Jameson, who wore a pretentious bow tie, wanted to know.

"Economics," Talbot said.

"And what sort of friends did you have in England?"

"No one who ended up in Moscow, if that's what you're wondering. I was part of the other clan, the New Right. Speaking of friends, I'm seeing one of my old classmates in a couple of days."

That got Jameson's attention.

"What's his name?"

"*Her name*, actually," Talbot said. "Margaret. She dropped me a note last week, saying that she was really looking forward to seeing me again at the G7 summit."

He knew he was being bad, but he couldn't help it.

"Margaret who?" Jameson asked.

"Margaret's last name was Roberts, when I knew her," he said, stretching it out until he could hold back the punch line no more. "Now it's Thatcher. Heard of her?"

That sure shut up this Mr. Jameson.

Game, set, match.

Talbot chuckled at the memory. He couldn't wait to tell his best friend, Charlie Keon, the chief of police, this story.

He pulled out his watch fob from his tartan vest. Two minutes to three. Everything right on schedule. Good time to go for a stroll over to the front door reception. He liked to be there every day at this time. He happened to know that Felicia, one of the three students who lived on the third floor, would be coming back from her afternoon run.

Talbot smiled at the thought. Red Running Hood, that was his nickname for the pretty woman, who always wore a red hooded sweatshirt when she went out jogging.

She'd told him she'd be away for a few days. Hopefully she'd be back. Then he would chat with her, flirt for a minute or two, and then maybe . . .

As he flicked off the light in his office and headed out into the wood-paneled hall, Aubrey Talbot was giddy with delight. Could things possibly get any better?

MAMA BEAR

45 HOURS MORE

MAMA BEAR SAW THIS mysterious woman close her eyes, shake her head violently for a moment on the pillow, then open them wide. She had such beautiful eyes.

She looked disoriented, shook her head again. "I can't sleep," she said.

"Stay here and rest," Mama Bear said, rising to get off the bed. "I'll go get the girls."

The Beauty, as Mama Bear had named her in her mind, smiled. "Not yet," she said, touching Mama Bear's back. "Lie with me for a minute."

"How could I refuse you?" Mama Bear whispered, settling her weight back onto the mattress.

"Let me go pick up the twins," the Beauty said, moving away from Mama Bear and sliding off the bed. "It will be a treat for them."

"I'll come with you."

"No, stay here."

Mama Bear lay back and watched the Beauty as she went over to her backpack, which Mama Bear had left in the corner. Slowly, she dressed herself. Once she put her shoes on, the Beauty looked squarely at Mama Bear.

Mama Bear was entranced by her deep, dark eyes. She noticed now that the left one was not quite right. It drifted off to the side.

She wanted to thank her again for saving Bethy. She was about to speak, but something made her pause.

The Beauty pulled out a piece of cloth. Never taking her eyes off Mama Bear, she moved to the bedside table and wiped the surface clean.

What was she doing?

The Beauty's eyes had turned to cold steel. Without saying a word, she moved methodically around the room, wiping.

Mama Bear remembered the roadblock. How the police were checking every car.

The Beauty got to the door and she cleaned the handle.

Mama Bear felt a chill roll down her spine. She's erasing her fingerprints so there won't be any trace of her. Mama Bear remembered the old cop poking under the bed in the van. He had been looking for someone.

The cops were looking for her.

Mama Bear's body shook involuntarily, the way it did when she was falling asleep. Tears formed in her eyes.

"You can have the van. The keys are in the kitchen. Take it. I won't move from here. I promise. I'll call my neighbour and have her keep the kids."

The Beauty reached into her backpack again and pulled out something else. Mama Bear saw what it was.

Now she understood why the police were looking for this woman. The huge roadblock. The car searches. This woman was a killer.

Mama Bear looked around the room. There was no way to escape. She looked back at those cold eyes.

"If you kill me, their father will take the girls away. He'll ruin their lives," she said. Tears were flooding down her cheeks, but she kept eye contact.

This woman, this killer. She seemed frozen.

Mama Bear had to keep talking.

"Please, you saved Bethy. Don't hurt the girls, please, please."

Mama Bear couldn't breathe.

At last, this woman, whoever she was, motioned her head toward the phone beside the bed. "Call your neighbour," she said in a voice that was entirely different. Cold. Guttural. "I need half an hour."

Mama Bear picked up the phone and dialed.

"Hi, Hanna, it's Jan," she said, staring at the woman and keeping her voice sounding upbeat. "How are my twin buttons behaving? Great. Listen, I still have a lot of unpacking to do from this trip, so can you keep them for another half hour? Perfect."

She hung up, stared back at the Killer, no longer the Beauty.

The Killer hesitated. Then, so slowly that it seemed she was hardly moving, she put her hand with her weapon back in her pocket, pulled it out, and there was nothing in it. "I don't exist," she said in a voice that would turn boiling water to ice.

"I won't move," Mama Bear said. "We never met. I'll never tell a soul. The girls are so young, they'll forget. You can trust me. I owe you my life. You know I'd do anything to—"

The Killer put her hand up to silence Mama Bear. "If I ever have to return here—"

"I understand," Mama Bear said. "I understand."

She stared at Mama Bear. Didn't move.

Mama Bear whisked the tears across her face with her arm. "Thank you," she said, her voice down to a whimper.

The Killer turned from her, gave the door handle one last wipe, and disappeared.

Precisely thirty minutes later, Mama Bear got out of bed. Her palms, her hair, even the skin behind her knees was filled with heavy sweat. Slowly, she ventured out into the hall. The house was eerily silent. Everything seemed perfectly in place.

When she got to the kitchen, she saw something on the grey

Formica-topped table. The ripped photo of the twins had been precisely pieced back together and perfectly repaired with invisible tape.

She felt her legs falter. Her head began to spin. She tried to hold herself up on the kitchen table, but fell hard on the cold linoleum floor.

She seemed to convulse. Got up, looked at the picture, and saw her tears fall on it like rain. She was heaving in great, uncontrollable sobs.

The back door opened. "Mummy, Mummy," the twins called out.

She took the photo and rubbed it hard on her sleeve, front and back, opened her shirt and tucked it under her bra.

"I'm here. I'm right here, babies," she said, wiping her eyes with the back of her hands before the twins ran into the kitchen. "Give Mama the biggest hug ever."

GREENE

45 HOURS MORE

IN THE PHONE BOOTH, Greene fished a quarter out of his pocket and called the number he'd known his whole life.

"Yitzhak Shoe Repair, how can I help you?" his father said, picking up after the third ring. He'd answered the phone at his shop the same way since Greene was a baby, growing up in their apartment above the store.

"Dad, I'm off duty," Greene said.

"Your mother was worried. You didn't call yesterday or the day before."

"Busy day with all the traffic," Greene said.

"Because all the big shots are coming to town," his father said, with his usual note of skepticism. "So?"

"I'll be there in about half an hour, I need you to fix the sole of my shoe. I stepped on a nail."

"I'm just finishing a Ukrainian woman's pair of boots."

Greene hung up and looked around to see if anyone was watching or following him. He didn't see anyone as he hopped on an oncoming streetcar just as the doors were shutting.

Soon he was on Dundas Street West, the commercial street where his father had his shop. He looked around, but there was no one in sight. Stop being so paranoid, he told himself.

"You look tired," his father said when he walked in the door, the bell on it tinkling the way it always did.

"Been a long few days," he said, slipping in behind the counter where, on the inside, his mother had marked in red pen his height every year on his birthday. He pulled off both of his shoes.

His father examined the hole.

"Directing traffic must be hard work," his father said with a cynical glint in his eye, looking at Greene's unshaven face and disheveled clothes.

Greene knew his parents had many secrets. What had they done to survive in the camps? And after the war? How about the three years they were stuck in the displaced persons camp in Europe before they were allowed to immigrate to Canada? How had they lived through it all?

"It was heavy traffic," Greene said with a shrug.

It was impossible to pull the wool over his father's eyes. He'd been through too much in his life to not see through his son's white lie, and was smart enough to know when he should not pry.

"Both shoes need to be cleaned up," his father said and went right to work.

Twenty minutes later he held the shoes up, examining them with practiced skill.

"You know, Ari," he said, "I've fixed thousands of shoes, from every country you can name. I always find that no pair, no matter how well made, is ever completely identical."

He handed them to Greene. "You're going back to work, aren't you?"

"I am," Greene said, putting the shoes on.

"Hard, isn't it," his father said, "this directing traffic? With all the world leaders here? You police have to keep them safe, don't you?"

Greene smiled, kissed his father softly on the cheek. "Don't worry," he whispered, "I'll be careful."

GABRIEL

44 HOURS MORE

THERE ARE NO SECRETS in small towns, Gabriel had learned in the last two years he'd been in Brockville. By the time he got back to the station, everyone knew that Osgoode was dead, and that Wayne Krupp had been on his Donzi with some naked woman when it almost rammed into the dock at Sand Island Resort and killed a boy. Speculation was rampant that Krupp was dead.

Gabriel knew he had to hurry. He changed into a fresh uniform and drove right over to see Jennifer North, Krupp's fiancée. He wanted to talk to her before the rumors got completely out of hand.

"It isn't true. Please, Brian, tell me it isn't true," Jennifer said when she saw Gabriel walk up the concrete steps to her parents' house, where she lived. "They're saying Wayne drove Osgoode's boat with some naked woman on it and . . . well."

Gabriel opened the screen door she'd been standing behind and took off his OPP hat. The gesture was enough to confirm her worst fears.

Jennifer clutched his arm. Her voice was barely a whisper. "He's gone, isn't he, Brian?"

Gabriel nodded, and saw the last vestige of hope dim from her eyes.

"We tried to save him," he said. "You can't imagine how hard we tried. That woman. All I can tell you is that she hijacked the boat. Wayne was in the wrong place at the wrong time."

"Oh, Brian," Jennifer cried. "Wayne was the sweetest thing on earth, you know that."

Gabriel wrapped his arms around her shoulders and rocked her.

"Our wedding is in nine days," she said.

She was speaking in the present tense about her now late fiancé. Gabriel knew this was typical of people in shock.

"He loved you, Jen," Gabriel said. "Don't ever doubt that."

"I know, I know," she said, releasing her hand from his arm and bringing it down to her stomach.

"I'm . . . I'm . . . "

She was a fit woman, but Gabriel could see a small bump down there. "I see," he said. "Did Wayne know?"

She shook her head. "I was going to tell him on our honeymoon. He would have been so happy to be a father."

She planted her head on his wide shoulder and began to heave great gasps of sobs.

He held her gently.

"Why would anyone want to hurt my Wayne?" Jennifer wailed.

Gabriel could do nothing but rock her and hold her and wonder himself.

Why?

WEDNESDAY

JULY 6, 1988

BERING

28 HOURS MORE

YESTERDAY, BERING HAD USED all of her leverage over Keon to get him to convince the G7 committee to throw up roadblocks on both the major highways around Mallorytown Beach. It was a bold move, especially in July with all the tourists flooding in. No one had been happy about it, and when they'd come up empty, as far as all those hotshots were concerned, Keon had egg on his face.

To his credit, Keon had taken the blame, claimed it was his idea, and sheltered Bering and Greene.

When Keon told Bering that the roadblocks were coming down, she'd had another idea. "I need the notebooks of every cop who stopped each car," she'd told him.

"This your needle in a haystack, Nora?" he'd said.

"Only way to find the needle is to jump on the stack," she replied.

"Okay," he'd said. "You know how cops hoard their notebooks. That's a lot to ask."

"Tell them this is a national emergency. I'll keep personal custody of them until the world leaders get on their planes home."

Keon had pulled strings, and now here she was opening a newly arrived

FedEx box filled with notebooks. And there were a lot. It took her about ten minutes to unpack and stack them in piles—Highway 401 East, 401 West, Highway 2 East and West. She counted fifty-six notebooks.

This would be hours and hours of work. Like any effective police investigation. Nothing high profile, nothing high tech, nothing fancy. Just boring old grunt work. It was going to be a slog.

She decided to start with the Highway 401 East pile and counted twelve notebooks. Opening the one on top, her heart sank. So many police officers had illegible writing. Sometimes when there was a trial they were required to type their notes out—which they hated to do—before disclosing them to defence lawyers.

The joke was—and it was true—since more women had come on to the police force, the quality of the handwriting had improved.

The notebook had an elastic band around the first page of relevant notes. Most officers did that. It took Bering almost three hours to go through the whole first pile, read each notebook for . . . for what? She wasn't quite sure. But it was her last chance at finding that elusive needle in the haystack.

She looked at the three remaining piles of notebooks. Might as well stick with the ones from Highway 401, she thought. She hit the floor and did her push-ups before she dug into them.

QUAN

25 HOURS MORE

WORKING AT ROOTS WAS the greatest. Everyone at the store was young, hip, and beautiful. The clothes were comfortable and easy to sell. And the new flagship store, where Barry Quan was a top salesman, was so cool.

The owners had befriended a famous Parisian designer, and she'd created a store that was minimalist in the extreme: bare floors, simple wood shelves held up by long thin metal wires, lots of windows.

The best part was the dressing room doors—talk about minimalist. Instead of a long door, there was a thin band of wood at midriff level. So cool. Barry loved to see women change there. They'd try to act casual as they pulled their clothes off, their private parts barely hidden.

Still, Barry enjoyed wonderful views of their legs, shoes kicked off, pants tumbling down, and even better, their naked shoulders and arms. There was something about a woman disrobing, especially taking a shirt off over her head, that drove him wild.

He knew all the mirrors and angles. On a good day, he could catch a few pairs of breasts. But being a Peeping Tom was a bore. The real fun thing to do was to walk right up to the dressing room, hand over shirt after shirt, talking away, and watch garment after garment slide off onto the floor.

The women loved it too. How risqué. Being naked with a thin piece of wood separating them from this unusually tall, handsome Asian man. And today it was so nice and warm out. Delicious. Women in short summer dresses. Women in sandals. Women in thin T-shirts. Women in baseball caps.

Quan looked out the front window. He saw a stunning woman crossing the road, heading toward the store.

"Melissa, my love," he said to the other salesperson on the floor. "When that gorgeous piece of protoplasm walks in the door, please vamoose downstairs to the kiddies' section. I'll get you a cappuccino on my break. Deal?"

Melissa, a preppy brunette with what Quan liked to call "field hockey thighs," smiled at her floor partner. "Sure, Barry, if you promise to introduce me to a hunk from your triad." And with a click of her teeth she was gone.

Quan turned his attention to the Protoplasm, the name he'd given her in his head. She had the most remarkable eyes, even if one of them wasn't perfect.

"I want two hooded red sweatshirts," she said. "Medium."

"Hey, I'm sure we can do better than that," Quan said, turning on the charm jets. "We sell a ton of the reds every day. I bet you want something different."

The Protoplasm smiled politely, but she was firm. All she wanted was two boring red sweatshirts.

Quan shrugged and pulled out the sweatshirts from the stack behind him. "You can try one on in the dressing rooms," Quan told her.

She didn't move. "I know my size. It'll fit," she said, and took out a pair of crumpled fifty-dollar bills from her pocket.

He made change as slowly as he could. "We've got some new ones in a cool black colour. They'd be terrific with your dark eyes, if you want to try one on for fun."

No luck. She didn't respond. Took her change and in a moment she was out of the store.

When she was gone, he hit the intercom button.

"Horny Asian Brute to Randy Private School Girl, over," he said, sotto voce.

He heard Melissa's deep laugh as she picked up the handset downstairs in Children's Wear.

"What happened, lover boy?"

"The coast, sadly, is entirely clear. The Protoplasm is gone. She bought the most boring red sweatshirts in the store right off the shelf. I couldn't even get her to try one on."

Quan turned off the speaker. He heard the front door brush open and looked up to see a gaggle of girls enter the store. He knew the type: down from the suburbs, right out of high school on their first shopping trip of the summer. All arms and legs and hair and skin. Every single one in a sundress and sandals. Now, this will be fun.

"Can I help you, ladies?" Quan said as he approached. Madame Protoplasm was ancient history.

This job, he thought. I love this job.

GREENE

25 HOURS MORE

"OFFICER BERING IS EXPECTING you," the police constable outside her hotel room said to Greene as he approached.

"Thanks," Greene said. "You are?"

"PC Mudhar. Chief Keon has assigned me to be on call for Officer Bering."

"Good work," Greene said as he knocked on Bering's door.

"It's open, Greene," he heard Bering call out. Inside, he could see she'd transformed the hotel room into her workspace. She was at a desk looking out the window onto the street, her back to him. On the desk were stacks of papers and what looked like piles of police officers' notebooks.

She whirled around and jumped to her feet.

"Am I ever glad to see you," she said, walking up to him. They'd always been formal with each other, but this time she embraced him for a moment before standing back to look at him.

"You go see your family?" she asked.

"My father fixed my shoes. Don't worry, I didn't tell them anything about this."

"Why do I think I hear a 'but' there."

Greene chuckled. "My dad survived four years in a concentration camp and three years in a displaced persons camp. After all he's seen, it's almost impossible to fool him about anything. I might be trying to save the world leaders, but he'd never forgive me for walking around in broken shoes."

They both laughed.

"Here are the two red cotton balls I told you about," he said.

"I checked with the police in Quebec who found the clown suit. As you thought, two balls were missing from it."

"I've got something else for you," Greene said, pulling out Wayne Krupp's map and holding it by the edges to show it to her. "A map of the Thousand Islands. In fact, there are a thousand eight hundred and sixty-four of them."

He explained to her how he'd extracted it from the dead man's hand on the sinking boat. "There's blood splatter all over it. Some of it might be hers. Maybe we can test it. A few weeks ago, I read about a new thing they have in Britain where they can find someone's molecular structure from their blood."

Bering had heard of it too. It wasn't in Canada yet. "I'll send it to the lab and have them preserve all the blood samples. You never know. But come look, I've been working on something."

She led him over to her desk and pulled out a pad of paper and a map. "Let's assume our pretty young friend got off the boat around 1:00 p.m. I checked with your helicopter pilot—he's a barrel of laughs—and got the coordinates of where you saw Osgoode's boat. It was right here."

She pointed to a small red X she'd drawn near the north side of the St. Lawrence River.

"And this second X marks the spot where you jumped on board. It took five minutes for the boat to go, let's see . . . " Bering put her old wood ruler down to take the measurement. "One inch. Good."

She pulled out a battered metal pencil and, with it and the ruler, drew a straight line between the two Xs. Then she continued the line all the way up to the north shore.

Greene looked on in silence.

"And here is where she landed." Bering's ruler crossed squarely at Mallorytown Beach.

"We came so close," he said at last. "I should have gambled and flown straight to that beach, maybe then—"

"Greene—"

"I know. Stop the 'I should haves.'"

"Listen to me. Our people ripped the park apart limb to limb. There's no way she was hiding there. We searched every car on Highways 2 and 401. I've got all the officers' notes from the roadblock. I'm halfway through them and there's nothing there. The current in the river is rough, but assuming Wonder Woman survived the swim, where did she go?"

"Yet again the lady vanishes," Greene said.

"Let me show you the summit timetable for the next twenty-four hours." She pulled out a detailed chart. "This afternoon the leaders meet at the convention centre."

"That's a sealed-off underground bunker. It should be secure," Greene said.

"Tonight there's a dinner at the Hunt Club, a golf club out on the Scarborough Bluffs overlooking the lake. They'll have so many police helicopters overhead it will look as if they're filming a Vietnam War movie."

"Should be secure," Greene said.

"Tomorrow there's the final photo op at Hart House. Seven minutes. Live broadcast. No helicopters overhead, no armed guards in view. The only time in the summit they're totally exposed."

There was a knock at the door and the composite artist came in, introduced himself, opened his portfolio, and fished out a tin box filled with black artist's pencils and put it on the table. He opened a pad to a fresh sheet. For the next half hour, as his hands flew across the paper, working and reworking the image, he questioned Greene about every detail of the woman's face: The nose—was it longer, wider, flatter? The hairline—was it higher, was her forehead deeper? The chin—was it thinner, rounder?

With each answer, the artist drew, rubbed things out with an eraser, or used his right forefinger to soften a line, then drew some more. Slowly an image emerged, like a black-and-white photo being developed in a dark-room. The woman in the picture was beautiful and aloof. Some parts of the drawing were remarkably accurate—the mouth, the chin, the nose—but he couldn't get the left eye quite right.

"It's close," Greene said, "but something's missing."

"Don't worry," the artist told him. "That's typical. I don't think we can do any better than this." He gave the paper to Greene, packed up, shook hands, and left.

When the door closed, Bering picked up the composite. She stared at it for a full minute, put it down, and riffled through a stack of papers. She extracted a green spiral notebook and flipped through the pages. She stopped, and jabbed her finger at something.

"Greene, the first time you told me about the people on the bus to Montreal, you said, 'Next was a young woman sitting on the left-hand side of the bus. Wearing a hippie-like flowery dress, wearing sunglasses. She was reading a book.'"

"Right," he said.

"We've just been focusing on that. I forgot the other thing you said. Here, listen:

"'She looked like a typical university student.'"

Bering looked up from her notebook. They stared at each other and said in unison: "Hart House."

BERING

24 HOURS MORE

BERING HELD THE SKETCH pad close to her chest and kept her voice modulated. "We're about to show you a composite picture of a young woman," she said to Aubrey Talbot, the warden of Hart House. He was perched on a chair behind what looked to be an old wood desk. He extended his arms, exposing a pair of gold cuff links.

"It won't be an exact likeness," Bering said, "but we would like to know if the face looks familiar."

"I'll help in any way I can," he said.

Bering took a close look at Talbot. The guy dressed like a real English fop. Oversized tweed jacket, striped tie, French cuffs. He had the complexion for it too, with his pasty white skin. To top it all off, he wore his yellowish brown hair flipped up in a ridiculous pompadour.

"You know, I see hundreds of female students every week," Talbot said.

"This woman is striking," Greene said.

Bering saw a flicker in Talbot's eyes. The twit looked nervous. She placed the composite in front of him. "Do you recognize this face?"

Talbot went a full shade whiter. Bering was amazed that the man could be so colourless. His eyes widened, but he didn't say anything.

He knows, Bering thought. "Who is she?"

"She's . . . Felicia. We call her Little Red Running Hood . . . " The words spurted out of Talbot as if he were under the spell of a sleazy TV hypnotist.

"She's at the university?" Bering raised her voice.

"She lives, she lives . . . " The blood rushed back into Talbot's face and his skin turned crimson red. Pools of sweat gathered on his forehead.

"Where?" Greene jumped in.

"Here. Here." Talbot's voice was hollow now. "She lives right here, at Hart House."

"What do you mean she lives here?" Bering was leaning over Talbot.

"Up . . . upstairs," Talbot said.

"What are you talking about?"

"Upstairs," Greene interrupted. "There are three rooms where students live on the third floor."

"Greene, have you been up there?" Bering stared at him.

"When I was a student, I lived there for a term. The rooms are on the west side." He gestured out the window. "They look right out onto the quadrangle. Which one does she live in?" he asked Talbot.

"The middle one," Talbot said.

"Where she'd have a perfect shot," Greene said.

"You've got to be kidding." Bering turned back to Talbot. "Where's she now?"

"She usually jogs every afternoon," Talbot said. "We nicknamed her Red Running Hood because she always wears a red hooded sweatshirt. Because Hart House is being shut down today for the security check, I saw her at the front desk about an hour ago coming in from her run, so I know she's back already."

"She should still be in her room," Bering said.

Talbot pulled out a fob watch from his vest pocket. "It's one o'clock. She might have left. All the residents and staff have to be out of the building this afternoon."

As if to confirm the time, the clock tower bell started its hourly four-part chime. There was a long pause, and then the bell rang once.

Bering took the phone from Talbot's desk and began to dial.

"What's this all about?" Talbot protested. "Felicia is an undergraduate student."

"We have to stay off our radios or the press will be all over us," Bering told Greene, ignoring Talbot. After a moment, she nodded at Greene, to signal that someone had answered the phone. "Carol, I need the chief right away."

Bering looked over at Talbot. He looked awful. Too bad. The fool. He was about to speak. She held up a finger for quiet.

"I'm in your friend Aubrey Talbot's office, here at Hart House," Bering told Keon when he got on the line. "We have a match for Greene's composite of the woman on the train. Get this. She lives right here, at Hart House, right under our noses."

"Are you sure?" Keon said, his voice registering surprise.

"It gets worse. Her room looks right out onto the quadrangle. You better hurry up and get over here."

Bering didn't wait to hear Keon's response. She smashed the phone down and seized Talbot by the arm.

"Let's go," she said. "Lead the way."

KEON

24 HOURS MORE

KEON BANGED THE PHONE down. "Aubrey, Aubrey, Aubrey," he cursed under his breath as he jumped from his chair, threw his gun holster over his shoulder, and muscled his way into his sports jacket.

"You fool," he muttered as he buttoned up his jacket and dashed to the front door of his office. "You goddamn fool."

"Miss Rose," he called out. "Call the prima donnas at the daily meeting and tell them I can't make it."

"Certainly. What should I tell them?"

"That I'm out doing some real live police work."

"Where are you going, sir?"

"Out," Keon said, sounding like a belligerent teenager.

Miss Rose smiled. "Don't forget this," she said, passing him the portable phone.

Keon looked down at the ugly hunk of plastic.

"You never know when I might need to club someone on the head or poke someone in the eye," he said, waving the phone in his hand. "That's about all this thing is good for."

GREENE

24 HOURS MORE

GREENE AND BERING MARCHED Talbot across the polished-tile main floor, took the wide marble steps two at a time to the second floor. At the top of the stairs they turned left, and Talbot pointed to the small winding staircase leading to the third floor. Greene nodded and broke into a run, Bering right behind him.

Greene remembered that the staircase was so steep it was difficult to take the steps without slipping. But his resoled shoes gripped them well. His footsteps echoed off the stone walls. He rushed past a small bathroom on the landing and down a hallway with a carpeted runner.

The doors of all three rooms were closed. Greene ran up to the middle one and examined it as he waited for Bering and Talbot to catch up. It was a plain wood door with a bronze door handle and an old-fashioned keyhole. Greene took out his gun and looked back down the hall.

Bering and Talbot were at the top of the stairs. "Get moving," Bering hissed at him. Talbot hesitated. His body jerked forward. Greene saw Bering had shoved him with her gun.

"Knock on the door," Bering whispered to Talbot when he got to the second room. Greene squatted low, with his gun pointed and ready.

Talbot gave the solid wood door a soft tap. "Excuse me, Felicia, it's Warden Mr. Talbot. Are you there? I need to speak to you for a moment."

There was no reply.

"Felicia, are you there?"

Again no reply.

"Do you have the key?" Bering whispered.

"Yes, I do, but it's against Hart House rules to—"

Bering wasn't listening. "Greene, shoot the lock off the door." She motioned at him with her gun.

"Okay, okay," Talbot said. "I'll open it." He produced a key ring and selected a metal key that looked like something out of a Dickens novel.

Bering positioned herself, gun poised. There was a metal click as the old lock moved and a loud squeak as the door opened inward.

"Felicia?" Talbot said as he entered the room.

There was silence. Greene and Bering moved in behind Talbot, guns drawn. The room was small. To the left there was a single bed against the north wall with a Gustav Klimt poster above the headboard. Beside it was a small night table with a black dial phone and a copy of Albert Camus's novel *L'Étranger* on it. A chest of drawers sat at the foot of the bed. All along the south wall to the right there was a bookshelf made of planks of wood separated by stacks of red bricks. It was crammed with books and binders. On the top level was a stapler and a cup filled with pens and pencils. In the corner of the room, a pile of dirty clothes spilled out of a straw basket. Typical detritus of a student in a typical student room.

Greene stooped down and looked under the bed. There was nothing there. Bering kicked over the laundry basket and the pile of clothes fell out, including a red hooded Roots sweatshirt.

The dominant feature of the room was the slanted ceiling on the east wall and the window cut out of a recessed bay. Bering went up to it, looked out, whistled, and shook her head. She turned back to Greene. "You're right. From here she would have had a perfect shot."

Greene looked around the small room. There was no cupboard, or anywhere else someone could hide. Once again, he thought, gritting his teeth hard, she's gone.

BERING

23.75 HOURS MORE

BERING PUT HER GUN in its holster, picked up the black phone beside the bed, and dialed.

"Carol, patch me through to him again." Bering put her hand over the receiver and looked at Talbot. "Where else could she be?"

"Anywhere. In the building, on campus."

"Nora, where are you?" Keon's voice came through on the phone. It sounded faint.

"Hold on a moment," Bering told him. She turned to Talbot. "If she was in the building, where would she go?"

Talbot blushed. The man looked awful.

"Where, Aubrey?" Bering demanded. "You know, don't you?"

Talbot sat down on the bed and buried his head in his hands. "I'm such a fool. Please, can I talk to Charlie?"

Bering threw Greene a "See, I told you so" look.

"Can you hear me?" she said into the phone to Keon.

"Not bad. I'm rushing over there and on this damn new phone."

"Well, listen up. We've got Talbot here, and he wants to talk to you."

Bering glared at Talbot. "He's on his way over. Talking on a portable phone. The reception is terrible."

Talbot nodded as he took the phone. "Charlie," he said, "I've made a grievous error. This woman, Felicia. She's a resident here at Hart House. She's quite, well, beautiful, and when she goes swimming every man in the pool ogles her. The women too. Charlie, I gave her a copy of the master key to the athletic wing."

There was a stunned silence in the small room. Bering glanced at Greene. He looked as if he were about to smack Talbot.

"I know, I know. You're right," Talbot said. "But it's even worse. Her other hobby is guns. She has the keys to the firing range."

Before she could even consider what she was doing, Bering grabbed Talbot by his arm and hauled him to his feet. Talbot winced.

She seized the phone.

"You heard all that?" Bering said into the phone, her eyes boring in on Talbot like a diamond-bit drill. She listened. "Right. The basement. If he doesn't cooperate, we'll deal with him accordingly. Get over here fast."

She slammed the phone down, pulled out her gun, and pointed it at Talbot.

"You're leading the way. If she's down in the range, you're going to talk to her as if you had never met us. And I'll have this pointed right at your head."

"Are you mad?" Talbot asked. "Surely this is improper—"

Bering shoved Talbot out the door. She kept her gun in constant contact with his back, making sure he could feel the hard metal.

"Will one of you please tell me what's going on?" Talbot said, making one last stab at keeping his dignity intact.

Bering looked at Greene. She gave him a slight nod.

"Your young friend is a cold-blooded killer," Greene muttered. "She's responsible for at least five deaths. That includes a fellow who was about to get married. She killed him by tying him up and chopping his arm off. The G7 leaders are her next intended targets, twenty-four hours from now."

That shut Talbot up. He looked as if he were in shock. He better get over it fast, Bering thought as she goose-stepped him down the hallway toward the staircase.

KEON

23.75 HOURS MORE

KEON KNEW THE FASTEST way to get to Hart House was on foot. It would take longer to get a squad car and try to get through the midday traffic. Even worse, all the streets around Hart House were barricaded off. A few years earlier, a bomb blast in Blackpool had almost killed Margaret Thatcher. No civilians were going to get within half a mile of Hart House until the summit was over.

Besides, Keon didn't want anyone to know where he was going.

He'd walked from his office to Hart House hundreds of times to meet Talbot. Often they'd have lunch in the Great Hall. In the summer they'd sit out on the spacious stone patio. Keon, who hated fancy restaurants, always enjoyed the collegial comforts of the university he never got to attend.

On a typical day it was a pleasant fifteen-minute walk. Keon's route wound through the stone arches and green fields of the University of Toronto, where it felt like he was at an ancient university, not right in downtown Toronto.

Today there was no time for a leisurely stroll. Keon rushed down the back stairs of police headquarters and burst out the fire exit onto Jarvis Street. He wouldn't be able to do this at the fancy new building, he thought as he rushed down the leafy residential street, crossed on a yellow light at Yonge Street, and hurried in a half walk, half run to Bay Street.

The sun was hot and the streets were clogged with traffic. Keon felt perspiration form under the back of his collar. The ugly plastic phone grew sweaty in his palm and he felt like tossing it into a garbage can.

In another few minutes he'd made it to University Avenue. He paused to catch his breath and looked across Queen's Park Circle and the Parliament buildings there. Beyond that he could see the clock tower of Hart House.

All about, people had laid out blankets and were picnicking. Smiling, laughing, playing. The people, the city, it had been his lifelong mission to protect.

Aubrey, how could you be so stupid, he thought again as a black squirrel ran across his path. And to think you pulled me out of the river, and now this.

GREENE

23.75 HOURS MORE

THE HART HOUSE ATHLETIC wing was a throwback to a more gentlemanly time. Completed in 1919, women were not allowed in until 1972. Before that, naked men strode casually through the brick-lined sports facility and played squash in their jockstraps without a thought.

Greene knew the place well: the bustling sound of crashing metal weights mixing with the pounding of runners on the track and the swish of basketballs hitting their mark, the pungent aroma of seven decades of baked-on perspiration and creaky wood floors, the old-fashioned tiled bathroom, and the fluffy white towels usually dispensed by a proud World War II vet.

Today it was eerily quiet. Greene and Bering led Talbot through the main door past the weight room, down the brick-lined stairs into the basement, and then down a passageway to the subbasement. A discreet sign with the words FIRING RANGE written in tight script pointed the way.

"Keep it simple," Greene whispered as they descended. "Tell her you're doing a final check of the building before it's closed down. You understand she may have lost track of the time. Get her out into the hallway and we'll take over. And no matter what, don't enter the room. If you so much as take one step inside, I'll shoot you right through the head. Got it?"

Talbot nodded grimly.

At the bottom of the stairs, Talbot led them along a narrow hallway. Near the end a thick metal door was slightly ajar. Talbot pointed at it and Greene nodded. Bering positioned herself at the top of the doorframe. Greene squatted below her.

Greene motioned Talbot forward. Talbot took a deep breath, tightened his back, straightened his tie and, like an actor making an entrance onstage, strode confidently up to the door.

Greene could hear the regular *pop, pop* of a rifle being fired. The shooter's timing was constant, like a metronome. It was a sign of someone who was experienced with a high-powered gun.

"Hello, knock, knock, Felicia," Talbot called from the entranceway.

"She's wearing earmuffs," he muttered under his breath to Greene and Bering. "This might take a few minutes."

"Hello, Felicia, hello," Talbot yelled much louder and rapped on the door with his knuckles. In a few seconds his face broke into an angelic smile.

The guy deserved an Oscar, Greene thought.

"I'm so sorry to disturb you, but the building is being cleared out on the hour."

"Oh, I lost track of time," Greene heard the woman say. It was the first time he'd heard her speak. Her voice was surprisingly deep. "I came straight down after my run. I'm shooting really well. Come see my targets."

Greene looked up and saw Bering ready her gun right at Talbot's temple. Talbot toed the metal threshold like a trapeze artist, but didn't cross it.

"You really must hurry," Talbot said. "Show me them later?"

"I'll see you upstairs," she said.

Greene saw Talbot falter. His Adam's apple slid up and down twice.

"That's not a good idea, I'm afraid," Talbot said. "No one knows about the master key I've given you, and, with all the security coming into the building, it would be better if we went out together. I need to lock up the whole athletic wing."

"Okay. It'll take a minute for me to clean out my rifle."

Talbot smiled his sweetest smile and Greene understood why. She sounded normal, guileless, like a friendly university student. Could this whole thing be a massive misunderstanding? Talbot had identified her in the composite drawing, but how accurate was that?

Time seemed to slide slowly forward as Greene heard the familiar sounds of cartridges being emptied from the rifle, the weapon being opened and swabbed. He wanted to whisper to Talbot, "What's happening?" but he didn't dare. He heard the click of the gun case being shut and footsteps approach the door. As the woman came closer he tightened his grip on his gun.

"Here is my best target, Aubrey," she said. Greene was surprised to hear her call Talbot by his first name. She was moving fast. For a horrible moment he thought she was going to run up and give Talbot a hug. Then her body popped into view.

"Freeze. Hands up. Don't move!" Bering shouted. She was on the woman's left side. She jammed her gun into the side of her face. Felicia raised her arms immediately, the paper target still in her hand.

Bering wasted no time. She pulled out a second gun and pointed it straight at Talbot.

"Talbot, down on the floor, spread eagle," she barked. "Arms all the way above your head!"

Talbot stared at her in alarm.

"What's the meaning of—"

"Down, Talbot, in three or I shoot both of you. I'm not taking any chances."

"But—"

Bering didn't wait. She shot at a spot slightly to the left of Talbot's head. The bullet ricocheted off a brick, raising a plume of dust. The boom of the gun echoed through the hallway.

Talbot scrambled to the floor like a scared rabbit. Bering turned to Greene, who was crouched on the woman's right side.

"Is this her? Greene, can you make a positive ID?"

Everything had happened so fast. Greene started to rise as he looked at Felicia. She kept looking straight ahead. He could see the side of her face. Did he recognize her?

"Mr. Talbot, I don't understand," Felicia said. "What's this about?"

Bering kept her gun trained on the woman's head. Greene looked at the target. The bull's-eye was shredded. Not one miss. Felicia began to lower her hands.

"This is about you keeping your arms in the air," Bering said.

The lighting in the hallway was dim. The air stank of permanent musk, now mixed with the smell of fresh gunpowder.

Talbot was curled up into a ball. "No, no," he moaned. "There must be some kind of mistake."

"Talbot, shut up," Bering said, like a mother trying to cut off a petulant child.

"Greene," Bering said. "Can you make her?"

Greene was standing now. The woman was shaking. He could only see one side of her face, and it was covered with tears. It was her. He was almost certain. But she looked so helpless. He lowered his gun and stepped closer to get a better look.

"See, he's not sure," Talbot said, lifting himself off the floor.

"I told you, Talbot, shut up," Bering screamed. "Greene! I need an ID. Yes or no," she demanded.

Footsteps clattered behind them on the stairs. "Nora, it's Charlie," a loud voice boomed out. "Are you okay?"

Felicia turned away from Greene.

Bering shouted: "Greene, down!"

He ducked.

Bering's gun exploded. The blast shattered the tense silence. The gun rang out again two more times in rapid succession. Blood and skin and bone flew against the wall. The booming noise echoed in his head.

"What!" Talbot screamed. "What have you done?"

"Stand back, stand back," Bering said, her voice high and strained.

Greene had seen Felicia's head jerk back when she was hit by the bullets, and now she lay on the ground, the left side of her face shattered.

"Don't go near her hands!" Bering yelled.

"Are you crazy?" Talbot said. "You killed her!"

"Nora." Greene heard Keon's voice right behind them.

Bering was breathing heavily.

"Hands?" Greene said, dazed.

Bering still had her gun drawn. Felicia lay on the concrete floor, inches from Talbot, the target still gripped in her hand. Bering deftly put her right toe on the corner of the paper and pried it loose. Hidden beneath, in the dead woman's hand, were three small needle-tipped arrows.

"Nora, Greene, are you all right?" Keon asked, gasping for breath.

Bering nodded. "Look at those needles. Poison. One for each of us."

Greene looked up at Bering. She'd saved his life.

Talbot moaned, writhing on the floor.

"That's how she killed all those people," Bering said as she carefully worked one of the needles from the dead woman's hand. "Look at the torque on this thing."

She aimed it at one of the remaining targets at the far end of the firing range.

Greene heard a click and a loud whistling sound as the small arrow tore across the room and slammed into it, right on the bull's-eye.

Bering met Greene's eyes. "Do me one favour."

"Anything."

"Never lower your gun on a suspect again." Bering allowed herself a slight smile. "Okay, partner?"

"Deal," Greene said.

TALBOT

21 HOURS MORE

TALBOT CROSSED HIS ARMS in front of his chest and shoved them into his underarms. He began to rock back and forth on the hard steel chair. He stared at the locked door, fixated on the handle.

He'd lost all track of time. Back in the basement of Hart House, after Nora Bering shot Felicia, events happened so fast his head was still reeling. Blood was everywhere. His clothes, his face were covered. Then he'd seen Keon run down the hallway.

"Charlie!" he had said.

"Don't say a word, Aubrey," Keon answered, not even looking at him before he turned and grasped both police officers by the shoulders. "Great work, are you two okay?"

"We're fine," Bering said, before pointing to the poison needles in Felicia's hand. "It must be strong stuff. Have it tested right away."

"That's probably why everywhere she goes people drop dead of heart attacks," Greene said. He looked at Talbot. "What should we do with him?"

Keon looked at him. Talbot tried to smile. He'd never seen Keon look so angry. There was a rumble of noise down the hall, and a row of police officers rushed toward them. Keon looked away.

"Bring this man to headquarters immediately," Keon said. It was as if he were some kind of criminal. "He doesn't need to be in a cell, but put him in the isolation room in the basement."

"But, Charlie?" Talbot tried to get to his feet.

Keon shook his head. "Officers Bering and Greene, I want you to interrogate him. And take your time."

Talbot watched Charlie Keon, his oldest friend, walk away without looking back. He was so shocked, he didn't even call out. Two burly officers took him by the upper arms, and the next few minutes were a blur: he was handcuffed, his arms behind his back, rushed out the side door, shoved into a squad car with two men on each side, driven to the sally port under police headquarters, brought down to the basement in a dingy service elevator, and deposited in this room, where he'd waited.

Finally a man wearing a bow tie walked in. Talbot recognized Jameson from their interview the day before.

"I don't think your old Oxford chum Margaret would be too impressed if she heard about this, do you, Mr. Talbot?" he said.

"I don't know what you're talking about. I thought Felicia was just another undergraduate student."

"Just another student with a key to the firing range twenty-four hours before the G7 leaders arrived. What was your girlfriend doing with the master key?"

Talbot felt like he'd been slapped in the face. Don't be ridiculous, he wanted to scream, she's not my girlfriend! But he went limp; his mouth sagged open, no sound came out.

The man looked squarely at Talbot. He had a young-looking face. But his eyes were angry and hateful. "You're the kind of fatuous twerp who puts every security operation in grave danger. I hope you're cleaning toilets in the janitor's office when this is all done." He turned and walked out the door, slamming it behind him.

Talbot didn't know how long he sat in the room after that. He didn't even bother to try the door. He knew it would be locked.

Eventually Bering and Greene came in. He told them the whole story. Although there were forty-five thousand full-time students at the University of Toronto, only a handful knew that there were rooms available for them to rent at Hart House. He kept it that way. Last year he'd received Felicia's application, and her letter of introduction had a certain sophistication that appealed to him. She was accepted, like all applicants, sight unseen.

Sight unseen, Talbot thought as he looked up at the two police officers. He didn't want to tell them that in all his years at the university, he'd never seen a sight like her. She tried to hide her beauty under bulky sweatshirts, pulled-back hair, and the occasional pair of glasses, but she was irresistible. That she was shy, perfectly mannered, and unceasingly polite added to the magic spell she had over him.

"One day, about three months after she arrived, she called down to the front desk," Talbot continued. "I took the call. Her sink was plugged and she'd tried for hours to unplug it. I went upstairs to fix it."

Talbot could still see her in the doorway. She said she hadn't expected someone so soon. She was wearing a red T-shirt and a pair of white painter pants.

He could tell she wasn't wearing a bra. Probably no underwear either. The moment was so intoxicating, even now. Thankfully these police officers couldn't read his mind, he thought.

"I went inside and turned off the water main, unscrewed the pipe, and cleaned it out. When I was done, I looked around. The room was Spartan."

Talbot looked down again. He wanted to ask for a glass of water, but he didn't have the nerve. "Maybe I wanted to impress her."

He began to cry. His tears turned to sobs. "I—I—I told her about the G7 summit and how the final photo opportunity was going to take place 'right there' and I pointed out into the quad. I—I never thought . . ."

Neither of the police officers moved. Talbot wiped his face with his sleeve.

"'I'd offer you a cup of coffee, but we're not allowed to cook anything in our rooms,' she said. I saw she had several books of Keats poems. I told her my thesis had been about Keats in Rome. She'd been to the museum at his last apartment at the bottom of the Spanish steps. And that's how it started. I would bring coffee up in Styrofoam cups and we would talk for hours. Just talk."

"What else happened?" Bering asked.

"Nothing!" He was angry. "I already told that Jameson fellow, she was not my girlfriend! This was not about sex, I swear."

He was breathing hard now, but was afraid to look up after his outburst. No one said anything. He felt cold.

Finally, Greene spoke. "What did it feel like when you were alone with her?"

The question took Talbot off guard.

"Very special, wasn't it?" Greene asked.

Talbot nodded. He put his head in his hands. "We'd read sonnets to each other. I know it sounds ridiculous."

"No, it doesn't," Greene said, much to his surprise. "The sonnets are beautiful."

Greene seemed bright, Talbot thought.

"She hated the way men were always watching her. I think she felt safe with me."

"I understand," Greene said, and he seemed to. After all these rough officers, it was nice to have a policeman he could talk to.

"When did you give her the key?" Greene asked gently.

"About three months ago."

"And why did she want it?"

"To go swimming. You won't understand. But, well, she loved to swim in the dark, when no one could see her. I had a copy made."

"It was a master key to the athletic wing, wasn't it?"

"Yes."

"And the firing range, that had a special key?"

"Yes."

"And when did you make her a copy of that?"

"About a month later. But I never . . . "

Talbot's shoulders started to heave as a fresh wave of tears streamed down his cheeks. The only sound in the room was his sobs.

Without saying another word, Greene and Bering got up and walked out, locking the door behind them, leaving him alone, rocking on his chair like an old man looking toward the end of his life.

GREENE

20 HOURS MORE

AFTER THEIR INTERVIEW WITH Talbot in the basement at police headquarters, Bering told Greene she was heading back to the hotel room. There were more police officers' notebooks she wanted to review.

Greene wanted to go back to Hart House to take one more look at the quadrangle. When he walked up the stone steps to the big oak front door, an officer stepped out and stopped him.

"Sorry, sir," the woman said. "The facility is closed."

"I know," Greene said, taking out his badge and ID. "I'm Toronto police."

The woman took Greene's credentials, examined them, shook her head. "My orders are no exceptions."

Greene heard a man's voice behind the cop. "You can allow Officer Greene through," he said. "I've given him total access to the building for the next twenty-four hours."

Greene saw Jameson, wearing a red, white, and blue bow tie today, approach.

"My apologies, Officer Greene," Jameson said. "This won't happen again. I've passed around the photo and the clearance for you and your partner, Officer Bering. Until we're done here, you can both come and go as you please."

"Thanks," Greene said, taking back his badge and ID. He went inside and headed to the Great Hall. Jameson walked beside him.

They kept going in silence. Greene was determined not to say the first word. Or to thank Jameson for letting him in.

"Good work," Jameson said at last. "Your chief Keon got it right to give you this mission."

Greene nodded, not willing to give Jameson the satisfaction of acknowledging his compliment, and walked into the Great Hall. It was being readied for tomorrow's big lunch. People scurrying all about working on the table settings.

Greene stopped and looked around. "I've studied the timetable for tomorrow," he said to Jameson. "After the leaders have their lunch here, they'll head to the quadrangle. I always loved walking out there after a meal."

Saying that, he pushed through the glass doors that led out onto the large stone patio. Jameson stayed with him until they came to the spot where the leaders would stand for their photo shoot.

On the lawn, workers were setting up chairs in long rows for the visitors and press.

The patio straddled the east side of the quadrangle. Greene went up to the low stone wall, peered across and up at the three dormer windows on the third floor. The middle room, where the woman had lived, was dead centre, right in line with where he was standing. The dormers cast a deep shadow. She could easily have hidden under the eaves on the north side, out of sight of anyone in the nearby clock tower to the south. He remembered Bering saying that for the seven minutes the leaders were on this patio there would be no helicopters overhead.

The clock tower bell finished its four-part chime, and then the bell rang five times: *Bong. Bong. Bong. Bong. Bong.*

Greene looked at his watch. It was five o'clock. He remembered his university days here, racing through the campus, late for some class, as the clock tower bell tolled out the hour, always perfectly in time.

As the sound of the bell faded, the sun came around the tower and struck him in the eyes. He turned away. Jameson did too.

Greene pointed to the tower. "The afternoon sun will blind everyone on this patio. I assume you've sealed off the clock tower."

"We'll have three marksmen there for protection, twenty men inside the building, and another twenty in this quadrangle."

Greene ran his hand along the stone wall. "When I was an undergraduate," he said, "I'd save up my money so once a week I could have lunch here."

"In the four years you were studying English literature," Jameson said.

Startled, Greene turned and looked at Jameson.

"Before you went to law school for a year, dropped out, and went to police college," Jameson added.

Greene turned back across the lawn and watched some technicians setting up stands for TV cameras.

"You investigated me?" he asked Jameson, without looking at him.

"We always do."

Greene laughed.

"As you and Officer Bering have demonstrated today, good intelligence is best done in the field, not in an office building."

"I'm not an intelligence officer, I'm a cop."

This time Jameson laughed. "But for how long?"

Greene turned and looked Jameson face on. "Are you asking me to apply to your agency?"

"You can't apply. The only way to join is to be asked."

"Lucky me. No one has asked me."

"Maybe I'm asking you now."

Greene shook his head. "How about you? You've never been a cop, have you?"

To Greene's surprise, Jameson pulled off his ever-present bow tie. "I bet you think I'm some trust-fund kid who went to an Ivy League school." His voice sounded entirely different. American Midwestern. No more faux-English accent.

"Princeton? Oxford?"

"Nope. Ohio State. Father was a truck driver, Mom died when I was thirteen. I got a full scholarship to Oxford for graduate school, turned it down, and went to the London School of Economics instead."

"Better scholarship?"

"No, better professor. Came back home. Was a street cop in Cleveland, recruited by the FBI. Spent ten years clawing my way up the ladder from a field office to headquarters in Washington before I got tapped on the shoulder by the agency for this job."

Greene looked down at the stone patio and found a small pebble. He picked it up and squeezed it between the thumb and forefinger of his right hand.

"In my line of work, I need people who never let their guard down, never give up," Jameson said. "I kept the bureaucrats away from you and your boss. I wanted to see how good you were."

Greene looked across again at the three dormer windows on the third floor. He tossed the pebble into the nearest flower bed.

"You were the mysterious source for the leak, weren't you?" he said.

Jameson broke into a wide smile. "Very good, Officer Greene. Or should I say Detective Greene? Yes, I had the intel and passed it along to Keon without him knowing where it came from. When he picked you, I had the agency do a complete background check."

"Well," Greene asked Jameson, squinting as the sun burst past the clock tower and full into his face, "did I pass your little test?"

BERING

14 HOURS MORE

BERING WAS BACK IN her hotel room, pacing. It was coming up to eleven o'clock, time to do her push-ups. But she was tired. So tired. And restless. They'd killed Felicia, and that should be the end of it.

Job done.

But . . .

Something still didn't quite fit. How had Felicia got through the roadblock? Why had Greene hesitated to make a positive ID? And most of all, tracking down this "Felicia" hadn't been that difficult. Hadn't it almost seemed too easy?

She looked out onto the street. This time of year it didn't get dark until almost ten o'clock. She saw a group of boisterous men stumble down the sidewalk.

"Hey, man, let's hit another bar!" she heard one of them yell.

"Party hearty!" another one yelled, and the rest of them laughed.

Huh, she thought. She should be so lucky. All afternoon and evening she'd been working her way through the police officers' notebooks. She'd been through the second set from Highway 401, nothing there. Same with the ones covering Highway 2 West. She was near the bottom of the pile of the last set of notebooks from the cops on Highway 2 East. Only two more to go. She still hadn't found a thing.

She yawned. A wave of exhaustion rolled over her. She looked at the final two officers' notebooks.

What the heck. Do them, then she'd be done. Push-ups and sleep.

"Officer Scott Cobalt," Bering muttered to herself, looking at the cover of the next notebook. Great. Another male officer. Let's see how bad his writing is, she thought as she opened it up.

To her pleasant surprise, Cobalt had neat handwriting. He had a thick elastic band around his July 5 page. She flipped to the entry and started reading.

Right away she could see he was a thorough note taker. Must be a veteran. She read entry after entry about the cars he'd stopped. There was nothing of interest. She yawned, lifted her foot to the desk, and tilted her chair back. She got to the last entry and read:

> *Red Dodge Van—82? Lic: MAMABEAR. Name: Janice Wellman. AKA Mama Bear. Female, w, Addr: 22 Cadding Court, 26yrs. old, h.t, bl hr. Two gs, tw, 6–7. No a.c —v. hot. Ch u bd w. e.b. in bk. Neg. Claims coming from Mtrl, but tls and kds b. suit v. w. Very a.s. Hates to be called "ma'am."*

She put her foot down on the floor and sat straight up. She read the entry again. "Wait a second," she said to herself as she checked her hand-made map for the location where Cobalt had been stationed. With a pencil and her ruler, she started doing calculations.

"Jesus." She called the Brockville OPP detachment and introduced herself. "It's urgent that I talk to Officers Brian Gabriel and Scott Cobalt immediately."

The cop on the other end of the line put her on hold for a minute.

Bering picked up the notebook and reread the entries. What did all this shorthand mean? Especially this entry: *Claims coming from Mtrl, but tls and kds b. suit v. w.*

"Scotty is going to be a problem," the officer said when she got back online. "He's at his cottage up north. No phone."

"How about Gabriel?"

"He just did a ten-hour shift, but we got him out of bed. I'll patch you through."

A tired voice came on the line. "Officer Bering?"

"Yes, hello, Officer Gabriel. Nora Bering, Ari Greene's partner. We spoke the other day. Greene has told me good things about you."

"Same about you. How can I help?"

"Do you know Officer Scott Cobalt?"

"Scotty? Everyone knows Scotty. Great guy, excellent officer, counting the minutes until he retires. What do you need to know?"

"Ever work with him?"

"Plenty of times."

"He makes the most detailed notes I've ever seen."

"That's a thing with Scotty. We kid him that he should teach penmanship."

"Or hieroglyphics. I'm looking at his notes from the roadblock the other day and trying to decipher some of his shorthand."

"You got me. No one can understand his notes."

"And I understand he's up at a remote cottage with no phone."

"With his wife and granddaughter. He's about to retire, and we're going to miss him. What do you need?"

Bering looked at the notes again. She remembered how Greene had jumped out of the helicopter to try to save Gabriel's friend Wayne Krupp.

"Officer, I know you just got off shift and it's been a long few days," she said, "but I've got a favour to ask you."

THURSDAY

JULY 7, 1988

WHITECASTLE

1 HOUR MORE

THIS WAS GOING TO be the longest day of Whitecastle's life. And he'd had his share of long days—marathon exam-marking sessions, late-night cabinet meetings, an unceasing list of campaign rallies, and the famous night of his election, when the final results weren't confirmed until sunrise.

Those had all been public days. Today the exquisite agony of waiting was something he could share with no one.

This afternoon, he'd taken his daily walk to the town to get his copy of the *Times*. He also purchased the *Daily Telegraph*, the *Guardian*, and even the *Independent*.

That provoked a comment from Tom, the tobacconist who ran the shop and always kept a copy of all the papers for his special customer.

"You sure you want to read that liberal fish wrap, Mr. Prime Minister?" Tom joked.

When he was in office, the *Independent* had been Whitecastle's most vocal critic, and it was an ongoing joke between the two men that the former prime minister shared the same disdain for the newspaper that it had had for him.

"It's for Mrs. Whitecastle," he said. He must avoid any behavior out of the norm. "She wants to read all about this G7 summit in Canada."

"That Mrs. Thatcher seems to be turning into a red Tory, doesn't she?" Tom said, pointing to the prominent headlines in all four newspapers: "'I can do business with that man,' Thatcher says of Gorbachev."

Whitecastle swallowed hard. It was the kind of thing that Alisander and he had predicted. The reason they were taking this drastic action. Keep your emotions under control, he told himself. You must stay calm. Look as if you are disinterested, even to Tom.

"Next thing you know they'll be inviting the Chinese to join their club," Tom said. "Then who? India? Any old country that has the bomb I should think will soon get in."

"Now, Tom," Whitecastle said as he bundled up his newspapers. "I'm certain the prime minister knows what she's doing."

"She knows, all right," Tom said. "Trading with the enemy. Her rich friends will make lots of money from all that Russian oil. And before you know it, there will be some commissar down the road handing me my weekly ration of rubles."

He couldn't have said it better himself, Whitecastle thought, as he patted Tom on the shoulder. "Well, think of the cheap vodka we'll be able to drink," he said with a chuckle.

"I'm serious, sir," the tobacconist said. "You have to think about getting back in the game."

"Oh, Tommy," Whitecastle said, letting out a booming laugh. "Nothing could be further from my mind."

BERING

1 HOUR MORE

BERING STARED AT THE clock. It was noon. One hour more until this G7 thing was all over at last. Time to hit the floor again for her push-ups.

But first she looked at the phone, wishing it would ring.

This Officer Gabriel, who Greene had worked with, was a good guy and he'd done his best. On their call late last night, she'd asked him to drive up to Scott Cobalt's cottage to get him to decipher his notes.

Gabriel had driven up early this morning and called Bering on the radio from his cruiser to report in. He'd arrived at the cottage only to find that Cobalt had already left to go fishing with his granddaughter. According to Cobalt's wife, this was their usual thing and there was no way of knowing when he'd be back. Or where he'd gone.

"She says he has all sorts of secret fishing spots."

"Well," Bering said, "thanks for trying. I'm sorry about your friend Wayne."

"We tried. Frustrating part is I'm sworn to secrecy, can't tell anyone about any of this."

"I know. Listen, I owe you one."

"I'll wait to see if he comes back, but don't count on it."

Bering hit the floor and had just done her tenth push-up when the phone rang. She lunged for it.

"Bering," Gabriel said without even saying hello. "Scotty came back. He's here in the cruiser with me. You ready?"

"Give me a second." She jumped up and grabbed Scotty's notebook. "Thank you, Officer Cobalt."

"Please, call me Scotty. Everyone does," he said with a laugh. "I understand you need me to translate my notes. Don't worry—after all these years I'm used to it."

"Can you please tell me: What does 'h.t, bl hr.' mean?" Bering asked him.

"Heavy-set, black hair."

"I see that. Maybe that's why she has the license plate MAMABEAR."

"I thought so too," Cobalt said.

"What about 'Two gs, tw,'?"

"Twin girls."

"Makes sense, but I can't figure out: 'Ch u bd w. e.b. in bk.'"

He laughed. "I was getting tired at the end of my shift. Means 'checked under the bed in back that the mother said she'd built. C.b. is my expandable baton. I stuck it in to make sure no one was hiding under there."

Bering thought of how the woman they were chasing had curled herself up in the luggage on the train to hide from Greene.

"I didn't feel anything," Cobalt was saying. "The kids were jumping up and down and their mother was yelling at me. That's what I mean by 'very a.s.' Very anti-social. At police college we had this detective who had a theory that fifteen percent of the people will lie to the police about any and everything. Doesn't mean they're guilty, just natural-born liars. Genetically anti-social."

"Is that why you wrote about the towels . . . ?"

"Yeah. She claimed she was coming from Montreal, but the towels and bathing suits were wet. Typical. Lie about something unimportant just because I was a police officer. She was hassling me the whole time to stop poking around and let them get going."

Bering stared at the veteran police officer's notes.

She could picture the whole scene. Cobalt had been out in the hot sun for hours, his shift almost over. Along comes this overheated mother with a couple of screaming kids and she starts giving him the gears. He pulls out his baton, jabs it under the bed once or twice, doesn't feel anything, and waves them on. But he's a good cop. While he's working, he gets her talking. She tells him they're coming from Montreal. He notices the towels and bathing suits are wet.

"Thanks, Scotty," she said. "This was very helpful. Enjoy your time with your granddaughter."

She hung up and rushed over to her desk to look at her homemade map again. The towels and bathing suits were wet, Scotty, she thought, because your roadblock was the first exit west of Mallorytown Beach.

Bingo.

Mama Bear and her brood weren't coming from Montreal, they were coming back from the beach. She was hassling you to stop because she'd hidden the assassin under the bed.

She folded the notebook back up, stuffed it in her pocket, yanked the door open, and yelled, "Mudhar, get the cruiser!"

TALBOT

1 HOUR MORE

TALBOT WASN'T SURE HOW much more of this he could take. He'd been held a virtual prisoner in this windowless room all night, given only a thin blanket to sleep on the floor. They'd taken away his tie, his shoelaces, and even his watch. He had no idea now what time it was. Had he missed everything? All he could do was stare at the door, hoping it would open and someone would come in and get him.

When at last it did open, to his great relief he saw it was his best and oldest friend, Charlie Keon.

"I'm so very glad you are here," he said.

Keon pulled out a handkerchief and handed it to Talbot.

Talbot took it and wiped his eyes. He blew his nose. "Handkerchiefs. Charlie, I bet we're two of the last people who still carry around a handkerchief."

"Young people today think that everything is disposable," Keon said. His face was ashen.

"I'm a total wreck. What's going on? Why in heaven's name—"

Keon cut him off. "Aubrey. Do you have any idea what you almost did? The eight world leaders could have all been killed right on the terrace of your precious Hart House, to say nothing of you and me."

"I know, I just—"

"You just what, Aubrey? Put your brain in your pants?"

"There was no sex with her."

"I don't care."

"Is it, the ceremony, is it over?"

"No, it's an hour from now."

After twenty-four hours of hell, Talbot felt some hope.

"An hour? Can I—"

"The Americans want you drawn and quartered. But I've convinced them that if you're not out there on that patio it would look wrong after all the publicity you've got. So here's the deal. You're getting out of here to clean yourself up. I called your house, and Gwen brought you a change of clothes."

"Thank you. She must be so worried—"

"No, she isn't. I told her that you and me and all of us have been on lockdown by special order of the head of security. What I didn't tell your wife is that her husband is a bloody fool, though believe me, I was tempted."

Talbot felt a sense of relief wash over him.

"You've got ten minutes to wash up, then we'll go over to the Great Hall. We'll be there in time for dessert, then you and me, two boys from the East End of Toronto, will escort the seven G7 leaders out onto the patio. You'll lead the way. Gorbachev will come last and I'll be behind him. The eyes of the world will be upon us and we'll be all smiles."

"Thank you, thank you, Charlie." Everything was going to be okay, Talbot thought at last. Everything was going to work out.

"Don't thank me." Keon took two pieces of folded paper from his breast pocket. "Sign these."

"What are they?"

"First one is a nondisclosure agreement. You ever breathe a word about this to anyone, and that includes Gwen and—"

"Okay, of course, okay," Talbot said. "I promise, you know I won't—"

"Sign."

Keon took out a pen, clicked it, and handed it over.

Talbot took it. He could see his hand was shaking. He'd always been so proud of his penmanship. This time all he could do was scratch out his name.

He looked up. "What's the second paper?" he asked.

"Your letter of resignation." Keon's voice was flat.

"Resignation? But, you know—"

"I know. This is your dream job. You've told me that a million times. You have all your plans of things you want to do here. Make Hart House a world-class centre for the arts and literature."

Talbot nodded. He looked at Keon hopefully. "You know how important that is. With the whole world turning away from the value of a strong liberal education."

But Keon shook his head.

"It's over. Sign or I'll have no choice but to feed you to the wolves."

Talbot saw Keon scratch that old wound on the back of his head. From the rock in the river, where Talbot had saved him.

"Aubrey," Keon said. "Until today, I thought you were the smartest person I'd ever met."

"I'll sign." Talbot could hear how meek his voice sounded.

He tried to steady his hand when he signed the second document. But it was no use. He put down his signature as best he could and handed the paper back.

"Charlie, I would never have made it through public school without you," he said.

Keon frowned, turned toward the door. Talbot grasped his arm, but Keon broke free and barreled out of the room, slamming the door shut behind him.

Leaving Talbot alone, Keon's pen the only thing in his hand.

BERING

35 MINUTES MORE

BERING HAD INSTRUCTED PC Mudhar to park the police cruiser a block away from the town house so that she could approach it without any visible police backup. She didn't want to scare the woman off.

She approached the small cement porch and pushed aside a collection of tricycles and sand toys, opened the aluminum screen door, and knocked on the plywood door. She checked her watch. It was 12:25. Thirty-five minutes more.

Bering hadn't brought anything with her. No gun, no notebook, no baton, not even her radio. She was out of uniform. Her badge was tucked into her front-left pocket. In her back-right pocket there was a piece of paper, folded neatly into three parts.

"Be there in a second," a husky female voice said from inside. "Bethy, I thought I told you to put your towel out on the railing."

The door had a peephole, and Bering expected she'd be inspected before it opened. To her surprise, she heard footsteps approach and the door opened right away.

"Hi! What can I do for you?" The woman standing there was wearing a billowing T-shirt with the words MOTHER OF ALL MOTHERS on the front. Stringy hair hung over her puffy face.

Last night Bering had researched Ms. Janice Wellman, a.k.a. Mama Bear. Wellman had no criminal record, but there had been two police contacts—both times when her ex-husband, a jerk named Randy Kline, assaulted her. When he got out of jail the second time, Kline tried to get access to Wellman's twin girls. When she wouldn't let him near them, Kline ran to the Children's Aid Society and alleged Wellman had abused the kids. A few days later, welfare and public housing both got anonymous tips that Mama Bear had a man in her house. None of it was true. Luckily, she had a good social worker, Ellen Brightstone, who took her side and closed the file. The joys of being poor, Bering thought—you get to have all these professionals snooping in your washroom to see if the toilet seat is up or down.

"My name is Nora Bering," Bering said as she slipped her foot in the doorframe.

"Look, if you're a Jehovah's Witness or something, I've got two kids and—"

"Janice, I need to talk to you." Bering kept her voice low. "Don't worry, it isn't about your kids and it isn't about Randy. It's about that beautiful woman you picked up at Mallorytown Beach. I'm a police officer and it's urgent."

Wellman took a moment to take this all in. "Look, lady, I don't have a clue what you're talking about and my girls are expecting me to take them to the swimming pool and Dairy Queen."

"Bethy and Barbie can wait." Bering pulled out her badge. "If you try to close this door I'll strong-arm it open, and I'll have Ellen Brightstone down here so fast you won't see your kids for a year."

Wellman looked at Bering in horror. "You couldn't. They closed the file."

"You're still on the register. One more anonymous tip and the CAS would be all over you. I'd hate to do it, but . . . "

"Yeah, right. You cops are all the same," Wellman said, backing up ever so slightly.

"I know that Randy was a total shit and his claim against you is nonsense," Bering said, putting the rest of her leg through the doorway. "Janice, talk to me for ten minutes, that's all I ask, and I'll get your record expunged for good. I can do it. One hundred percent clean."

Wellman took a deep breath, weighing her options.

Bering thought she'd lost her, until Wellman's shoulders slackened.

"Okay, come in," she said with as little enthusiasm as she could muster. "I'll send the kids out back. But I don't know a thing about any Mallorytown Beach."

KEON

35 MINUTES MORE

"CHIEF KEON, WHERE'S THAT phone you've been carrying around all week?" a familiar voice asked Keon as he stood alone by the French doors that opened onto the Hart House quadrangle. He'd arrived with Talbot five minutes earlier and had no appetite. No interest in eating.

Keon looked around and saw Jameson had come up behind him wearing a green bow tie.

Keon pointed to the tie. "You're looking very Irish today," he said.

"In honour of Ronald Reagan and your prime minister Mulroney. You have a brush of the Irish too, don't you?"

Keon laughed. "Just a touch." He pulled the phone from his briefcase. "The stupid thing never works properly. I screwed it up. The battery is dead yet again."

"How convenient for you," Jameson said.

"You kidding?" Keon said. "This phone cost the force thousands of dollars and every time I go into a tunnel it cuts out. The reception is terrible and you have to fiddle with the battery before you recharge it, or some such nonsense. When I really need it, the darn thing never seems to work. I feel naked without my radio. You call that convenient?"

"Very," Jameson said. "You used it as an excuse so the committee couldn't get in touch with you."

"Why would I want to do that?"

"I asked myself that same question. How about this for a short list?" Jameson began to slowly count off on his fingers. "One, by giving the committee the impression that you were some local cop who couldn't even find his way to a phone booth; two, you didn't have to give the committee detailed reports about Greene and Bering's progress; which, three, meant no other police forces were involved; which, four, means the whole thing didn't get messed up by a bunch of half-assed cops who have all the toys and none of the street smarts to get the job done; so that, five, you could protect your people in the field."

Jameson held out his now open palm. "Chief?"

Keon looked back at the quadrangle and allowed himself a wry smile "My mother once told me there are two types of people, Mr. Jameson. People who bitch about things and people who do something about the things the other people bitch about."

Jameson laughed aloud. "My mother also told me there were two types of people. Those who brown their marshmallows and those who burn them."

Keon chuckled. "Jameson, I thought you had me pegged days ago. Why didn't you make me come clean with the committee?"

"Because, sir, even though I don't have a uniform, I'm still a cop. There's one thing any good cop can spot right away."

"What's that?"

"Another good cop."

"You mean Greene?" Keon asked.

Jameson nodded. "The last thing I'd ever do is get in the way of a good officer in the field."

"Why did you ride him so hard?"

"I wanted to confirm I was right."

"And?"

"I think you know the answer."

35 MINUTES MORE

"HERE'S MY BADGE," BERING said, sitting on a plastic chair in Mama Bear's galley kitchen. "Get me a pen and paper, and I'll write out my name, my home address, home phone number—you name it."

"Here." Wellman reached up to a shelf above the table and brought down a red coloured pencil and a piece of yellow construction paper.

"There. You have all my information," Bering said once she'd finished writing. "You'll be glad to know this is against regulations."

"So why do it?"

Bering glanced at her watch. "Because I have about thirty minutes to try to save eight lives. Listen carefully."

She told Wellman everything: the tip about the assassin coming to Toronto to kill the world leaders; how Greene had started following her; the dead bodies in Vermont and Quebec; the lawyer, Wayne Krupp, and the child at the resort; the massive roadblock and fruitless search; and how she'd gone through hundreds of police officers' notebooks and found the entry about Wellman and why it was suspicious. She told Wellman she was acting on her own. And that at one o'clock everyone would be out on the patio at Hart House, and if the killer was still out there, it could be catastrophic.

"All of this information is classified, top secret," Bering said. "If it ever gets out I told you this, there goes my badge, my pension, everything."

"This is all interesting, lady—"

"Nora."

"Fine, Nora. What does it have to do with me?"

Bering kept on talking. "This woman you picked up from Mallorytown Beach has eluded everyone. I don't know how she does it, beyond being exceptionally, highly trained. But she does."

"Look, my van was searched by that old cop. Ask him. There was no one there but me and the twins."

"Officer Scott Cobalt. He took perfect notes. How the kids were acting up in back and how messy the van was. How hot it was. How he was at the end of his shift. How you were giving him the gears. How he poked his baton under the built-in bed one time and how you started wailing at him to hurry up."

"Right. I told him to search all he wanted."

"You made it as difficult as you could. Look how neat your home is. You told your girls to mess up the van and act up. You saved the life of a good man. His daughter is a hooker in Toronto, so he and his wife are raising their granddaughter."

Silence descended on the kitchen. Wellman had crossed her arms in front of her chest. She wasn't going to say another word.

"Thirty minutes to go," Bering said, looking at her watch.

"No, five minutes. You said you wanted to talk to me for ten minutes. Five more to go." Wellman tightened her lips and pointed to the digital clock on the microwave. "If you aren't out the door by twelve thirty-five, I'll call the cops."

GREENE

30 MINUTES MORE

IN HIS SECOND YEAR at the University of Toronto, the idiosyncratic charm of Hart House took hold of Greene. At lunchtime he ate steam-tray meals in the magnificent Great Hall, after class he exercised in the dilapidated, brick-lined gymnasium, and at night he'd drink English draft beer and play darts in the underground pub.

Or he'd go up to the second-floor reading room, where first editions lay casually on shelves and open-mouthed students fell asleep on the overstuffed red cushioned chairs and sofas. He loved the eccentric clubs at Hart House. Where else would you find crossbow, fencing, revolver, and rifle clubs—plus a barbershop, a chapel, two grand pianos, and a full gym—all under one slate roof? The place became his second home. And in his third year, he'd moved into one of the three rooms on the third floor.

After lunch one wet November day in that third year, he drifted into the reading room and discovered a standing rack full of newspapers from all over the world. They were displayed on long wooden reading poles, through which pages of the papers were weaved.

He put down his knapsack and picked up a day-old copy of the London

Times. He read it through, then the *Washington Post*, the *Melbourne Journal*, and the Cape Town *Standard*. Before he knew it, it was almost six o'clock and it was dark outside. He'd missed three afternoon classes, but he didn't care. Looking up, he noticed a dark-haired woman sitting on the other side of the round wooden table. She was reading the same edition of the London *Times* he'd read. Plucking up his courage, he started a conversation. Her name was Meredith. They ended up having dinner in the Great Hall. Over a tray of overcooked vegetables, which she critiqued mercilessly, their romance began.

It was hard to believe that was almost seven years ago, Greene thought as he wandered into the Reading Room. He eyed the two chairs in the corner, the spot where he'd first seen Meredith sitting, reading.

He smiled to himself. Too bad he didn't have a Polaroid camera so he could take a picture of the chair to show her tomorrow when he drove up to her at the cottage. But then again, if he had a picture, how could he explain what he was doing in Hart House during the final G7 meeting when he was supposedly out on the street directing traffic?

Well, the conference was almost over. The clock tower bell had just rung. Greene had looked at his watch: 12:30. Why bother wearing one? he thought. The old clock still works like a charm.

He'd synchronized his watch with Bering when she'd called him half an hour earlier to tell him about the police officer's notes she'd read about a woman in a van the cop had stopped during the roadblock.

"Something about it feels wrong," she said.

"Go check her out," he said. "But hurry. Not much time left."

He unhooked the radio from his belt and looked down at it, as if by staring at it, he could will Bering to report back to him.

"Keep the radio on at all times," she'd instructed him. "I'm not taking mine with me when I meet with her. That would be too intimidating. Who knows if she has anything to tell me, or even if she'll talk to me? But be ready just in case."

He got up and walked over to the newspaper racks. On the front page of the London *Times* there was a photo of Margaret Thatcher on the green lawn of a golf course in Toronto, carrying her purse. The front page of the *Washington Post* showed the Canadian prime minister kissing Nancy Reagan on the cheek. The *Globe and Mail* had the headline "Leaders Make Overture to Soviets," featuring a photo of Gorbachev shaking hands with the German leader Helmut Kohl.

He headed back out of the room. Walked past the front desk and went out into the quadrangle. A guard on duty nodded at Greene and let him by with a smile.

Jameson had taken Greene around and personally introduced him to all the security personnel.

"This is Officer Greene of the Toronto Police Force," he had told them. "We owe him a great debt of gratitude. He has one hundred percent clearance until the summit is over. Let him pass anywhere at any time." He'd done the same for Bering.

No one outside the security community would ever know what he and Bering had done, but inside this small world they were the celebrities of the moment.

The sun was creeping down the east wall, illuminating the broad stone patio where the G7 leaders would soon be. Behind it, a panel of glass French doors shimmered in the light. The door on the south side would open soon. That's where they'll walk out in a few minutes, he thought.

Assembled on the lawn below the patio, members of a brass band were warming up. Every player had been searched by hand. Their instruments were taken apart and reassembled. Their cases checked for false bottoms. Behind them between rows of black folding chairs, scores of reporters, photographers, and cameramen stirred restlessly. Each had also been hand-searched.

Greene crossed through the crowd of talkative reporters, and peered back up at the third-floor window of the room where Felicia had lived. The Hart House roof was a steep affair made of overlapping green slate tiles. The dormer windows looked like three small sentry boxes, plunked on top of the roof. Even if someone was in there, with the sun in your eyes you'd never see them.

Give it up, Greene thought. You've done your part. Jameson had assured him that they'd double-checked the room.

There was nothing else he could do.

The world's best security people had spent months making sure this place was safe, Greene told himself. So why did he feel so uneasy? He checked his radio again. It was still on.

Bering still hadn't called.

BERING

28 MINUTES MORE

BERING HADN'T MOVED FOR two whole minutes. Neither had Wellman.

"That threat I made at the door about Children's Aid was bullshit," she said finally. It was 12:32. "I'd never call the CAS on you. I only said that so you'd let me in the door. No matter what happens, I'll get your record expunged."

"Nice." Wellman dove into her pack of Exports, lit a cigarette, and tossed the pack back on the table.

Bering picked up the pack and pulled out a cigarette. Wellman eyed her with surprise.

"I used to work morality squad, the Jarvis Track." Bering jumped to her feet, flexed her hips, and popped the cigarette into the side of her mouth. "Hey, buddy! Got a light? It's cold out, isn't it? Want some warmth? How much? Come on, mister, I need three more tricks for my man to make my night. No, I haven't seen the cops around here for hours."

As quickly as she'd put on her act, Bering dropped it. She took the cigarette out of her mouth, put it back on the table, and sat down.

Wellman looked over at her. The silence between them hung heavy. Finally she smiled. They both started to laugh.

"I was good," Bering said, picking up the cigarette and twirling it in her hand.

"I can see that."

"Too good."

"What do you mean?"

Bering rolled the cigarette tightly between her forefinger and her thumb. "I was the best on the force. The toughest, the smartest and, well, the prettiest. They recruited me for a special job. There was a judge down at Old City Hall courts. Japanese Canadian. The first so-called ethnic judge in Toronto. A war hero—in Europe. Believed in civil liberties, prisoner's rights. And the police hated him because, unlike the other judges who would always take the cops at their word when they testified, if he thought they were lying in his courtroom, he'd say so. On the record."

Bering noticed that Wellman was looking at her now, but she kept concentrating on the cigarette, which she was slowly squishing flat.

"They wanted to get rid of him. I didn't want to do it, but the chief of police talked me into it. Said the force needed me. I got myself 'arrested,' with all the girls down in courtroom 125 at Old City Hall. Once the judge released me on bail, I went back to his office, wearing high heels and a real low-cut blouse. Five cops were waiting outside the door. When I saw him, I thought I couldn't go through with it. I was about to whisper to him it was a trap. Before I could say a word, though, he pulled off his black robes and unzipped his pants. He did it so fast. 'Suck it, here, suck,' he told me. I can still hear him saying those words. That was it. I stomped three times on the floor—that was my signal—and all hell broke loose."

A piece of tobacco fell from the end of the cigarette. Bering kept squishing it thinner.

"What happened to the judge?" Wellman asked.

"They arrested him. It was front-page news. All the racists loved it. He had a wife and two daughters. You ever drive over the Danforth bridge?"

"Hundreds of times."

"Next time you do, stop on the north side where there's the lookout point halfway across. Look straight down. That's where he jumped, three days later."

Wellman exhaled a puff of smoke. "Shit." She touched Bering's arm. "You must have been pissed at the chief of police."

Bering lightened her grip on the cigarette and began to roll it back into a cylinder.

"I didn't talk to him for three years, until this week when I got assigned to keeping the world leaders safe. I don't care a fig if they're the eight most powerful people in the world, or eight runaways on Yonge Street. I'm a cop. My job is to save lives."

Over Wellman's shoulder, Bering could see the green digital clock on the microwave clock: 12:35.

"There you have it. The chief and I are the only ones who know the whole story. He owes me big time. He'll do anything I tell him to. When I say I'll get your record expunged, I mean it. Once you have someone's blood on your hands, it doesn't wash off."

Bering's words hung between them. The microwave clock had clicked to 12:37.

She looked over at Wellman. Their eyes met.

She pulled a folded piece of paper from her back pocket. She laid it on the table, face-side down, and slowly unfolded it.

"I got the Children's Aid reports about you this morning. Some things Officer Cobalt said don't fit. He says the girls were ill-behaved and the back of the van was a mess. Every report speaks in glowing terms about how well-behaved your kids are."

"The reports also say it's their compensation for the anti-social attitude of their mother," Wellman snapped.

"So why were they acting up in the van?"

"It was hot, man."

"The reports say you're an extremely neat and clean person. Look at your home. You've got two kids running around, yet it's spotless."

"Fucking social workers," Wellman said. "They all think they're Margaret Mead studying us like we're apes in the jungle."

Bering smiled. When you're interrogating a subject and they don't deny the information you put to them, but attack the source, you know you've got them. Keep talking.

She pulled out the composite drawing.

Her trump card.

"This is a police composite sketch. We think it's close, but the eyes aren't quite right. Apparently the left one was slightly off-centre."

Wellman tried not to look at the piece of paper. Instead, she picked up a stray crayon and scratched off some of the frayed paper near the tip.

Bering waited.

At last Wellman's eyes drifted to the composite.

"This woman killed a five-year-old boy who was in the water and just beyond his mother's reach." Bering allowed an edge of anger into her voice and pointed to the drawing. "This woman ran the boy over with a boat; the propeller sliced his femur and he bled to death before they could get him onto land."

Bering stared back at Wellman. Waited until the woman lifted her head.

"Same age as the twins, wasn't he, Janice?"

Bering saw Wellman's eyes widen. Then, ever so slowly, she nodded.

It was no time to let up. "My partner was in a helicopter when he saw the child's mother covering him up with a sheet on the shore," Bering said, holding her eyes. "It had started to rain, which by my calculations is the time you and the twins left Mallorytown Beach." Bering stabbed the composite with her forefinger. "With her under the bed in your van. Want me to get a search warrant and rip up your handiwork?"

The crayon slipped out of Wellman's hand. They both reached for it at the same time. Their hands touched.

"Janice," Bering said, grasping her wrist. "The kids were acting up in the van because you told them to. And to throw their stuff all around. You wanted that old cop to hurry up his search. No one is blaming you. I'm sure this woman told you some story that made you think she needed your help. It's not your fault. You didn't know."

Wellman didn't resist Bering's grip. "I always thought *Macbeth* was a better play than *Hamlet*," she said.

Bering was stunned. Then she got it. Wellman had picked up Bering's reference from *Macbeth* to the blood not washing off. She'd been doing this job for five years now, she thought, and she still hadn't learned to never, ever, underestimate people.

"She saved my Bethy."

Wellman's voice was such a soft whisper that Bering could hardly hear it. Wellman started to cry. "I promised her . . . "

This was the moment. Wellman's hard shell had cracked. Now Bering had to get inside it and dig for everything that lay there.

"What did you promise this woman?" Bering's voice was quiet now, parroting Wellman, her finger still on the drawing.

"That I'd never tell. Anyone. If I did, she'd kill me. She wiped off all her prints before she left."

"We will move you, Janice. New location, new identity, enough money so you don't have to worry. Ever. Every record, every trace, will be erased. She'll never find you."

Wellman put her head in her hands. "This is all I know, and it's not much."

She told Bering how the mysterious woman had saved her daughter, how the woman's body was so badly scratched and bruised, how the woman told her she'd been abused by a rich man and she'd believed her, how they hid her in the van and brought her home, and how when she left the next day, she warned Janice to never tell a soul. Or else. "And that's all."

"Her eyes?"

Wellman smiled. "Yes. The left one was kind of off-centre."

"Did she tell you her name?"

"No. I never asked."

So close, Bering thought, yet so far.

"Did she leave you a note?"

"No."

"Did she say goodbye to the girls?"

"No."

Bering looked at the microwave: 12:40.

"Did she leave you anything?"

Wellman paused. Bering stared at her.

"There was one thing."

"What?"

"The kids had a fight over a picture of the two of them. They wanted to show it to her and, well, you know how kids are with their 'gimme gimmes.' They ripped it and she fixed it." Wellman reached inside her shirt and pulled out the photograph.

Bering took the picture and held it by the edges. It was chilling to touch something the killer had touched. It was a picture of the twins with their arms around each other. She had to look close to see the rip, which had been carefully repaired with invisible tape.

Bering took a plastic bag from her rear pocket and slipped the picture into it. "I'll get this back to you as soon as I can," she said.

Wellman looked plaintively at the picture as it disappeared into Bering's pocket.

She got up to leave. Wellman really was a Mama Bear, she thought. She'd been honest, told her everything. Too bad it hadn't led anywhere.

Still, Bering had this sense that something didn't fit. But maybe it was sheer exhaustion, maybe it was mental fatigue, maybe there was nothing to it. She'd come to the end of her ability to figure it out. There was nothing more for her to do.

"Thank you so much. I'd like to bring you and the girls up to my father's farm for the time being. He's an old goat living alone up north. He'd love to have them around. I'll shred all your records Monday morning. I appreciate your time. And your honesty."

Bering put the cigarette back in the package and got up to leave.

Wellman got up with her.

"Did this help?" she asked.

"Help? I don't know. It helped me because now I know I've done everything I could. I'll let myself out. I'll call you tomorrow."

Bering closed the door behind her and blinked into the midday sun. The assassin with the heart of gold, she thought, shaking her head. At least for those twin girls.

She walked down the street toward the cruiser. Mudhar had parked it at the bottom of the hill with the tinted windows rolled up. Bering had always wanted to have a sibling, especially a sister. Her mother died when she was young, and she was an only child. All she'd ever had was her father. Imagine what it would be like to have a sister. A friend for life.

Bering stopped right in the middle of the road. The thought hit her so hard it almost knocked her over. "At least for those twin girls," she whispered to herself.

She started to run, frantically flapping her arms. She could see Mudhar look up from the driver's seat with a stunned expression. He started desperately trying to lower the car window.

Bering screamed at the top of her lungs. "Mudhar! Mudhar! The radio, the radio! Mudhar, give me the radio!"

MARINA

15 MINUTES MORE

EVERYTHING IN HER LIFE had been about preparing for this moment, Marina thought as she slid the tip of the rifle through the window and focused the sight down on the patio at the other end of the quadrangle.

She heard the clock tower bell begin to chime. Fifteen minutes to go. Perfect.

The way Alisander had planned it. Everything had worked. The tip he'd planted about an assassin coming across the border had set the trap. Killing the border guard had been the ideal way to announce her arrival. But when that policeman Ari Greene showed up on the bus and her sunglasses had slipped off, she hoped he hadn't noticed her left eye.

Alisander hadn't counted on someone being as persistent as Greene.

Getting off the boat had been a close call. Still, the years of training Alisander had put her through paid off. Besides, it was essential to the plan that she create havoc. Kill enough people all along the way so she left a trail.

"Think of the mother killdeer bird," Alisander had instructed her. "When a predator is nearby, she will fake an injury to her wing and limp away from the nest to protect her young."

Marina thought back to how easy it had been to get into Hart House yesterday. Wearing her hooded red sweatshirt, she'd jogged in the front door. Everyone who saw her—the clerk at the front desk, the janitor in the hall, the regulars in the Reading Room—they all waved.

She ran up to the third-floor room, softly knocked three times, waited, knocked three times again. The door unlocked and she slipped inside. A moment later she was looking at the only family member she'd ever really known. Her twin sister. Her bird with a broken wing.

Marina was amazed at their exact resemblance, after so many years. Her sister's face, her hair, her skin, her body. Everything except her left eye because of the fire so long ago. The doctor had fixed everything else about her face.

"I'm sorry, the optic nerve has been damaged irreparably," he'd said.

"Will she be able to see from it?" Alisander had asked.

"Oh, yes, but it will drift to the side. That we can't change."

Marina and her sister fell into each other's arms. Lay down on the bed in a warm embrace, the same way they'd done when they were children sleeping together in their mother's small shed. They were four years old when, after the fire that killed their mother, Alisander took them. Their training started when they were five, and her sister left for North America when Marina was fourteen.

They held each other and talked in urgent whispers, like schoolgirls on a sleepover. They tried to remember things about their mother, their lives before they were trained to be North American, when they were allowed to speak in the old language.

"Do you ever think in it?" Marina asked.

"Sometimes in my dreams," her sister said. She began to sing a child's lullaby in the language. Marina joined in and they sang it through. Then they laughed and hugged each other.

They had just a few hours together. Marina and her sister went over the final stages of the plan step-by-step.

Once that was done, they drifted in and out of sleep. Too soon, it was nearly morning. Time for Marina to hide. They held each other for a long last moment. As her sister was about to pull away, Marina took a short breath and pulled her near one last time. Speaking in their lost language, she said: "Did we have a brother, or is it something I dream of?"

"I have the dream too. In my dream he's older."

"Yes, much older," Marina said. "And a baby sister? Did we have a little sister?" She needed to know. This was her last chance to find out.

"I think Mother hid her. I think she got away."

Marina thought back. The fire, the roof red like the sun over the sea, the heat, the burning pieces of wood falling on them, and from somewhere, a baby crying. She was pulling her twin sister out into the air, then she was running onto the sand, rolling and rolling, the heat going away, her left eye, the searing pain, a man's hands taking her, plunging her into water, holding her down until the red light was gone and all that remained was the hurt.

Marina held her sister for as long as she dared. She wanted to say: I saved you once, I'll do it again. But she knew that was impossible.

"I'll succeed, for you I'll succeed." Those were her last words to her sister. Then it was time for her to slip into her hiding place.

Marina peered down the gun sight at the glass door that led onto the patio.

The second quarter chimed. She inhaled deeply through her nose. Steadying her breath, the way Alisander had trained her.

The third quarter. She exhaled in a constant steady stream.

With her forefinger, she caressed the gun's smooth metal trigger and felt it warm to her touch. She focused on the long door handle. She was ready and waiting for it to turn.

GREENE

15 MINUTES MORE

GREENE OPENED THE ORNATE wood-and-glass door of the Hart House library. He'd had never been in the room alone. He started looking at the book titles. Each shelf had a neat, handwritten sign: DRAMA, COMEDY, BIOGRAPHY, POETRY.

Romantic poetry, he thought. Talbot said that Felicia liked Keats. Greene had taken a course in romantic poetry when he was a student. He ran his hand along the spines of the books and pulled down a volume of Keats's poetry collected by J. E. Morpurgo. On the bottom of the cover the price was listed: "Two shillings and six pence."

He flipped it open. A poem he remembered from his undergraduate days, "O Solitude," caught his eye. He shrugged his shoulders and began to read:

> *O Solitude! if I must with thee dwell,*
> *Let it not be among the jumbled heap*
> *Of murky buildings; climb with me the steep,—*
> *Nature's observatory—whence the dell,*

He put the book down and looked out the south window. Below was the old University of Toronto observatory, its round green copper dome slowly corroding black. He smiled at the coincidence and kept reading:

> *Its flowery slopes, its river's crystal swell,*
> *May seem a span; let me thy vigils keep*
> *'Mongst boughs pavillion'd, where the deer's swift leap*
> *Startles the wild bee from the fox-glove bell.*

Greene looked up from the book again. Flowery. Like the dress that the woman on the train had been wearing. The wild bee startled by the deer in his headlights. That sure sounded like Frank Osgoode, that lawyer she'd killed in Brockville. He finished the sonnet:

> *But though I'll gladly trace these scenes with thee,*
> *Yet the sweet converse of an innocent mind,*
> *Whose words are images of thoughts refin'd,*
> *Is my soul's pleasure; and it sure must be*
> *Almost the highest bliss of human-kind*
> *When to thy haunts two kindred spirits flee.*

He put the book down on a long table. "To thy haunts two kindred spirits flee," he whispered.

"Two kindred spirits."

He thought of what his father had said: "No pair of shoes is ever exactly the same."

His heart started to speed up. "That's it," he said aloud.

He grabbed his radio. Before he could push the transmit button, it cackled to life.

"Greene, Greene." It was Bering. She was screaming. "She's a twin! She's a twin!"

"Yes," he said. His heart was pounding. "I just figured that out."

"Identical twin." Bering was struggling to breathe.

"We got the wrong one," he said, raising his voice in the usually hushed library. "That's why I hesitated to ID her."

"We killed the decoy."

Greene looked around the rows of bookshelves in the ornate library. "The books! She must have hidden behind that wall with the bookshelf. That means she was in the room the whole time. She'll have a perfect shot from the window."

Greene ran out of the library, radio in hand.

"Are they outside yet?" Bering asked.

"Any minute now."

Greene raced up the third-floor staircase, taking the winding steps as fast as he dared. It was so clever, he thought. All one sister had to do was cut a hole in the wall, hide her twin behind it, plaster it up, and replace the bookshelf. A perfect hiding place, especially when everyone assumed the original occupant had been killed.

Greene pulled out his gun as he hit the last step and charged along the corridor. He could hear the band outside tuning their instruments.

He got to her room. The door was closed. He tried the handle and it was locked. He shot it off. The gun echoed in the confined space as the latch flew off. He smashed his shoulder into the heavy wood door. It opened a few inches, then stopped. She must have moved the bed to block it. He threw himself at the door again. It moved, but the opening still wasn't wide enough. He shoved it a third time. There was barely enough space for him to squeeze through.

The room was empty. There was a gaping hole in the drywall on the south wall and the bookshelf was in disarray. Her hiding place. Greene ran to the window that faced the quadrangle. It was open.

She'd planned to shoot from here. But, he realized, she must have heard him running down the hall and knew she had to get out the window. She had to be somewhere on the roof.

He looked down. Through the glass doors he could see Talbot standing beside Prime Minister Mulroney, who turned back and waved to the others to come join him.

The clock tower bell began to ring. Right on cue the band struck up "O Canada."

"Stop, stop," Greene yelled, but his words evaporated into the vast space below.

GABRIEL

1 MINUTE MORE

"SALLY, YOU DON'T MIND if I change the channel, do ya?" OPP Officer Gabriel asked as he walked up to the TV at the end of the counter and turned the dial.

"And miss *Days of Our Lives*? Now that is calling for a real sacrifice," Sally said as she gave him a glass of cold milk. She touched him lightly on the arm. "Are you going to eat at the counter today, up here near me?"

Gabriel smiled, keeping one eye on the TV set. "Sure."

"And what's your pleasure today?" she asked, her fingers still touching him.

"The usual, sweetheart," he said, rubbing his thumb and forefinger through his moustache.

"You're in for a treat. I brought in some fresh tomatoes from my garden. The first crop is early this year thanks to the hot weather."

"Grilled cheese with tomato sounds great," Gabriel said. He peered around Sally at the TV. A reporter was broadcasting live from the quadrangle at Hart House. The camera panned and showed a field of journalists. Gabriel saw there were armed police officers in each doorway. He looked up at the plastic clock above the cigarette display. It was 12:59.

"People in town are saying nice things about you, Mr. Brian Gabriel."

It was Sally. Gabriel hadn't even noticed she was still at his side.

"Oh, don't believe everything you hear," he said. "Just rumours."

"And that handsome policeman from Toronto who was in here with you the other day, I suppose he was a rumour too."

Gabriel tore his eyes from the TV and looked at Sally. "How'd you know he's a Toronto cop?"

"Oh, come on, Brian. He didn't buy those fancy shoes at the Zellers."

Gabriel looked back at the TV. The reporter was still babbling away. Sally moved nearer. Her breast brushed lightly against his forearm.

"Tommy's going to his dad's house for two weeks, starting tomorrow," she said, her voice now a whisper.

"I thought his dad only got one week in July," Gabriel said.

She leaned down so her mouth was close to his ear. "Honey, I decided to give him more time," she said.

"That's good," Gabriel said, still looking at the TV.

"You don't sound very excited," she said, pulling back up.

Gabriel sighed. "Sweetheart, I need to watch this for a few minutes."

"It's that meeting of all the big shots in Toronto, isn't it?" Sally said. "I read where the French prime minister brought his mistress with him."

"Yeah, and rumour has it he brought his wife too," Gabriel said. The cameras turned to show the doors where the leaders would come out. He picked up his glass of milk.

"I know. You put in for that transfer, didn't you, Brian?"

Gabriel took a quick gulp of his milk. People were coming out of the door, and they started walking onto the patio. The first was Prime Minister Mulroney with a man Gabriel didn't recognize. Next came President Reagan and Prime Minister Thatcher.

"Didn't you?"

"Sally, please. I need to watch this." The rest of the leaders came out. They were smiling away and waving. Flashbulbs were popping.

Gabriel gulped down the rest of his milk in one swallow. They all turned and Gabriel could see the Russian leader Gorbachev walk out to meet them.

"Where are you going? Ottawa?"

Another man Gabriel didn't recognize came out and walked swiftly up to Gorbachev. The Russian leader turned back to go inside.

What was going on? Gabriel squeezed his empty glass.

"It's Toronto, isn't it?" Sally said. "You're going to be a big shot, aren't you, Brian Gabriel? Great. And I just gave up a week with Eddie for nothing."

Gabriel couldn't believe what he was seeing.

He heard a loud popping sound.

Like a gunshot.

Startled, he looked down at his hand. He'd squeezed the glass so hard it had shattered. Shards of glass lay over the counter spattered with his blood.

He looked back at Sally. "I'm sorry, honey," Gabriel said. "I'm sorry."

GREENE

1 P.M.

GREENE HAD TO GET out onto the roof. If she saw him now, he'd be dead, Greene thought as he crawled out the window and struggled to find a footing on the thin outside ledge.

He found a perch on the eave's trough and scanned the roof. He didn't see her. She could be behind any of the three dormers jutting out onto the roof. He looked back over his shoulder at the quadrangle below. Talbot, Mulroney, and Reagan were already out on the patio. They were looking back and Margaret Thatcher was stepping through the door, wearing a bright white outfit, in stark contrast to the dark suits the other two men wore.

Made her a perfect target, Greene thought. He wanted to yell again to tell them to go back, but there was no point. The music was too loud. He was too far away.

Greene looked at the clock tower to the south. Two marksmen were stationed there. They would have seen her if she was hiding behind the dormer on the south side. She must be behind the one on the north side.

He looked down again. Thatcher was out and now Mitterrand was next. Four out, four more to come, including Gorbachev.

Greene had to find her. His only chance was to crawl to the side of the dormer and hoist himself over to the north side. That way he could come in behind her and catch her by surprise.

He leaned into the steep slant of the roof. The slate shingles were as slick as ice. His right foot slipped and he lunged for the eave's trough on the dormer, reached it. He levered himself up as best he could and pulled himself on top. He looked over the edge. She wasn't there.

Again he looked down. The Italian prime minister was walking out.

What if he was wrong and she had gone the other way? He was almost out of time. He hoisted himself up as high as he could on the small dormer roof, then, like a cowboy hopping onto a horse's back, threw himself over it and landed squarely on the roof. It was a dangerous move. His feet began to skid as soon as they hit the slate.

But miraculously his shoes held. He had a momentary thought. Thank goodness his father had fixed his shoes, or he'd have fallen right off the roof.

His hip smashed into the side of the dormer and his radio broke loose. It tumbled down the roof and lodged in an eave's trough. He grabbed for the rooftop ledge. If he couldn't get a grip he'd fly right off, onto the stones below.

He dug his hands into the eave's trough. The metal sliced through his skin. He squeezed harder and blood spurted out of his fingers. He was going over, he thought, as he clawed for a purchase.

He stopped sliding. Ignore the pain, ignore the pain, he told himself, or all will be lost. He pulled his knees up and righted himself.

Where was she? He'd expected to land on top of her, but she wasn't there. Another look down. There was the Japanese prime minister.

Greene looked around frantically.

At last he spotted her. She was tucked into a small crevice where the corners of the roof met. She had a rifle pointed down at the patio. Why hadn't she pulled the trigger yet? She must be waiting, but for what?

He looked back down. All seven of the leaders were now out on the patio. They all turned to applaud and Greene saw Gorbachev start to walk out. To Greene's surprise, Chief Keon emerged from the door two steps behind the Russian leader and quickly moved to stand beside him. He was carrying the big new phone he'd been complaining about.

Greene looked back at her. She was about ten feet away. He saw her tuck in her elbows and suck in her cheeks. She was about to shoot.

There was no time to get his gun. Greene took two gigantic steps and dove.

BERING

1 P.M.

MUDHAR HAD DRIVEN LIKE a bat out of hell, with the squad car's sirens wailing full out, but now there wasn't an inch of space for the cars to get out of the way. They'd ground to a halt in a Gordian knot of traffic on Bloor Street, still blocks away from Hart House. Bering had tried to call Keon from the cruiser. He didn't have his radio anymore. All he had was the portable phone and every time she tried the damn thing, it went blank.

Only one thing for her to do. Abandon the cruiser—the vehicle of the devil according to her father's strict Mennonite family—and run. Hope you're satisfied, Gramps, she muttered under her breath to the grandfather she'd never known as she slammed the car door shut and took off. She was on the south side of Bloor, beside the old University of Toronto football field. The sidewalk was wide at this point, but crowded with families out shopping, students with piles of books under their arms, and tourists clutching maps.

She zipped past the Royal Conservatory of Music, a hulking stone building set well back from the street, and almost collided with a man rolling along a double bass.

She got to two stone pillars and a wide staircase heading down toward a well-tred path called Philosopher's Walk, one of the secret gems having a university in the city offered. It was also the shortest way between Bloor Street and Hart House.

Bering flew down the stairs. The noise and fumes of the street fell away. To her left was the university's graduate music building. In front of her, a couple was walking slowly, holding hands. Another couple was under a weeping willow, a wicker picnic basket opened beside them, abandoned now as they lay intertwined in a passionate embrace. From an open window in the music building she heard a female opera singer practicing her scales.

Bering emerged from the south side of the path. A group of armed RCMP officers in full uniform were manning a barricade. She flashed her special-clearance badge that Jameson had given her and kept running.

Bering rushed headlong through the side door of Hart House and down the wide hallway to the Great Hall, where the leaders were about to go out onto the patio. She'd spent three years avoiding Keon, and now she had to get to him before they all walked outside.

She was running into battle, the way her father had done so many years before.

GREENE

1:01 P.M.

GREENE FELT HIS HANDS touch her skin. He'd smashed into her just as the shot went off. But he'd lost his balance. He needed to grab her and hold on. The fingers of his right hand wrapped around her left forearm. He squeezed as hard as he could until he stopped his free fall. She barely sustained his weight.

The killer had become his life raft, Greene thought. If she slipped, they'd both fall to their deaths. His feet scrabbled frantically for a foothold to take his weight.

His foot found a ledge. He got his other hand on the rifle and slammed it down on the roof. She held on. He slammed it down again. The weapon broke loose from her grip and skittered below them into the eave's trough.

But Greene's effort threw his balance dangerously off-kilter. She pulled up her leg and kneed him square in the stomach. His grip on her loosened. She ripped her arm away from his grasp and with her free leg kicked him right in the solar plexus. He gasped, and grabbed for her ankle, managing to get enough of a grip to keep himself on the roof.

If she kicked him again, Greene thought, he was gone. He tried with every ounce of strength to throw himself up out of the range of her legs. Their eyes met. Greene saw the deep brown eyes and the left one drifting off-centre.

This beautiful face, those hypnotic eyes, they were going to be the last things he'd see before he died, Greene thought as she kicked him again. But this time he was ready. He deked out of the way and twisted back underneath her leg. He grasped her thigh. Using her pant leg as a brace, he heaved himself up until he was practically on top of her.

She glared at him. "You," she said in an odd, accented voice that seemed to go right through him. She kneed him hard in the chest. It was a direct hit. His lungs heaved, knocking the air out of him.

She'd gained room to maneuver. She jumped up and, moving like a cat, scampered away. Greene felt underneath his body for his gun. He got his hand on it and rolled over. He looked back at the spot where she'd been seconds ago, but she'd disappeared over the peak of the roof.

One more look down at the quadrangle. He expected the worst. Prime Minister Mulroney was holding the door open, making sure everyone else went inside before him. He could see the chief's big phone was a shattered mess on the stone patio.

Breathing hard, Greene pulled himself up and ran after her. In seconds he was on the north roof. She was about five long strides ahead of him.

I have her trapped, he thought.

He saw her tug at something. It was a rope, painted the same green colour as the slate roof. It was looped around a chimney stack. She'd planned her escape route, Greene realized. She was about to go over the side.

Greene charged across the roof, ignoring the steep slant, and propelled himself at her. He had to get his hands on the rope before she slipped over the edge. She looked at him and, pulling hard on the rope, backed up.

Greene was three steps away now. He felt the gun hard in his hand.

She gave him one final look and leaned on the rope.

He wasn't going to make it in time to stop her. There was only one thing he could do.

He raised his gun, took careful aim, and fired.

WHITECASTLE

1:01 P.M.

WHITECASTLE HAD GIVEN UP all hope of stopping his hands from shaking. He had fantasized about this moment for so many years, now it was here.

He rehearsed in his mind yet again the story he'd soon tell the press: "I was working in my greenhouse, listening to the BBC, when the news bulletin came in. Horrific, unbelievable news. I rushed to the house, took my darling wife, Deborah, in my arms and, as she began to cry, I told her, 'In the coming days, we will all be tested.'"

He had walked in front of the potting table, mouthing the words, getting the intonation right. Britons would like this image: the ex–prime minister at work alone, he heard the horrific news, and then stoically delivered it to his wife, all the while calmly thinking of his duty to his country.

Calm. Ha! He was anything but calm right now. He tried to rearrange a pot, but his hands were shaking uncontrollably. He fiddled for the hundredth time with the volume on the radio. It was just after six o'clock now. The news on the hour broadcast. The presenter was going live to a reporter in Toronto at the photo opportunity. Perfect.

Whitecastle grew still, listening in reverent silence.

"The French doors are opening now. Here comes the Canadian prime minister, Mr. Mulroney, accompanied by a gentleman who I'm told is the warden of this historic building."

This is it, this is it! Whitecastle thought, his body rigid, his eyes glued to the radio.

The announcer droned on: "Mr. Mulroney is waving to photographers. Now he's motioning for the others to come join him. Here comes President Reagan, a big smile, a big wave. Now our prime minister Thatcher. A smile upon her face as well."

Whitecastle's temples were pounding. He could feel the blood throbbing through his fingers.

The announcer became more animated: "All seven leaders have now appeared out on the patio, waving to the crowd. And clearly this is pre-planned, they have turned together to the door, and there he is. The Russian president Mikhail Gorbachev. Quite a moment. He's smiling, waving, his arm extended to shake hands with the world leaders."

Whitecastle tried to calm his breathing. But how could he? This was it.

"Wait," the announcer said. "A man has come outside. He's walking swiftly up to Mr. Gorbachev. I'm told . . . "

What? What were you told, dammit? Whitecastle thought. Clearly someone was whispering into the announcer's ear.

"I'm told apparently this is the chief of police here in Toronto. He wasn't on our program—a last-minute addition, I assume. Now he's standing beside the Russian leader."

Whitecastle grasped one of his favourite geranium pots, like an owner stroking his dog at a time of crisis.

"This is extraordinary," the announcer was saying. "The police chief I just mentioned was holding one of those new portable phones and I can see it seems to have shattered. He's walking over to the Canadian prime minister. Now Mr. Mulroney is motioning the world leaders back inside. Like a good host, Mr. Mulroney is holding the door open as, yes, one by one, the most powerful men and woman in the world are going back indoors."

Whitecastle seized the radio in disbelief. "What are you saying!" He squeezed it with all his might. "What? What! No! This cannot be!" he screamed, as if the radio itself were responsible for what he was hearing.

"The Canadian prime minister is the last one. He's waving to the reporters, and now he has left the patio as well. There is no one left outside. Wait, excuse me, yes, we've just received word." The announcer was speaking slowly. "Yes, it appears that the leaders wish a few more minutes to finish their final communiqué." The twit was reading as he was talking. "The BBC has learned that an additional clause has been added welcoming Russia to the G7."

The radio slipped out of Whitecastle's hand, plummeted off the side of the worktable, and smashed onto the concrete floor.

At that moment, Deborah walked in.

"Oh dear, my love, I hope I didn't startle you," she said with a chuckle. "I finished that Agatha and thought I'd pop down for a surprise visit. I was going to invite you into your own house for supper. Oh dear, it looks like you're bleeding. Must have cut your hand when your radio fell. Angus, you look white as a ghost."

GREENE

1:03 P.M.

IT WAS A PERFECT shot.

Greene saw the dazed look on her face. She saw he'd hit his target. And she stopped.

The bullet had cut right through the rope. It was now hanging by a thin thread. If she put any more weight on it, it would break, and she'd tumble to a certain death.

Greene kept moving. Two steps, one step. Her eyes flared at him. She knows she's trapped.

Greene saw her look over the edge. She glanced back at him. He was almost there. He heard a loud sound. The rope had snapped. Her body jerked. He saw a flash of fear cross her face.

Fear of falling, Greene knew, is one of the most primal of all instincts.

The rope was slithering down the roof, like a chain with the anchor thrown overboard. She was about to tumble over.

He lunged for the rope. He held the end with his left hand, while with his right he circled the chimney pipe. He looked up and saw she was gripping the rope for dear life. He'd saved her.

Greene gritted his teeth and tugged hard at the rope to pull her up.

Her balance was precarious. If he slipped, she'd tumble to the ground. He hoped the chimney could hold all this pressure. If it didn't, they were both going over.

He dug the heels of his shoes into the roof and pulled. She took a step forward. If he could pull her closer, she'd be able to sustain her weight.

He heard a creaking sound. He looked down. The chimney was cracking.

He pulled again. She took another step toward him. He heard another creak. The chimney was about to go. He gave the rope a final tug. She regained her balance and the pressure on the rope eased.

The chimney gave out another groan in protest, but it held.

"Come slowly," Greene said, training his gun on her. "I don't want to use this."

She moved cautiously up the precarious slate.

"Just two more steps," he said, "then sit with your back to me."

She nodded, not saying a word. She took a step. And a second step. Then she pounced.

Greene shot at her, but he missed. She was too fast. He felt her grab his left arm tight. Instinctively he pulled it back, but not in time.

Her nails dug in. Right on his childhood scar. He felt a searing pain. An old pain, from long ago. "Mommy," he was saying in his mind, "it hurts. Daddy help."

She squeezed harder.

He dropped his arm. The only way to break her hold on him was to reach down with his right hand, grasp his trapped left hand, and yank it up in one rapid motion. Basic training.

He pulled fast and hard. Taking her by surprise and breaking free of her grip. He grabbed her, jumped up, twisted her around, and kicked her hard behind the knees, driving her down onto the roof, and then jerked her arm high up her back.

It was a classic takedown move he'd learned in his first week at police college.

She began to buck under him, frantically trying to kick him and hit him with her left hand. Greene's positioning was perfect. Her feet and free hand could do no real damage. He yanked her right arm hard, higher up her back. Slowly, he began to feel her energy diminish. It was impossible for her to escape.

He smelled a powerful, acrid stench. Her body began to convulse. Was this a trick? Then he realized what she'd done.

He loosened his grip. She didn't react. Frantically, he rolled her over. She gave no resistance. He forced her mouth open. A horrible smell burst into his face. Her tongue had turned a greenish-yellow colour.

It was cyanide.

He felt her neck. There was a faint pulse, but it was fading.

Her arms went limp. Her eyes were wide open. She was dazed, but still alive.

"Who sent you?" Greene shouted at her as loud as he could, as if that would help him be heard.

Her eyes flickered at him. She took a deep breath and he felt her body rise underneath him. Her lips formed into a deformed sneer. She shook her head.

Greene seized her by the shoulders.

She reached up and touched his face. She looked right at him. Her face broke into a grotesque smile.

"Who?" he yelled.

Her breathing stopped. Her body went limp in his arms.

"No," Greene shouted.

But there was no one to hear him. He held her, as if that simple human gesture could bring her back to life.

In the distance he heard the beating of helicopter wings. Like fast-approaching thunder, the rhythmic pounding grew louder. Greene looked up and saw the chopper approaching.

"Greene, Greene," a voice was calling from behind him on the roof.

He turned and saw Bering rushing toward him.

"Ari," she called out, "are you okay?"

He raised his arm and waved.

The helicopter was now right overhead. Greene looked up to the endless blue sky punctuated by the blazing yellow sun as a long rope disgorged from the chopper's belly. He watched it slowly unfurl, like a gigantic umbilical cord, hovering above him just out of reach.

FRIDAY

JULY 8, 1988

GABRIEL

1 DAY AFTER

GABRIEL HAD LEARNED THAT anyone in town who knew anything about sailing or boating knew about the Krupp family's map of the Thousand Islands. Passed down from generation to generation, it was a local legend, and now, thanks to the Toronto cop Nora Bering, it had been passed to Gabriel.

Bering had called him last night and told him the lab had taken blood samples from the map. They'd been able to confirm that there were two different blood types on it, but nothing more. She told him that apparently there was some new science coming out of Great Britain, and one day they might be able to trace the identity of a person by testing their blood. They said it would be even better than a fingerprint. But the lab couldn't do this test yet, so for now they were preserving both samples.

Bering said they cleaned the map up as best they could and had given it back to her. She'd called to say she wanted to return it to him.

"How quickly can you get it to me?" he'd asked her. "I'd like to have it as soon as possible."

"I'll drive it over there tonight," she'd said. "I owe you."

This morning he was going to pass it along to the person who would be its new rightful owner.

Once again he'd put on a fresh uniform and once again he'd driven over to see Jennifer North at her parents' home. He'd called her in advance and told her he had something of Wayne's for her. She was waiting for him on the front steps when he pulled up in the driveway.

"Thanks for coming," she said, walking down the steps to greet him.

"You don't have to thank me."

"What do you have?"

He didn't wait. He had the map in his hand and he handed it to her.

It took her a moment to realize what it was, then she gasped. "The Krupp family map. It was his grandfather's, and his dad's, and then Wayne's."

She looked up at him.

"And now you can pass it on to the fourth generation," he said.

She clutched the map to her body, wrapping her arms around it as if were a long-lost treasure that she'd found at last.

"I will," she whispered. "But, I mean, the boat sank and Wayne never went out on the water without his map. How did you ever find it?"

"It's a long story," Gabriel said. "All I can tell you is that it was worth the effort."

SATURDAY

JULY 9, 1988

GREENE

2 DAYS AFTER

GREENE UNTIED THE ROPE that held the canoe to the dock, tossed a life preserver into the boat, laid his paddle across the gunnels to brace himself, and lowered his body into the stern.

Meredith was doing the same thing in the bow.

It was Saturday, so it was his turn to be in the stern. Sundays were her turn. An equitable arrangement that had served them well every summer since they'd started dating, and he had been coming up to her cottage.

"You really missed something a few nights ago," she said as they shoved off and began to paddle in unison. "All the Americans on the lake were excited because the Fourth of July was on our holiday Monday this year and so everyone was up."

"Must have been fun," he said as he sank his paddle, the cedar one he'd bought from a local craftsman, deep into the water.

"More fun than what you were doing, I'm sure," she said, stretching far out with her paddle and doing hard, consistent strokes. She'd spent every summer of her life either at camp or her family cottage and had canoe tripped all over the Canadian North. "Pretty bad planning, if you ask me. What's with the Toronto police, having to call you in at the last minute to do traffic-control duty?"

"Comes with the territory," he said, sinking his paddle back into the water, finishing his J-stroke to steer the canoe in the right direction, and lifting it back out. "In their eyes I'm still a relatively new recruit. Hopefully this is the last time."

It had been a matter of seconds and inches, he thought as he sunk his paddle back into the water. Bering had made it to the Hart House dining room just as Gorbachev strolled out onto the patio, and warned Keon that the assassin was alive and on the roof. Keon went outside and caught up to the closest person to him, Gorbachev. Cop instincts. All Keon could do to protect him was cover Gorbachev's heart using the only thing he had. The portable phone.

But as Keon was lifting his arm, the bullet shattered the phone. The shot had barely missed. Greene had got to the gun just in time.

"Switch," Meredith called, and without missing a stroke, fluidly swung her paddle from the left side of the canoe to the right. Greene mirrored her move, switching from right to left.

"I need northern Ontario like I need air," she'd told him the first time she brought him up to the cottage with her. "I'm more comfortable in a canoe on a clear lake than anywhere else in the world."

Who was the mysterious assassin and where did she come from? Greene wondered. Bering had told him that they'd come up empty about the blood on the map. Maybe one day they'd be able to identify who she was.

"This assignment they gave you, it reminds me of my law firm," Meredith said, paddling as consistently as a musician keeping time in perfect four-part harmony: paddle forward, in the water, pull hard, all the way back, lift. Repeat. "This is the first year I don't have to photocopy!" she said with a laugh.

"Ari, you ever regret quitting law school?" she asked, after maybe a hundred strokes. They'd gone to law school together. He'd quit after a year to become a cop and she'd gone on to a promising career as a corporate lawyer.

"No," he said. This time he was the one laughing. "I was always lousy at photocopying."

"True," she said, laughing along with him.

Now he had new career decisions to consider. Last night, after the leaders left Toronto, the chief had announced he was renewing his contract for another five years. An hour later he called Greene.

"I've talked to Bering and congratulated her," he said. "I'm promoting her to the homicide squad."

"She'll be an excellent detective," Greene said.

"I'm making you the same offer."

Greene thanked the chief and asked for a few days to think about it. Jameson had phoned him before the chief's call. "Come join the agency. It's an opportunity of a lifetime, and by the way, you can call me Jimmy," Jameson said. "You'll see the world in a way few people ever get a chance to."

"Look at the loons," Meredith said in a loud whisper, lifting her paddle and pointing to two birds moving seamlessly across the water. All their hard work unseen, below the surface.

"Keep your paddle up," he whispered back. "I'll use silent strokes to see how close we can get."

They drifted near enough to see the complex back-and-white geometric pattern on the back of the loons. Then, by some unseen signal, both ducked down at the same moment and disappeared.

It made him think of his parents, and how they did everything together.

Before he'd come up north, Greene had dropped in to see them. He smiled at the thought.

"How were the shoes?" his father asked.

"Perfect," he said. "They made all the difference."

Dad, he so wanted to say, if you hadn't fixed my shoes, I would have slipped off that roof. You, the Jewish man the Nazis couldn't kill, just saved eight world leaders. Instead, Greene hugged his father. Somehow, he thought, Yitzhak Greene, who'd seen things his son could never even imagine, knew.

"You would have loved it," Meredith said as they rounded the corner, bringing their secret beach into view.

"Loved what?" he asked.

"The show over the lake. It was an amazing display."

"I'm sure I would have enjoyed it," Greene said, smiling as he stretched his arm out and sank his paddle again into the clear blue water. "Maybe next year I won't miss the fireworks."

AUTHOR'S NOTE

World leaders at the 1988 G7 Summit at the
University of Toronto's Hart House.

"Of course he was not always accurate . . . But does it matter? I don't know why fiction should be hampered by fact."

—**W. SOMERSET MAUGHAM**,
Far Eastern Tales, "Neil MacAdam"

BLAME MY GRADE EIGHT teacher. Or perhaps John Keats.

All through my school years in Toronto, I was blessed with inspiring English teachers. In grade eight I learned a truth that I carry with me to this day: that a writer could, sometimes even *should*, bend the facts to make the words work on the page.

We were studying the Keats's sonnet "On First Looking into Chapman's Homer," about the first European explorer to see the Pacific. The teacher focused on the line:

Or like stout Cortez when with eagle eyes

She told us Keats had got it wrong. The explorer wasn't Cortez, it was Balboa. "Why," she asked the class, "did he use the two-syllable name *Cortez* instead of the three-syllable *Balboa*?"

The answer was stunning.

"Cadence. Look at the sentence: eight syllables, perfect iambic pentameter. *Balboa*, with its extra syllable, didn't work."

There's more. After Keats had completed the sonnet, his best friend pointed out the mistake. Undeterred, Keats kept Cortez in knowing it was not historically accurate. Making the words work was more important than getting the details right.

The lesson applies to this, my eighth published novel. About thirty years ago, I started the work on this manuscript (which I then titled *Hart House*) on the portable typewriter I got as a present for my bar mitzvah. It took me ten years to write. I did my research by looking through old newspaper microfiche at the Toronto Public Library. When it didn't sell, I started on what would become my first-published novel, *Old City Hall*.

Decades later, when I picked up this manuscript again, I assumed that I had the facts right. I didn't. The G7 Summit was held in Toronto in 1988, but not on the July 4 weekend. And Mikhail Gorbachev did not attend. But I needed the July 4 parade. I needed Gorbachev to be there. These were my Cortez to the historically correct Balboa. (Having said that, most of the 1988 references in the novel are correct: the white Motorola "brick" phone, the emergence of DNA, Cyndi Lauper's song "Girls Just Want to Have Fun," police officers needing quarters to make phone calls, Margaret Thatcher liking English breakfast tea, etc., etc.)

Without a doubt, I have made other historical mistakes. And I've had to do some geographical shifting around at times. I'm sure my readers will write me about them—as you always do. Please do. Always fun to see my own foibles.

I trust you can forgive me, and agree that making the words and the story work is more important than getting every so-called fact right.

As one of the many commentators on Keats's poem has written: "in poetry, one looks for truth in human nature rather than for historical truth."

———

P.S. In case you are wondering why there are eight people in the photo when there were only seven world leaders—the man on the left is, of course, not Mikhail Gorbachev. Nor is he a world leader. He is Jacques Delors, president of the European Commission.

ACKNOWLEDGMENTS

I WAS A MAGAZINE editor for almost a decade before I became a published novelist.

Those years have given me a special appreciation for editors. I've worked with many terrific editors, but for the last few books I've had the good fortune to work with Laurie Grassi. The best editor I've ever had.

Top editing requires two very different skills. The macro—seeing the arc of the story line, the whole of the novel. And the micro—having an eagle eye for every repetition, flabby sentence, unnecessary word.

There's a third ingredient, I call it "the magic." Passion for an author's work. That extra gear.

Laurie has all three skills. Plus a great sense of humor. Lucky me.

As always, eternal gratitude to my supportive family, friends, law partners, and readers who write me continually about my novels. (It may take some time, but I always write back.)

Being a criminal lawyer for decades, I've worked with many police officers. As a writer, I've had the assistance of three former Toronto homicide detectives. Del Chatterson, now a successful crime writer, saved me from misnaming the Toronto Force the Toronto Police Service—not its name in 1988. Mark Mendelson, who works out of the same office building as I do, is a well-known TV and radio commentator. He confirmed for me that back in 1988, "we used to drive around with a bag of quarters so we could make phone calls." Most of all my good friend Tom Klatt, now a top private investigator who I work with on my cases, has been my source for all things to do with policing since book one. His experience working with other police forces led to the line about Greene and Gabriel: "In the few hours they'd worked together, they'd transformed themselves from strangers to partners."

Many writers have "alpha readers" who have the patience and skill to read early drafts. Since my first novel, I've been blessed with two. Gloria Cassidy and Katherine McDonald have been reading, commenting on, and suffering through innumerable early drafts of all eight novels. I'm grateful to both of them beyond words; please excuse the pun.

Last, but not at all least, a special thanks to my agent, Michael Levine. Every writer should be so fortunate to have an agent such as Michael standing at their side, having their back and, most of all, leading the way.

On to book nine.

Toronto, November 8, 2024

ABOUT THE AUTHOR

ROBERT ROTENBERG is the author of several bestselling novels, including *Old City Hall*, *The Guilty Plea*, *Stray Bullets*, *Stranglehold*, *Heart of the City*, *Downfall*, and *What We Buried*. He is a criminal lawyer in Toronto with his firm Rotenberg Shidlowski Jesin. He is also a television screenwriter and a writing teacher. Visit him at robertrotenberg.com or follow him on Facebook, LinkedIn, Instagram, and X @RobertRotenberg, and Bluesky @robertwriter.bsky.social.